PRAISE FOR
HELEN HARDT

"I'm dead from the strongest book hangover ever. Helen exceeded every expectation I had for this book. It was heart pounding, heartbreaking, intense, full throttle genius."
~ Tina at Bookalicious Babes Blog

"Proving the masterful writer she is, Ms. Hardt continues to weave her beautifully constructed web of deceit, terror, disappointment, passion, love, and hope as if there was never a pause between releases. A true artist never reveals their secrets, and Ms. Hardt is definitely a true artist."
~ Bare Naked Words

"The love scenes are beautifully written and so scorching hot I'm fanning my face just thinking about them."
~ The Book Sirens

Burn

STEEL BROTHERS SAGA
BOOK FIVE

Burn

STEEL BROTHERS SAGA
BOOK FIVE

WATERHOUSE PRESS

DEDICATION

For my nieces,
Lauren and Anna Staab.
Aunt Sissy loves you.

WARNING

This book contains adult language and scenes, including flashbacks of child physical and sexual abuse, which may cause trigger reactions. This story is meant only for adults as defined by the laws of the country where you made your purchase. Store your books and e-books carefully where they cannot be accessed by younger readers.

PROLOGUE

Melanie

I had no idea how long I had been in the room. The man in black had brought me food once, and though I hadn't been hungry, I ate. I had been over every inch of the room, trying to find an escape, but it was impossible. Whenever I was thirsty, I drank from the sink in the tiny bathroom. I still had no idea what my fate would be.

As if in answer, the man in black unlocked the door and entered. "Good morning, Doctor."

Did that mean it was morning? I had no idea. I had slept...I thought. Or had I just relived sessions with Gina in a semi-hypnotic state?

"Today's your lucky day," he said. "You're getting out of here."

Though the thought should have made me ecstatic, I sat there grimly. The memory of Gina's session—*I'd rather die*—had numbed me again. Had I missed a cry for help? There'd been no other indication that she might be suicidal. She'd held down a job, done volunteer work at a local children's shelter...had been in a lot better shape than Talon Steel had been when he first came to me, and he hadn't been suicidal. To the contrary, his overwhelming will to survive had completely overshadowed his desire to die.

The man in black interrupted my thoughts by pulling me from the bed and turning me around to face the wall.

He bound my hands behind my back, this time with duct tape. "Can't have you trying anything funny," he said.

Anything funny? As if I could. The room held nothing that could be used as a weapon, and this man had already demonstrated that he was much stronger than I was.

"Don't you want to know where you're going?"

"Not particularly," I said.

"Okay. Have it your way."

We walked out the door, and I realized I was in a house. This little room with no windows had been built in the middle of the basement. He led me up the stairs, through a laundry room. To the left was a kitchen. We went to the right. Into a garage. It was a large garage, big enough for three vehicles. However, only one old car sat there.

"This is a very special car, Dr. Carmichael."

It was huge, like an old pimp car from a few decades ago. "It doesn't look that special to me. It looks like a piece of crap."

He laughed. "Yes, it is that. It belongs to someone you knew, and the funny thing about this car is that it's an older model. I can start it and then lock it so no one can get in while the motor is running."

"So?"

And then it hit me.

"No!" I tried pulling away from him.

"So you figured it out?"

He pushed me into the garage, against the car, and then jiggled a set of keys in my face. "You won't be able to open the door and turn off the ignition without these. And guess what? They'll be locked inside the car."

My heartbeat raced as cold fear pulsed through my veins. "Let me go! Let me go!"

"I'm afraid not, Doctor. You're going to die. In this garage, at the mercy of this car. Just like Gina Cates did."

CHAPTER ONE

Jonah

Still facing Bryce, Larry curled his lips into a sleazy half smile, his blue eyes creeping eerily toward me while his head stayed still. "Keep looking if you want to, kid, but let me give you a piece of advice. The truth is overrated. Once you open the door to that dark room, getting out is damn near impossible."

My body went cold. Larry was addressing Bryce, but only I knew what he was referring to.

The truth.

The truth—that Bryce's father was one of the men we were searching for.

The truth was indeed a dark room, and I knew who would have to open that door for Bryce. And it wasn't Larry.

Larry was still being steadfast in his refusal to name the other two culprits. But now more than ever, I was certain of what I had inferred earlier from Larry. Bryce knew one of the abductors.

And that abductor was his own father.

"Tell me, Uncle," I said. "You seem to think that Bryce here knows one of the abductors. Why don't you save him and my brother a lot of heartache and tell us, right now, who it is?"

My demand to Larry wasn't altruistic, and I knew it. If Larry told Bryce about his father, I wouldn't have to.

Larry's expression remained stoic. "I said no such thing."

"Maybe not in so many words," I said. "But you certainly implied it."

"Again, I did no such thing."

Bryce sat next to me, his face pale, his countenance rigid. Larry's words had gotten to him.

"Then what is all this bullshit about the truth being a dark room?" I stared into my uncle's blue eyes.

"Do you really think you can handle the truth?" This time Larry was looking straight at me, not Bryce, whose eyes were focused forward.

"I've been forced to handle things no human being should have to handle since I was thirteen years old." I gritted my teeth. "I can deal with anything you throw my way." Especially since I knew already what "truth" he was referring to.

Larry continued staring me down. "And your friend here? A new father? You think *he* can handle the truth?"

Those words catapulted Bryce out of his stupor, the color gradually returning to his face. "I can handle anything you have to dish out."

"Think long and hard before you go there, kid," Larry said, turning his gaze to Bryce.

"I can handle it," Bryce said again through clenched teeth.

"We're grown men, Uncle, despite the fact that you like calling us kids. Now, do all three of us a favor and tell the goddamned truth. Who were those other two men?"

Larry shook his head, chuckling. He turned to the guard standing next to him. "We're done here."

Bryce stood, his hands fisted. "We're far from done here. You're going to tell Joe and me who abducted his brother and who killed my cousin. Right now."

Larry stood as well, his half smile snakelike. "You two don't hear very well. I'm not going to roll on anyone. That will never change."

The guard led Larry away.

Bryce's pallor had turned into ruddiness. He was angry. "Damn," he said. "We're never going to know the truth."

The truth. I already knew part of it. And I knew something else as well.

On my next trip to see my uncle, I would be alone.

★ ★ ★

"So who lives here anyway?"

I pulled up into a parking space near Melanie's building. All I had told Bryce so far was that I needed to check on a friend.

A friend.

God, she was so much more than my friend, and I had been ready to turn her away. But no more. I'd changed my mind. I was going to be there for her, or at least I would try. My own head was such a mess I wasn't sure I was much good to her, but surely just being there would help.

I didn't want to lie to Bryce. I was already keeping so much from him. "My friend is...a psychotherapist. Dr. Melanie Carmichael."

"Isn't that..."

I nodded. "Talon's therapist. Yeah."

"So she's a friend of yours?"

"Yes. Sort of. I mean—"

"Christ. You're screwing her."

I shook my head with a chuckle. How in the hell had Bryce

and I been separated for so long yet he still knew what I was thinking? "That's none of your concern."

Bryce gave me a broad grin. "Joe, I have known you your whole damned life. You can't hide that shit from me. I can read you like a book."

Apparently, he could, which wasn't necessarily a good thing. I didn't want him guessing what I suspected about his father, not until I had better proof. Once I did, I had to tell Bryce before I could tell Talon. I owed Bryce that much. This was his father, after all. I wasn't looking forward to it.

"Okay," I said. "You got me. We've fooled around a few times, but we're really just friends."

"Yeah? Then why are we coming here to check on her? Why not give her a call?"

"Because she's not answering my calls."

After Melanie had sneaked out of my house a few days before when Talon and Jade found us swimming naked in my pool, I'd been angry. When she called me a few hours later, I hadn't answered. When I'd finally tried to call her, she gave me the same treatment. She didn't take the call. I deserved it, but now I was starting to get worried. Melanie wasn't the type to hold a grudge. She was a good person—a person who preached against grudges, a person who helped others.

"Have you considered the possibility that she doesn't want to talk to you?"

"Yeah, I've considered it. Maybe she doesn't. It's been a few days."

"Did you leave everything fine?"

I let out a sigh. "Unfortunately, no. I was mad at her for a while. But I'm over it."

"What did she do?"

"It's a long, dull story. The gist is that Talon and Jade walked in on us while we were naked by my pool. She was embarrassed, and instead of staying, like I wanted her to, she got dressed and sneaked out without telling me." I opened my door.

Bryce left the passenger seat and followed me. "Nice building."

"She has a great little loft here. Fourth floor."

"You want me to stay down here?"

"Yeah, if you don't mind."

"Not at all. There's a tavern across the street. After talking to Larry again, I need a beer."

"Sounds good. I just want to check on her, and then I'll meet you at the bar."

Bryce waved good-bye and walked toward the tavern. So much for him reading me like a book. I knew damned well that if Melanie was home, I wouldn't be meeting my friend at the bar in a few minutes.

I'd be fucking the sexy woman's brains out.

CHAPTER TWO

Melanie

My body went numb. No. This could not be happening. *Use your head, Melanie. There has to be a way out of this. You can kick open a car window. No problem.*

So far he hadn't bound my ankles. If I distracted him, maybe he would forget.

Keep him talking. Keep him talking.

"Is this actually the car that Gina used to kill herself?" I didn't really want to know the answer, but I had to prolong this for as long as I could. Every second made a difference at this point. I had to throw him off balance.

"Do you really care?"

Did I? Whether or not this car had killed Gina, it could very well kill me. "Of course I care. She was my patient. I care about all my patients."

"Do you, Doctor? Then why did you let her die?"

He might as well have sliced my guts open with a sharp knife. "I didn't let her die. She killed herself."

"Because you didn't help her."

My wrists burned as he applied another layer of duct tape tightly around them. My legs were still free. What if—

I turned quickly to face him, the black glint of his gun apparent in his waistband. He could easily grab it and kill me before I could do anything. But I had to try. I had vowed I would get out of this mess, go back to Jonah, and confess my love to him. I drew a deep breath and quickly kneed him between his legs.

"Oof!" He doubled over.

I raised my leg again, ready to axe kick the small of his back, but he turned over quickly, grabbing my ankle.

I screamed as pain shot through me when he twisted the fragile joint.

"You dumb bitch. I know enough to wear a cup when I'm working. Why the hell did you try that?"

He kicked my sore ankle, and another shard of pain lanced through me. I squeezed my eyes shut, trying to will away the tears. But I was weak, both in mind and body. I had no idea how long I'd been here, and although he had fed me, it hadn't been much. How much more would I be forced to endure? Would I have been smarter to have waited until he started the car?

No. I had to take every chance I had. Unfortunately, this one hadn't panned out, and now I had the added debilitation of a sore ankle. I could move it, so at least it wasn't broken. I might have quite a sprain, though.

"Dumb cunt. I ought to kill you and be done with it. But that's not the plan."

"What is the plan?" I asked. "Who sent you to do this to me?"

"Not at liberty to say."

"Rodney Cates? Gina's father?" It couldn't have been Gina's mother. She was still hospitalized.

"Still not at liberty to say."

"Why keep me around for so long? Why didn't you just kill me when you took me from my home?"

"That wasn't the plan."

"Screw the goddamned plan!" My ankle was throbbing. "Just tell me what you want. Money? I'll get it for you."

"I've got plenty of that. I charge a lot in my line of business."

I coughed. So this man wasn't my enemy. He was simply a hired killer. Someone Rodney Cates had employed. But Rodney Cates was a college professor. He wasn't a rich man. Gina had said her upbringing was modest. Hired guns didn't come cheap, at least as far as I knew.

"Who hired you?" I gasped out, wincing at the pain in my ankle.

"I've had enough of your talking. Shut up, or I'll duct-tape your fucking mouth!"

I pinched my lips together. No, he couldn't take away my ability to scream. I needed that. It might be my only tool once this was underway.

He tied my ankles together with rope instead of duct tape, and I grimaced and groaned again at the pain.

"Hurts, huh? That's your own damned fault."

I wanted to scream at him, but I remembered his threat about the duct tape. I needed my voice.

"Funny thing. These days, with modern cars, it takes a damned long time to die this way. Newfangled catalytic converters reduce carbon monoxide emissions by quite a bit. This old thing, though... You won't be so lucky."

It was a big garage, and that was in my favor. I'd have to stay as high as I could, where the air would remain clearer. The room was bare but for some old metal shelving. I'd climb on the shelving if I could somehow get myself unbound. If my ankle would support me.

If I couldn't get unbound, I still had my head. Surely my

head was hard enough to break a window. But if I knocked myself out, I'd lose consciousness and die anyway.

The man finished binding my ankles. "Time's running out, Doctor."

"How long does it take?" I asked. "To die, I mean." I knew the answer to that question, of course, being a doctor. But I needed to stall.

"Each case is different. How long do you think it took Gina Cates to die?"

Always the knife, every time someone mentioned Gina. Every damned time. "I don't know." And I didn't, though I could surmise.

"Doesn't really matter now. She's dead. A fucking corpse because of you."

"Did you know her?"

"Fuck, no, I didn't know her."

"Then why does this matter to you?" Of course I knew why. Money. But he was talking, and that was good.

"Not your concern."

"Whatever they're paying you, I'll double it."

"Sorry."

"Are you saying you can't be bought?"

That got a laugh out of him. "You know better than that. But I wouldn't stay in business for long if I weaseled out of a job for more money. No one would trust me."

A hired gun with ethics. Interesting.

"Besides," he continued, "you don't have any money. You're bluffing."

I *was* bluffing. I made a good living and had a good retirement account started, but I didn't have the kind of money he wanted.

However, Jonah Steel did.

Would he give it to me to ensure my safety? He was obviously mad at me for running out on him, but he'd wanted me to stay.

I let out an audible sigh. I had no way to get in touch with Jonah. His number was in my phone, but I didn't have it memorized. I couldn't call him even if I had the capability. The masked man certainly wasn't going to help me.

I was on my own.

Alone.

Just like Gina had been as a child. Just as Talon had been, in that dark, cold basement.

The masked man opened the car door and started the engine. Instinctively, I took a deep breath—my last breath of clean air.

He reached toward the passenger door, locked it, and then stood, locked the driver's side door, and slammed it shut. "Time's up, Doctor." He pushed me toward the car.

I fell against the driver's door, unable to keep my footing. I slid down, the door handle jabbing into my back, and ended up on the floor, my ankle burning.

He stared at me from the door leading to the house. "All locked up tight. Good-bye. See you in hell."

The door shut and clicked quietly.

I closed my eyes and inhaled, going back to the essence of life...breathing, and—

No! This was one time when the essence of life wouldn't help me. The more I breathed in, the quicker I'd lose consciousness from the carbon monoxide.

I trembled, still lying on the concrete floor next to the car. No time to panic. I had to act, and I had to act quickly. My ankle still throbbing, I scooted on my ass toward the shelving on the other side of the garage.

And then I saw it.

CHAPTER THREE

Jonah

"What the fuck?"

A chill pulsed through me. Melanie's door was roped off with police tape and locked with a padlock. What the hell was going on? Had her home been burglarized? I hoped that was it. She had to be all right. I quickly pushed the doorbell.

No response.

Don't panic, Joe. This didn't necessarily mean anything. She could be at work. Her office wasn't too far from here. No—she wouldn't be at work. She had taken a three-week leave of absence. She could be out on an errand. Or—

A swift spike of envy gored me. Maybe she was out with Oliver Twist.

I shook my head. God, yes, I'd rather she be out with Oliver than in some kind of trouble. As much as I didn't want to face it, police tape meant trouble. Was she hurt? Was this why she hadn't returned my calls?

I'd thought she was punishing me for not returning her first call. What had she expected when she sneaked out of my house after I'd invited her to stay? Hell, I'd *wanted* her to stay. I heaved a sigh and then pounded on the door. No one answered, but a door several yards down the hall opened.

"What's all that racket?" A young woman with short hair

stood in her doorway, wearing jeans and a T-shirt that said "Kiss me, I'm Irish."

"I'm sorry if I disturbed you. I'm looking for Melanie Carmichael. Do you know what's going on here? Why is her door taped off? What happened to her? Is she all right? Have you seen her?"

"Slow down with all the questions. No, I'm afraid I haven't seen her. She wasn't here when the police came."

My heart pounded. Okay, that was good. It was probably a simple burglary, and Melanie was okay. Still, where *was* she?

"What happened? Why were the police here?"

"I'm not really sure. They forced their way in and then taped off the place. I was around, and I came out when I heard the noise, but I couldn't find anything out. They weren't here for long. I figured her alarm went off or something."

The young woman was, well, young. She was a cute little thing, wearing that T-shirt. She looked Irish. She had blondish-red hair and blue eyes. She was also no help at all.

"When were the police here?"

"Two nights ago."

"*Two nights ago?*" The night Talon and I had driven to Denver. "Have you seen her since then?"

"I haven't, but she and I don't exactly run in the same circles."

Damn. If she'd needed me, she would have called, right? I kept telling myself that. "If you do see her, could you tell her I'm looking for her?"

The young woman smiled again. "Sure, I can do that. But you'll have to tell me who you are first."

"Oh, of course." I pulled my wallet out of my back pocket, opened it, and pulled out one of my business cards. "Jonah

Steel." I handed her the card.

"And will she know what this is about?"

I nodded.

The woman held out her hand. "I'm Lisa O'Toole. Nice to meet you."

"You too." I shook her hand quickly and then turned.

"Why are you in such a hurry?"

I turned back around, and she was smiling, her hips tilted in a seductive pose. Really? She was going to try flirting with me *now*?

"I have a friend waiting for me at the bar across the street. Please, just tell Melanie I'm looking for her. And that I'm worried about her. I need to know she's okay."

"Will do, Jonah Steel." Lisa winked.

She must have been a trust fund baby to live in Melanie's building. Or maybe she was older than she looked and had a job.

I was one to talk about money. My brothers, sister, and I had never had to worry about money. Still, we worked hard, running the ranch. We could've sold it if we'd wanted to and pocketed enough money to support the next several generations of our family. But both my grandfather and my father would no doubt be rolling over in their graves had we done so.

So her loft had been burglarized. She was probably staying at a hotel. She would have called if she wanted to, or at least answered my calls. Clearly, her sneaking out of my house had been a message. She didn't want me.

I'd live with it.

I had to.

Still, something niggled at the back of my neck—that

bizarre feeling when something wasn't right.

I swished it away with a gesture. Nothing a martini couldn't solve. I walked to the elevator, descended, and then strode over to meet Bryce. I spied him right away sitting at a cocktail table, a beer in his hand. A martini sat at the empty spot. Good man. I ambled over to join him.

"How'd it go?" he asked.

I picked up the drink and took a sip. Not CapRock but not bad. "It didn't. She wasn't home, and her door was blocked off with police tape."

"What?" Bryce set his beer down without taking a sip. "Is she okay?"

"As far as I know. I talked to her neighbor. Melanie wasn't there when the police came, so it was probably a burglary. Why didn't she call me, though?"

"Didn't you tell me she sneaked out of your house a couple days ago? Maybe..."

"You can finish the thought. Maybe she didn't want to call me." I took a long drink of my martini. "I can fucking handle it." Though I wasn't sure I believed my own words.

"Well, just keep calling. She has to answer eventually. Maybe."

"I just can't shake the feeling that something's not right."

"So she's not home. She's probably at work."

"No, she's not. She took a leave of absence."

"Really? Why?"

"I don't know all the details."

I did, but I didn't feel at liberty to divulge Melanie's business. I hated lying to Bryce. I'd gotten pretty damned good at it, though. Here I was, having already convicted his father in my mind, and I hadn't told my best friend about my suspicions.

I needed some more concrete proof before I could act.

"I wouldn't worry about it," Bryce said. "She's probably out shopping or something."

Melanie didn't strike me as much of a shopper. She could get beige cotton panties anywhere. And though her clothes were nice, they were deliberate and professional. Sexy as hell on her, but not anything she couldn't get from an online catalog.

Of course, the woman did have to eat. She could be somewhere as simple as the grocery store.

"You're probably right."

Too bad I didn't believe myself for a minute. Maybe she truly didn't want to talk to me. If that was the case, I would make peace with it. Not like I had any other choice.

"So what did you think about today?" Bryce asked.

"What do you mean?"

"About our visit with Larry."

Of course. My mind was so full of worry for Melanie. I had all but forgotten about the visit with my uncle. "I'm not sure we got anything new."

"You still think I know one of the attackers?"

I wished I hadn't voiced this theory to Bryce after our first visit to Larry, but that had been before I found out about his father's potential involvement.

"I don't know, man. I'm not sure I know shit about anything right now."

"You could be right, though. His words did seem to indicate that. I just don't know who the hell it could possibly be. I don't know anyone like that."

I opened my mouth, not having a clue what was going to come out, when my cell phone buzzed. Saved by the bell, literally. I looked at my phone. "You mind if I take this? It's Marjorie."

"Go ahead."

I put the phone to my ear. "Hey, Marj."

"Joe, you have to come home." Her voice was high-pitched and shrill. Something wasn't right. "I have to talk to you now."

"What's going on? Are you all right?"

"I'm fine. I think." Now her voice shook. "I saw something today."

"What did you see?"

"I don't want to talk about it over the phone."

"Can't you talk to Talon and Ryan?"

"Ryan's too busy to get away, with all the winemaking. I can't ask him. And Talon... No, I can't talk to Talon. Not now. Not...yet."

"Where's Jade?"

"She's at work."

"I'm in the city, Marj. Bryce and I are—"

"Oh, God. Bryce..."

"What? Bryce is here. He's fine."

"He's with you?"

"Yeah, right here. We're having a drink."

"Then where's Henry?"

"Probably with his parents."

"Oh, God..."

"Marj, tell me what's going on."

"Ask Bryce if his mother has the baby. Now."

"Marj—"

"Now. Please."

I looked at my friend. "Henry's with your mom, right?"

Bryce nodded. "Yeah."

I got back on the phone. "Henry's with Evelyn. He's fine."

A heavy sigh met my ears through the phone. "Thank God..."

"Marj, what the hell is going on?"

"Just come home. I'll be waiting for you at your house."

This didn't sound good. And the fact that she was concerned about Henry... It could only mean one thing.

I ended the call, downed the rest of my martini in one swallow, and turned to Bryce. "I need to get home."

CHAPTER FOUR

M e l a n i e

A piece of white PVC pipe was lodged between the bottom of the shelving and the wall. If it was hollow—and pipe usually was—and if I could find a tiny crack somewhere in this seemingly impenetrable garage, I could breathe through the pipe and live. Better yet, I could use the pipe to break the car window and turn off the ignition. An older-model car like this one probably didn't have shatterproof glass. At least I hoped not.

The problem was unwedging the piece of pipe. All I could do right now was hop around with one foot pulsing with pain, and I had to use my hands.

My adrenaline was pumping, and energy surged through me. I was scared, as scared as I'd ever been, but I needed to act quickly. I hopped along one side of the garage, examining the walls as closely as I could, inspecting every crevice. I needed something—anything—that I might be able to use to unbind myself. Searching like a hawk, I looked for any type of hole in the structure where I could breathe in fresh air. When I got to the back wall, I examined the door to the outside. It was solid wood, as far as I could tell, with no windows, and locked, of course. No chance of escape there unless I had an ax, and free hands to use it.

I hopped next to the side of the garage that contained the door that led into the house. I knew that was locked. I couldn't try the knob anyway, with no hands. I scanned the wall as high as I could go. Something had to be there. Something had to give me a way to escape.

Still nothing.

I hopped to the front where the garage door was. It was painted white, and it looked solid. From what I'd been able to gather, this was an older home. The garage door was probably wood instead of aluminum. At least that's what it looked like from this side. I eyed it from all angles as best I could, looking for any deterioration, any crack that I could possibly get oxygen through. Any small crevice in the structure.

The weather stripping attached to the bottom of the garage door was a possibility. If I could pull it off, the seal would no longer be airtight. But I had no hands. I slid down to the floor, my back to the garage door, and tried to grasp the stripping.

Damn!

I'd need my hands free.

I gazed back at the garage door. Something was off. Three-quarters of the way up the door the color changed slightly from white to an even starker white. A closer look, and—

Glass! The entire inside of the door had been painted white to throw me off, but this wooden garage door had glass windows.

Glass that I could break to let in fresh air! My head was already starting to ache. Dizziness and nausea would come next, followed by confusion and drowsiness, and...

There had to be a way.

My adrenaline still pumping, I willed my mind to churn,

my synapses to fire. How could I get free and break this glass?

I hopped back around to the other wall and leaned against it.

Something poked into my lower arm.

What the hell? I turned, and—

A nail, no more than a quarter of an inch shooting out. Painted over, and nearly invisible to the naked eye. Whoever had gone through this garage had missed it. So had I, upon first look, and I would've missed it again if I hadn't leaned at exactly the right spot and felt it on my arm.

Quickly I turned around and started rubbing my duct-taped wrists against the nail. If only the sharp end was pointing out, but that would have been unlikely. Who would hammer a nail into the wrong side of the wall?

What a silly thought. My head was beginning to feel fuzzy.

The duct tape was thick, and nothing much happened except that I poked my wrists.

Damn.

I turned to the shelving next to me. It was old, cheap metal shelving, and upon closer look, it would never hold my weight, even if I were capable of climbing on it.

I slumped my shoulders. What had I been thinking?

I'd never get out of here alive.

I'd never be able to tell Jonah how much I loved him, how much he meant to me.

Numbness swept through me. I slid down to the floor, needles piercing my sore ankle, until—

"Ouch!"

Something bit through the gray fleece on my upper arm. I turned to the shelving once more. A jagged edge had poked me, enough to tear into the fabric.

If it could tear through fabric...

I stood, ignoring the pain in my ankle, and turned, my back toward the sharp edge. I rubbed the duct tape against it hurriedly. Nothing much happened except several gashes to my hands. But I felt no pain in my quest for freedom. Thank God for adrenaline.

I pushed my bound wrists against the edge and punctured a hole through the duct tape. Yes! I could pop it through and make little holes one after the other, cutting the tape.

Although the shelves were nailed to the wall, they weren't very stable. I had to act quickly and carefully. This had to work. It had to. I lowered my wrists slightly, punching another hole. I had to go quickly, and my heart was jumping out of my chest. *Come on, come on...*

This was taking too long. Quickly, I began rubbing the duct tape up and down, as I had when I began. Now, with several holes already in the tape, this worked better. I couldn't see what I was doing, and I scratched and pricked myself more than once, eliciting an "ouch." But after the initial shock, no pain, only my adrenaline rushing through my veins, making me work harder and harder to release myself.

I looked over my shoulder. My blood stained the silver-gray shelving. I didn't care. Carbon monoxide poisoning would kill me. A few cuts would not. I'd need a tetanus shot, but it was a hell of a lot better than dying here.

Faster and faster, I rubbed against the metal. "Come on, damn it! Come on!" When I could move my wrists farther apart, I screamed in triumph. With all my strength, I pulled my wrists apart, but it still wasn't enough. The tape was still connected at the top. Frantically, I rubbed some more, scratching my already bloodied hands and forearms.

Joy surged into me. I was getting somewhere! My arms were braced, ready to break free when—

My wrists suddenly appeared in front of me! I removed the duct tape quickly and then sat down and began to work on my ankles. No, it was more important to get fresh air. I stood again, and—

Whoa. I leaned against the wall. Dizziness, and now the headache, like a jackhammer. I hadn't noticed it when I'd been trying to free my wrists.

Need to sink against something...anything...

No! Need to get back to Jonah. Nothing matters but getting back to Jonah.

I looked to the car. It was fuzzy and blue. Needed to break the driver's window.

I wobbled, changing my mind. It was more important to break the garage window and get some fresh air in here. I could do that faster than I could break the car window. My wrists were already bloody. I hopped to the shelving and grabbed the piece of PVC pipe that was wedged underneath. Then I hopped over to the garage door and began banging on one of the windows.

I threw everything I had into my arms and the pipe. Finally, I threw the pipe down and crashed into the white glass with my bloody fists.

Until I heard a crack.

Yes! A small crack, barely visible beneath the paint. I picked up the pipe again and forced it against the glass until it finally shattered and I was able to push it outward.

"Help! Help! Someone help me!"

No houses were visible. Either I was in a rural area or suburban area facing a lot of green space. I stuck my head through the window and breathed heavily of the fresh air.

But who knew how long it would take me to get help?

I took a few more big gulps of the fresh air out the window and then went to work on unbinding my feet.

My ankle still throbbed from where I had twisted it and the man had kicked me. I hadn't noticed the pain so much while I was hopping around looking for an escape.

I certainly wasn't out of the woods yet. The man had tied a strong knot, and my hands throbbed in pain from the cuts, but I was determined. I looked to the fuzzy car again, my vision blurring. I should be breaking that window... Turning off the car... To hell with my feet.

But my hands kept working, and within a few minutes I was free and could walk.

I headed over to the car and started beating on the driver's side window with the pipe and my bare hands. Eventually the window shattered, and I pushed the glass through and onto the seat. I unlocked the door, opened it, and quickly disengaged the ignition, pulling out the key.

Then I ran back to the garage door and took several more deep breaths out the window.

Damn, my head. Things looked fuzzy. Just grass and dirt and tumbleweeds rolling in the breeze. Even though I now had an open window and the car was turned off, the garage was still full of poisonous gas. At least no more would be added.

I took a few more deep breaths out the window and tried to hoist myself up to go through. My hands were already full of cuts, and my ankle was sore, but I had to try. I jumped, screaming at the pain in my ankle and grabbing at the bottom of the open window. But I couldn't keep my hold.

I sat down, tears emerging in my eyes. All I had

accomplished was to cut my hands even more.

I looked toward the doorway in the back wall. The fuzzy blue car—was it moving now?—blocked my view.

And then I laughed out loud.

CHAPTER FIVE

Jonah

A little over an hour later, I was back at my house. Marj was sitting at the kitchen table, Lucy at her feet. My sister was visibly distraught. In front of her sat a lowball glass filled with what looked like bourbon or scotch. Marj wasn't normally a big drinker.

"Thank God you're back." She jumped up, nearly knocking her chair down, and ran into my arms.

I rubbed her back. "Everything is okay. I'm here."

"The baby? Is he okay?"

"Yes, he's fine. If he weren't, I would've heard from Bryce. I dropped him off, and I saw Evelyn holding Henry in the doorway."

"Thank God." She sniffled against my shirt.

I pushed her away from me, so I could look into her face. "What has you so upset?"

She shook her head. "Joe, it's just too terrible for words. I can't even imagine..."

"Come on." I led her back to the table. "Sit down. Take a drink of...whatever that is."

"Scotch."

"Since when do you drink scotch?"

"Since this whole fucking thing happened." My sister took

a big gulp.

I sighed. This had been particularly hard on Marj. After all, the rest of us had known about what happened to Talon for twenty-five years. We'd kept the truth from her, trying to shield our baby sister, until a month or so ago, when Talon decided it was time to tell her. I often wondered if we'd made a mistake. Because the horrible ordeal had happened to Talon, Ryan and I had always taken his lead in dealing with it. Looking at my baby sister right now, I wished she were still ignorant.

But she wasn't. Reality had been thrust upon her, the way it had been thrust upon the rest of us decades ago. She didn't deserve this, but neither did anyone else. Most of all Talon.

"Take another drink."

She did.

"All right. Now look at me, and tell me what happened."

She rubbed the back of her neck. "I went to the gym today."

"So you went to the gym. That's a good thing."

"I've been meaning to get back into my aerobics. There's a new step class over at the gym, and I wanted to try it. So I went over today, and I renewed my membership."

"And?"

"I had missed the class I wanted to attend, so I decided to get on the elliptical for a while."

"Okay."

"I did forty-five minutes, worked up a good sweat..." She gulped in a breath.

"Relax, honey. I'm here."

"So when I got off the elliptical, I went over to get a towel to wipe my face, and there was another guy standing there, his back to me. He had gray hair."

"Okay."

"He lifted his arm, and I saw..."

"What did you see?"

"A..." She choked. "A birthmark. Shaped like Texas, like what Talon described to us. Right on the underside of the arm. Just like he said."

My blood ran cold. "Who was it, Marjorie?"

But I already knew.

"It was the mayor, Joe. The mayor. Bryce's father."

My heart thumped against my sternum. I had all the evidence I needed. I had been racking my brain to find a way to get Tom Simpson to tell me where his birthmark was without alerting Bryce, and my innocent baby sister had discovered it unintentionally.

Although I hated what this was doing to her, I was glad to know.

"Calm down, honey," I said.

"It's him, Joe. And Bryce lives there...with that little baby."

"He's looking for his own place. He told me. He won't live there much longer, not if I have anything to say about it."

"Are you going to tell him?"

I cleared my throat. "I haven't told any of you this, but I've suspected the mayor for a while."

"Oh my God! Why didn't you tell Talon? And why didn't you tell Bryce? He's living there with his child!"

"Relax. Henry's fine. I didn't have any real evidence until now. I knew Tom had a birthmark like that, but I didn't know where. You've filled in the blank for me."

"But even to be suspicious... We have to get that baby out of there."

"Bryce grew up there, and nothing happened to him. And his mother's there. But don't worry. I'm going to tell Bryce."

"And we have to tell Talon."

I nodded. "Marj, I have to tell Bryce first."

"Why?"

"Because he's my best friend, and he's living there with his infant son. And this is his father."

"But Talon is your brother!"

"I know. But Talon is fine and needs a break. First I have to get Bryce and Henry out of there." I sighed. "Don't worry. I'm telling him tonight."

"Oh my God. You're not going there, are you?"

I shook my head. "No, I'll call him and tell him to come over here, that I have something important we need to talk about."

Marj shivered. "Make sure he brings the baby with him."

"I will."

I just hoped my friendship with Bryce was strong enough to withstand the accusation I was about to lodge against his father.

CHAPTER SIX

M e l a n i e

The car.

I had a car at my disposal.

My head was clouded and pounding, but how had this not occurred to me before now? As much as I didn't want to even think about turning that ignition back on and flooding the garage with more carbon monoxide, the automobile was the best weapon I had.

I opened the driver's side door, again ignoring the pain in my ankle, and pushed the jagged glass from the broken window onto the floor. I winced as several shards cut into my right hand. I sat down in the driver's seat and turned the car back on. Would I have a better chance of backing through the garage door? Or pummeling forward, attempting to knock the wooden back door off its hinges?

I could no doubt get better speed going forward than in reverse, and I needed everything on my side. All I needed to do was dislodge the back door so I could escape.

Then again...I had no idea what was back there. I could see out the front. It was a driveway, and surely I could get through an old wooden garage door.

I just hoped I could do more damage to the door than I would undoubtedly do the back end of the car at the same time.

No more time for thinking. I put my seat belt on.

I pulled as far forward as I could and floored it in reverse.

Took three times, but I finally busted through the old wooden garage door.

I laughed like a maniac as I drove in reverse out of the driveway and onto a dirt country road with a bashed back end. I put the car in drive and stomped on the gas.

I needed medical care. I needed a blood test to see how much carbon monoxide had gotten into my system, my ankle probably needed an X-ray, and my hands and forearms needed to be patched up.

And I needed oxygen. I was light-headed and dizzy, my vision was blurred, with objects coming in and out of focus. But I had no choice. I had to drive out of there.

I had no idea where I was. I glanced at the dash. A half tank of gas. I had no money and no ID, so this half tank had better get me somewhere.

I regarded the vast prairie as I drove down the road, a drum still pounding in my head.

And I laughed like a maniac again.

★ ★ ★

I'd been driving almost an hour, my mind still foggy, when I finally saw a sign. Delta, ten miles. Delta was a tiny municipality about forty miles away from Grand Junction. If I could get to Delta, I could get home. All I needed was for the gas to hold out, and it probably would.

I drove with all the windows open—not that I had a choice on the driver's side. I wanted only fresh air. I never wanted to inhale car fumes again. I was driving with a lead foot, and I reached Delta in less than ten minutes. Night had fallen, and Delta was a small town. Would their police station be open? Most likely, but I had no idea where it was, and I didn't want to waste the gas looking around.

So I hopped on US 50 to Grand Junction. I knew how to get to the police there, but that wasn't where I was going.

★ ★ ★

I had almost reached Grand Junction when a siren started blaring behind me.

Fine. I needed to talk to the police anyway.

I stopped the car, coughing. Out of habit, I reached for the glove compartment for my registration and insurance card, even though I didn't have any. I opened the glove compartment anyway. Maybe Gina still had her registration in there—if this was indeed her car, as the masked man had insinuated. That way I could show the officer something. But no dice. Nothing in there.

I shut the glove compartment and turned—

"Oh!" I coughed again.

The barrel of a pistol pointed at me.

My leg muscles tightened, and my clammy hands clenched around the steering wheel. *Jonah. I want Jonah.* God, would I never get back to him?

"Step out of the car, ma'am."

"Please, you don't need your gun." I opened the door and stepped slowly out, still feeling slightly dizzy, landing on my sore ankle. "As you can see, I'm in need of medical attention."

"Are you aware that this vehicle has been reported as stolen?" the police officer said.

"That doesn't surprise me. I'm Dr. Melanie Carmichael—"

"Hands on your head, ma'am."

I complied, wincing at the pain in my arms. "You don't understand. I'm Dr. Melanie Carmichael. I was abducted... I don't know when I was abducted. What day is it today anyway?"

"I'll do the talking, ma'am. I need to see some ID."

"I don't have any. Aren't you listening to me? I was kidnapped, knocked out, and then tied up and left in a garage with a running car."

"Sure you were."

"Look at me. Look at my hands. They were bound, and I got loose by cutting the duct tape with some sharp edges of metal shelving. See the injuries I've sustained on my hands and forearms?"

"Please turn around, ma'am."

I shook my head and turned around slowly. Was this truly happening? Why didn't he believe me? *If only Jonah were here. He would protect me.*

The officer frisked me quickly. I was still wearing the loose gray sweats, and I was barefoot. Where would I hide anything? If he still didn't believe me, I didn't want to think about where he might look next.

"You seem to be clean. You say you need medical attention? I'll call the emergency vehicle."

"Why? We're close to Grand Junction. I'm a doctor, and I have privileges at Valleycrest Hospital. Someone will be able to identify me if you just take me there. Please."

"I'm afraid not, ma'am. Policy is if a criminal requests medical attention—"

"Criminal? Are you arresting me?"

"This is a stolen car, ma'am."

"Oh, for the love of... Even if you arrest me, I'm innocent until proven guilty. I'm *not* a criminal!" My feet folded under me, and I collapsed against the wrecked car.

"Ma'am, ma'am! Are you all right?"

"Of course I'm not all right. I've been through a nightmare, and I need medical attention." My hands fell from my head. Some of the shallower cuts had clotted up. "All right, then. Follow your procedure. Call the ambulance. I inhaled a lot of carbon monoxide, and I need a blood test. Maybe oxygen."

"I'll cuff you, and you can sit in the back of my car."

Handcuffs? On my bloody wrists? Sounded like torture, but I had no more fight left in me. The paramedics would be here quickly as we were close to the city. He took my hands and forced them behind my back.

"No, no, please. Not behind me like that."

"Ma'am—"

"Please. The man who kidnapped me tied my hands behind my back like that. He bound my ankles too and then left me in a garage with a running car to die. Please. Just keep my hands in front of me."

The officer sighed. "It's not standard procedure."

"Do I really look like a flight risk to you? Look at my hands." I turned to face him. "I can barely stand on my ankle anymore."

His stern eyes finally softened a bit. "All right. In front." He clasped the cuffs around my sore wrists. "So you're telling the truth?"

I let out a sigh of relief. "Yes, I am. I know this isn't my car, but I didn't steal it. The person who left me in that garage did. I just used it to escape."

"I'll take your report later, when we get to the hospital."

He led me to the back seat of his car and opened the door. "Make yourself comfortable in here for the time being."

Comfortable? Well, it was a sight better than a concrete floor with my hands and ankles bound, breathing in poison. Still, I couldn't get into the car.

"Can I stay out here? I don't want to be...closed in. I need fresh air."

"I've already bent the rules for you, ma'am. In the car you go."

I trembled, my skin tightening around me. "You believe me, don't you? I didn't do anything wrong."

"It's not up to me to make that assessment."

"Look at me, for God's sake. I have no ID. I have..." *No fight left in me.* I sighed.

"You're in possession of a stolen car, ma'am. That's all I know for sure at the moment. Now get on in."

I relented. And when I sat down in the back seat, I passed out.

CHAPTER SEVEN

Jonah

"He's getting awfully fussy," Bryce said, rocking Henry in one of the recliners in my family room. "He'd be much happier at home in his crib. Pull the bottle out of the diaper bag, will you?"

I took a sip of iced tea. I hadn't opened the bar on purpose. What I had to say to Bryce needed to be said without alcohol. I fished through the diaper bag and found the bottle. "You want me to heat this up?"

"Nah, he doesn't mind it cold." He pushed the nipple between Henry's lips, and soon the little boy quieted. "He should be asleep soon."

"I set up a place for him in one of the spare rooms. I just arranged a few of Lucy's old doggy gates to fence him in and put down some soft blankets. He can sleep in there."

"You didn't have to go to all that trouble. But then again, why did you insist that I bring him? You knew he'd be nodding off soon."

"I'll explain it all in a little while."

A few minutes later, Henry had fallen asleep. Bryce took him into the other room and then returned. He walked behind the bar. "Can I get you something?"

"Nope." I cleared my throat. "And I'd rather you not drink

tonight either."

Bryce shuffled back a step. "Yeah? All right. What the hell's going on, Joe?"

God, where to start? Here was my best friend in the whole world, and I was about to tell him that I thought his father was a child molester and murderer. Was our friendship strong enough to weather the storm this would bring on?

Bryce had had a good childhood. He'd always lived in town, as his father was an attorney in Snow Creek before he became the mayor. The Simpson family wasn't super rich, but they were well off. Bryce had been a great kid—always smiling, always ready for any new adventure that the two of us could dream up.

"You going to talk?" he asked.

I nodded. "Remember once, how you said I'd changed? We were around fourteen, I guess."

"No. Wait...yeah. You got different after that summer. More closed off. Not as much fun anymore. You'd go days without talking. You never explained why. Of course, now I know why."

"Yeah. Now you know. But you don't know everything."

"What haven't you told me?"

"That we think we've found another one of Talon's abductors."

"Seriously? That's great!"

I closed my eyes and inhaled.

"You should be ecstatic, then."

"I should be, yes."

"Then why so glum?"

"Remember how Larry insinuated that you knew one of the others personally?"

"Yeah. But that can't possibly be true. I've racked my brain to come up with someone I know who might be such a sick person. And Joe, I've got nothing."

I breathed in, out, steadily, though my heart was beating a mile a minute. "Bryce, we have—"

The doorbell rang.

Saved by the bell again.

I shivered, relief overwhelming me. A five or ten-minute reprieve from telling my friend that his father was a psycho iceman seemed like a lifetime.

I stood. "Sorry. I'll be right back." I walked, more slowly than usual, to the door. I opened it.

Talon stood on my front deck.

"Hey, Tal. What's going on?"

He walked in, his eyes laced with fire. "Mills and Johnson matched another set of fingerprints on that business card of Morse's we found in Jade's old room."

"Great. Whose are they?"

He turned to me, meeting my gaze. "It's not good news."

CHAPTER EIGHT

Melanie

When I woke up, I was in an ambulance, an oxygen mask over my face, an IV in my arm. A paramedic was working on cleaning the cuts on my right hand.

I made a small croak.

"You're awake? How are you feeling?" The paramedic removed the mask.

"About how I look, I'm sure." I coughed.

He placed the mask back over my nose and mouth. "Don't try to talk. We're almost to the hospital. They'll take good care of you there."

"The cop?" I tried to choke out.

But he was clearly done listening to me. He didn't remove the mask.

When we arrived, I was laid on a stretcher and taken into the ER at Valleycrest.

"We have a female, twisted ankle, multiple lacerations on her hands and arms. Says she's been exposed to CO. No ID. We're guessing in her thirties."

"Thank you," a male voice said. "Get her in room five. We need to draw some blood."

Within a few minutes, I was in one of the ER exam rooms, and a nurse entered.

"Hello, ma'am, I just have to take— Dr. Carmichael?"

I looked up, my vision fuzzy. I recognized the nurse but couldn't place her name.

"Is that you, Dr. Carmichael?"

I nodded and moved to remove the mask.

"No, keep that on. I'm going to take some blood for testing. My God, what happened to you?"

I couldn't answer, and not because of the oxygen mask.

Blackness descended like a curtain around me.

★ ★ ★

I awoke again in a hospital bed. I quickly looked at my bandaged hands. No handcuffs, thank God. After the nurse— what *was* her name?—had identified me, I hoped the officer would believe my story. Seemed that he had.

I quickly pressed the button on my remote control to call the nurse.

A few seconds later, a young woman in green scrubs entered. "Yes, Dr. Carmichael?"

I removed my oxygen mask. "What day is it? How long have I been here?"

"It's Thursday evening. A little after eight p.m. Your doctor's here, doing his rounds. He'll be in to see you in a minute." She smiled. "Can I get you anything?"

I attempted a smile but couldn't quite get there. "Maybe a drink? I don't have much of a sweet tooth, but for some reason, I'm craving something with sugar."

"Of course. A soda? Maybe some fruit juice?"

"Apple juice, if you have it. Thank you."

"Sure thing. I'll be right back." She turned, and a young

man entered. "Here's Dr. Hernandez now. He'll update you on your condition."

The tall young man approached me. "Dr. Carmichael, I'm Mark Hernandez. How are you feeling?"

I cleared my throat. It was dry and scratchy. "Thirsty. Slightly light-headed."

"Not surprising." He picked up my chart and examined it. "You did have carbon monoxide in your bloodstream, although not enough to do any lasting damage. I'm surprised you remained conscious as long as you did, however."

"Adrenaline does amazing things."

He chuckled. "Indeed, it does. The CO should completely leave your system within the next twelve hours. We've X-rayed you. No lasting damage to your hands, and as for your ankle, it's bruised and swollen, but there are no fractures. Just a light sprain. It will feel much better in a few days."

Light sprain? It hadn't felt so light when it had happened or when I had been hopping around that garage. I simply nodded.

"Did the blood test show anything else in my system?"

He glanced at the chart again. "Nope. Why do you ask?"

"I was...drugged. Injected with something late Tuesday afternoon."

"Looks like they ran the standard drug panel. We can run it again, but if it was something like Rohypnol, it's probably left your system by now."

Of course. Rohypnol. The date-rape drug. It induced amnesia, impaired judgment, and left the system quickly.

I'd been wondering how the masked man had gotten me out of my apartment without anyone noticing. I hadn't passed out after all. I'd walked out of the apartment on my own. I just didn't remember. That was also why he hadn't given me any food until quite a bit later. I would have thrown it up.

"Run the test again anyway," I said. "Please."

He nodded. "Of course." He cleared his throat. "All we know from the police officer who wrote you up is that you said you were kidnapped from your home and then forced into a garage with a running car."

"Yes, that's correct. And if today is Thursday, I was gone for almost forty-eight hours."

"I see. Now that you're awake, we'll bring in a police officer, and you can make a statement."

"At the time I was pulled over, Doctor, the officer in question wanted to arrest me for grand theft auto. So you can understand if I'm not too excited about speaking to the police again."

"We've verified your identity," Dr. Hernandez said, "and your injuries are commensurate with what you described. I don't think you're going to be arrested." He gave me a big smile.

"Still, you don't know for sure."

"If the police thought you were any kind of risk, they would have someone posted at your door. Possibly have you cuffed to your bed. I'm pretty sure you're in the clear. Do you have any questions for me?"

"Yes. When can I get out of here?"

"I'd prefer to keep you overnight, for observation. We want to make sure the CO gets out of your system in a timely manner. But I don't see any reason why you can't leave tomorrow. We'll get you a soft boot for your ankle. You'll probably only have to wear it for a week or two. Maybe only a few days."

Since I had no idea what my loft would look like when I got there, staying another night in the hospital didn't sound too bad. "Can you get me some food?"

"Of course. There's no reason why you can't have a little something to eat."

"Great. Thanks."

The nurse entered. "Here you are, Doctor." She handed me an apple juice box, the straw already inserted.

I took it quickly and sucked down some of the cool juice.

"Betsy, can we find Dr. Carmichael something to eat?" Dr. Hernandez said.

She turned, looking at him with stars in her eyes. "Of course. Right away." She giggled and left the room.

Crushing on the doctor. I was too tired even to smile.

Dr. Hernandez was busy writing some notes in my chart. "Is there anyone we should contact? Are you married? Live with someone?"

He didn't ask if I was in love with someone. Of course he wouldn't. But I was. I was in love with Jonah Steel, and I might have lost him forever because I'd sneaked out of his home.

I shook my head. "No. And I've taken a leave of absence from my practice, so no one will be missing me."

Had Jonah missed me? He hadn't answered my call when I'd tried desperately to contact him while the intruder was in my loft. I had no idea if he even cared. And because I hadn't memorized his phone number, I couldn't get in touch with him.

"Things are looking good here." Dr. Hernandez put down my chart and turned. "Oh, and here's the police officer to speak to you." He looked at the woman in blue. "Not too long, okay? Dr. Carmichael needs her rest."

"For sure," the officer said.

My memory was fuzzy, but this definitely wasn't the officer who'd stopped me on the highway, since she was a woman. She was uniformed, her black hair pulled back in a severe bun from a pretty, although non-made-up, face.

She sat down in the chair next to my bed. "Dr. Carmichael, I'm Officer Ruby Lee. I just need to ask some questions about what happened to you."

"All right. I'll do the best I can."

"That's all I ask. If you start to get too tired, just let me know, and we'll continue another time."

I nodded.

"All right, just start from the beginning."

"I was in my loft, in the shower, on Tuesday, when I heard some scuffling. I got out of the shower, but left it running, and grabbed my purse on my dresser and ran to my closet. I tried to dial 9-1-1, but I got a busy signal. Twice. Why did that happen? Someone is supposed to be there to help in emergencies."

Officer Lee nodded. "I sympathize. It does happen sometimes, however."

"I have no way of knowing whether help would have gotten to me in time anyway, but it would've been nice to know someone was trying to help. No one knew what was going on."

"Someone did. Your call was logged, and the police went to your apartment. They recovered your purse and your phone, and there was evidence of forced entry."

I heaved a sigh of relief. "So you know I'm telling the truth."

She smiled. "Of course we know you're telling the truth. The officer who stopped you was being a little bit of a vigilante, and trust me, he'll hear from his superiors."

I closed my eyes and breathed in.

"The car you were driving was reported stolen by a Dr. Rodney Cates."

"That doesn't surprise me. But don't let that fool you. I'm pretty sure Dr. Cates was behind this attack."

"Why would you say that?"

God, I didn't want to go through the awful facts again, but I had to tell the truth to the police. "His daughter was a patient of mine. She ended up committing suicide, and Dr. Cates blames me for it, even though a practicing psychotherapist and an attorney reviewed my file and concluded that there was nothing in my notes to indicate she was suicidal."

"I'm very sorry," Officer Lee said, not making eye contact with me. "I'm sure it is very difficult to lose a patient."

I swallowed down the lump that had formed in my throat. "Yes, it is."

She paused, not speaking for a moment, and then cleared her throat. "So what happened next?"

"The intruder found me in my closet. I can't describe him, other than he had blue eyes. He wore a black ski mask and all black clothing. I tried to attack him with a shoe, but he outmanned me. He injected me with something in my neck, and the next thing I remember, I woke up, and my first thought was that I was in a hotel."

"But it wasn't a hotel room?"

"No. There was nothing on the walls. They were painted a very light blue. There was a bed and a bathroom with just a toilet and sink. And there was a desk."

"How long were you there?"

"I don't know. I was in and out of consciousness from the drug he injected me with. He brought me food a few times. But you can extrapolate the timing, I guess."

"How did you get out of that room?"

"He came in, bound my hands behind me with duct tape,

and took me out of the room. I realized why the room was built without windows. It was in the middle of a basement. He took me up a set of stairs, and I remember there was a kitchen and laundry room to my left, but he took me to the right to a door that led to a three-car garage."

"All right." Officer Lee scribbled on a pad.

"He opened the door to the garage, and an older-model car was in there. A tank of a car. I wish I could tell you the make and model, but I didn't notice at the time. Besides, if it was listed as stolen, you no doubt already know that stuff."

"Yes, it was a 1984 Cadillac Eldorado Coupe."

"Wow. No wonder I didn't have much trouble crashing through the garage door." I attempted a small laugh.

"So then what happened?"

"He told me that because the car was an older model, he could turn it on and lock the door, so I would have no way of getting in and turning it off. He..."

My God... The vivid details were coming back to me like an IMAX picture. I closed my eyes against the images.

But they were still there.

"Are you all right, Doctor? Should we resume this later?"

I open my eyes and swallowed. "No, I need to get through it now." I cleared my throat. "I tried kicking him, but it didn't work, and he twisted my ankle. Then he bound my feet with rope and pushed me onto the floor of the garage. He turned on the car and locked the doors with it running. Then he shut the door to the house and locked it behind him."

"What can you tell me about the garage?"

"Concrete floor, walls were painted white—like bright stark white, the kind that hurts your eyes. There was a little bit of metal shelving on the far side, across from the entry into the house."

"So how were you able to escape?"

"Honestly, Officer, it's such a blur at this point. My adrenaline was rushing through me. Let me think." All I could see in my mind's eye were images of ice-blue eyes as he turned me around and pushed me onto the concrete floor. Leaving me to die.

"Do you need to stop?"

I shook my head. "Let's get it over with. I knew I had to find some way to get air, so I hopped around, looking at every part of the garage."

And then it unfolded before me, like a Technicolor film. I related to the officer how I had found the pipe, discovered the nail and then the sharp edge on the old metal shelf, released myself, turned off the car, and then turned it back on and crashed through the garage door to my freedom.

It all seemed so unreal.

"You're a very brave woman, Dr. Carmichael," she said. "Brave and also resourceful."

"I didn't feel very resourceful at the time. But I suppose resource comes from gross desperation."

"Indeed it can." She smiled. "I have enough for my report now, so I won't bother you anymore tonight. I want you to get some sleep. If they release you tomorrow, drop by the station and we can give you your phone, your purse, and your identification. I'll leave my card here on the table for you. Is there anything I can do for you before I leave?"

I opened my mouth to say "no," but then shut it quickly.

Yes, there was something she could do for me.

CHAPTER NINE

Jonah

"Oh my God. Who do the fingerprints belong to?"

Talon cleared his throat. "They belong to Felicia."

Talon's housekeeper and cook. A young woman from the Dominican Republic who lived on the outskirts of Snow Creek in a small house with her ailing parents. Felicia had been with the family in one capacity or another for nearly ten years. This was unbelievable.

"There must be some mistake."

"That's what I thought too, but they're definitely hers. I had Mills and Johnson check them twice."

"When we all got fingerprinted, to rule out anyone with access to the house, did Felicia give you any trouble about being fingerprinted?"

"No. But that may not mean anything."

"That means she's not guilty. Or it's a pretty good indication. It's possible they could've planted her fingerprints on the card. Or, when Colin came over to see Jade, perhaps he handed Felicia his card when she answered the door. Do you remember?"

Talon shook his head. "I've been over and over it in my head. I don't remember Felicia ever interacting with Colin."

"Have you talked to Felicia?"

He shook his head again. "I don't know how to bring it up."

"You're going to have to. Maybe he stopped by when no one else was home, Felicia answered the door, he gave her his card, and she never thought to tell anyone that he had stopped by."

"Yeah, I suppose that could have happened."

"We don't know anything until we talk to her. You don't for a moment think that Felicia is guilty, do you?"

"God, no," Talon said. "She's been with us for...how long now? No, there's not a criminal bone in that woman's body."

"I don't think so either," I said.

I turned toward footsteps.

Bryce walked into the foyer. "Hey, Talon, what's going on?"

"Sorry," I said to Bryce. "We've got some new evidence that Talon came by to talk to me about."

"Oh, okay. Let me just get Henry, and we'll be on our way."

"No!" My voice sounded harsher than I intended. "I mean, don't disturb him. In fact, why don't you leave him here for the night?"

Bryce started laughing. "No offense, Joe, but I don't think you know anything about kids."

He had me there. "Then you crash here too. God knows I have the room. It'll be fun, like old times."

"You mean when you and I used to pass out in your barn because we were too drunk to move?" He shook his head, still laughing. "It's not even nine o'clock yet. It's early. Henry will be fine."

"Bryce, I really need to talk to you."

"Then call me later. Right now, I need to get my son home. He needs to be in his own bed."

I sighed. What could I say? Henry was probably safe at the Simpsons' house. After all, Bryce would be there.

"When are you moving out?" I asked abruptly.

"I don't know. Probably in a couple days. I was able to get an apartment right on the outside of town. I figure Henry and I can stay there until I find a place to buy. Frankly, I'm getting a little sick of living with my parents. My mom treats me like I'm twelve."

I tried not to sigh with relief. "You just say the word, bro. I will be there to help you move."

"No need. I rented the place furnished. All I need to do is move Henry's stuff."

"I'll help you with that. Can you get in tomorrow?"

"Calm down, Joe. Probably this weekend. What's your hurry?"

I pressed my lips together. I could not tell Bryce my suspicions about his father with Talon standing right here. Talon would go crazy...and rightfully so. Right now, I had to focus on my brother. He was distraught over this new evidence. Plus, Bryce was going to be home with Henry. He wouldn't let anything happen to his child. I knew that. I just had to make sure Henry was never left alone with his grandfather.

"So what did you want to talk to me about anyway, Joe? You said something about one of the—"

"It can wait," I said. God, if Bryce had finished that sentence, I would've had to spill the beans right in front of Talon. "I'll call you tomorrow."

"Sounds good. I'll just go get Henry." Bryce left us standing in the foyer.

In a few minutes, he returned with his son, still a sleeping bundle. "See you later," he said quietly.

"Yeah, thanks for coming over, man. We'll talk tomorrow."

Talon and I went into the family room. Time to open up the bar. I poured us each a drink, and then we sat down on the couch.

"I don't even know how to approach this," Talon said.

"I think you need to ask her. Talk to her first, before bringing the cops in."

"Yeah, definitely." Talon took a sip of his bourbon. "I just can't imagine how her prints got on that card."

I shook my head. "I sure don't know either, but there may be a logical explanation. So you talk to her. Maybe take Jade with you. Or Marj."

"It's just so weird at the house right now, with Brooke there. And I love Marjorie, but Jade and I don't get any alone time, except at night. And now this. I have to talk to my housekeeper about something really awkward." He sighed.

"Tal, you may not solve everything that happened twenty-five years ago, but maybe you can at least find out who got in your house and left that flower for Jade. You have to follow this lead. You know that as well as I do."

He took another sip of his drink and nodded. "I know that."

"You want me to go with you to talk to her?"

"Yeah, maybe. I need some time to figure out what to do."

"Understood."

He furrowed his brow, the wrinkle on his forehead creasing. "You don't really think Felicia could've had anything to do with this, do you?"

"Of course not. But we have to find out for sure."

"God, when will this all end?"

"I don't—" My phone buzzed.

"Go ahead and take it," he said.

"No, I don't have to."

"For God's sake, Joe, take the call. I've disrupted your and Ryan's lives enough as it is."

I grabbed my phone out of my pocket. It was a number I didn't recognize, with the Grand Junction area code.

"Hello, Jonah Steel."

"Jonah?"

The voice was soft, kind of parched. But it sounded an awful lot like...

"Melanie?"

CHAPTER TEN

Melanie

Just hearing his voice smoothed soothing lotion over my tired body and menaced mind. "Yes. It's me. Melanie."

"Are you all right? You haven't been returning my calls. I've been worried about you."

"I'm fine, Jonah."

"You don't sound fine. Where are you?"

"I'm in...the hospital."

"What happened?"

"It's a long story. But I'm going to be okay."

"Are you at Valleycrest? I'm coming to see you."

"No, it's late. They won't let you in."

"They'll let me in, by God."

I sighed. I wanted to see him more than anything. I needed to see him, to know that he still existed in the world. Even if he could never return my feelings, I needed to touch his hard body, like a pillar of rock in the whirling tornado of my life.

"Yes," I said, barely whispering. "Please come."

"I'll be there in an hour."

I rang for my nurse and let her know I was going to have a visitor. Of course I got the standard lecture on hospital rules, but she finally relented and said she'd show my guest to my room when he arrived. I closed my eyes, picturing Jonah's strong countenance.

I needed his strength right now. I needed *him*.

★ ★ ★

"Melanie?"

Something nudged my arm. I opened my eyes, and a blur stood in front of me.

Jonah.

My Jonah.

I opened my eyes wide. He was *not* my Jonah. At least not yet. It wasn't like me to be so presumptuous. But after the near-death experience I'd just had, I didn't want to waste one more moment not telling him about my feelings.

"God, Melanie, what happened? They wouldn't tell me anything at the nurse's station."

I was fatigued and groggy. "Give me a minute."

"I'm so sorry. I probably shouldn't have woken you. But I just have to know that you're all right."

I fumbled for my remote control and adjusted my bed so I was sitting up. I didn't even want to think about what I looked like. I hadn't had a shower in over forty-eight hours, and I had been to hell and back.

No. I had not been to hell. Gina Cates had been to hell. Talon had been to hell. I had not.

Jonah was seeing me at my worst right now, and that was as good a way as any to tell whether we had a future.

"What happened to your hands, sweetheart? Why are they all bandaged up?"

"I cut them. On glass."

His eyebrows rose. "How? How did that happen?"

I cleared my throat, which was still dry and parched. "Like I said. It's a long story."

He pulled up a chair next to my bed and took one of my bandaged hands in his. "Is this okay? It doesn't hurt, does it?"

"No. It's fine. They must be giving me lots of ibuprofen. I didn't want any narcotics. I wanted to be awake when you... you..." I yawned.

"I'll stay here. I'll sit here all night if you want, if this is too much for you right now. You need to sleep, so sleep."

"No, no. I want you here. I want to be awake. I want to look into your eyes, feel your touch. I need to know that you're here, keeping me safe."

"Keeping you safe? Melanie, what is this— Oh my God. I went to your loft. Your neighbor said you weren't there when the police came. I figured you were okay. What happened?"

"I'm so sorry, Jonah. I'm so sorry I sneaked out of your house the other day. I don't know what came over me. I was embarrassed, and a little bit frightened. But it was all so stupid."

"It's okay. I was angry at first, but I'm over it. I'm sure you had a good reason for leaving. But tell me what happened. Why are you here? Thank God you're—"

"Please." I held up a hand to stop him. "I need to say this. I didn't have a good reason for leaving. My reasons for leaving were stupid and infantilc. It was self-indulgent. I should have faced up to what we'd done, what I'd done. I was there of my own free will. I wanted you. I shouldn't have left."

"Look, Melanie, I accept your apology, okay? Just tell me how you ended up here in the hospital with your hands all cut up."

"I was...attacked."

He stood, his eyes burning. "What?"

"Please, sit down. I need to feel you next to me. I'm all right now."

He sat back down, his demeanor still tense and rigid. "What the fuck happened, Melanie?"

"When I got back to my place, I took a shower to wash the chlorine out of my hair. While I was in the shower, an intruder entered my loft."

"Oh my God, did he hurt you?" Rage flared in his eyes. "I'll fucking kill him."

I shook my head. "No. I mean, yes. He hurt me a little, but not in the way you mean."

"If he put one bruise on your beautiful body..."

"He only kicked my ankle after I twisted it. Other than that, the only thing he did was tie me up and inject me—"

"Inject you? Inject you with what?"

"I don't know. Something that knocked me out, or so I thought, anyway. My blood test didn't show anything, so whatever it was left my system quickly. My guess is that it was Rohypnol."

"Rohypnol? You got roofied?"

"Probably. We don't know for sure. But it's gone now."

"God." Jonah raked his fingers through his hair. "That's the date-rape drug. Are you sure he didn't..."

I shook my head. I'd wondered the same thing, but the doctor had done an examination, and there were no signs of sexual assault. Plus, I didn't have any pain down there. "I checked out clean."

"Thank God." He pulled at his hair again. "I can't believe any of this. How did you cut your hands? Is that why you're here?"

I let out a little cough. "I'm here because...I was exposed

to a lot of carbon monoxide."

"What?"

"The man who took me, he tied me up and pushed me into a closed garage with a running car. He..." My voice shook. Tears formed in my eyes. "He wanted me to die like my patient did."

Jonah stood again, his jawline tense. "Her parents are behind this. I'll fucking kill them."

"That's my thought as well, but we don't have any proof."

He sat back down. "I'm so sorry. That's not what's important now. What's important is that you're okay. Tell me, sweetheart, how were you able to escape?"

In my crackling voice, I relayed the story to Jonah. Several times he tried to interrupt me, but I gestured for him not to. Finally, I said, "Somehow I remained conscious. My adrenaline was really moving. Dr. Hernandez says that although I didn't inhale enough to kill me, I should've been unconscious."

"Oh my God, baby. Oh my God." He closed his eyes and then opened them. "Why didn't you call me?"

"I tried to. When I was hiding in my closet. I called 9-1-1, but it was busy. Can you believe that? Busy. Anyway, after that I tried to call you. It was Tuesday evening. But you didn't pick up."

His eyes widened into circles. "Oh my God," he said again. "Oh my fucking God."

"What? What is it?"

CHAPTER ELEVEN

Jonah

The call. The call from Melanie when Talon and I were about to leave for Denver to see Wendy Madigan.

I hadn't picked up.

I'd been angry at her for leaving.

"Oh my fucking God," I said once more.

"What is it, Jonah?"

How could I tell her? She was lying here in a hospital bed because of me. She could be dead right now. Only her own resourcefulness had saved her. I hadn't saved her. She had cried out for me, and I hadn't been there for her.

And then, when I'd gone to her loft and seen the police tape... Why hadn't I investigated further?

More guilt.

Guilt had been a way of life for me for the last twenty-five years. Why had I ever thought that could change? I had wondered why Melanie hadn't returned any of my later calls, after I changed my mind and wanted to speak with her. It was because she hadn't been able to. She hadn't had her phone. She had been locked up and then forced into a garage to die.

My God, I wasn't worthy of her.

I wasn't worthy of anyone.

"Jonah? Will you stay with me tonight? I know that chair

won't be the most comfortable in the world, but I... I need you here."

She didn't need me. She wouldn't want me there once she learned the truth. I would never be able to make this up to her. She would never forgive me.

"Yes." I nodded. "I'll stay."

She smiled, and her beautiful green eyes closed.

I still held her bandaged hand, and I sat next to her. I didn't sleep when the nurse came in to check her vitals.

I didn't sleep at all.

★ ★ ★

She was still sleeping soundly when a nice-looking young man with dark hair came in early in the morning. "Good morning," he said. "I'm Dr. Hernandez."

I stood, wiping my eyes. "Jonah Steel." I held out my hand.

"Are you a friend of Dr. Carmichael's?"

A friend? I hoped I was more than a friend. I'd dreamed of being way more than friends, but that seemed impossible now, given my oversight. I simply nodded. "How's she doing?"

He scanned the chart. "Everything looks good. She can probably go home today. I'd like to send in a lab tech to take some blood, just to make sure the CO is out of her system. After we get a clean check there, she can go."

I nodded again.

"No need to wake her up just yet. She'll wake up when the tech comes in to take her blood."

For the third time, I nodded, and then I sat back down in my chair, my body weak with fatigue. Melanie looked like an angel sleeping. Her hair was a mess, and she wore no makeup, but she didn't need it. She was so naturally beautiful.

I rubbed my forehead. What had I done? I rose and left the room, took the elevator down to the main floor, and got myself a strong cup of coffee. When I returned to Melanie's room, she was awake, and the lab tech was drawing her blood.

She attempted a smile when she saw me. "Oh good, you didn't leave."

"I would never leave without telling you I was going. I just needed some coffee."

"Of course. Isn't he wonderful?" she said to the lab tech. "He stayed here with me all night in that uncomfortable chair."

The lab tech smiled. "He's not the first one I've seen do that. It's what people do for those they care about."

Care about... Her words sank into my head. I had grown to more than just "care about" Melanie Carmichael. Was I in love with her?

And it hit me like a weight crashing down on me.

I was.

I was in love with her.

And it was a love that would never be returned. I had failed her.

I had failed her, just as I had failed Talon on that fateful day.

I was so fucking tired of failing the people I cared about. The people I loved most in the world. Was I doomed to a lifetime of failing the people I loved?

It would appear so.

"All set," the tech said. "Just please read the label on this vial, and make sure that I have your name and date of birth correct."

Melanie took a look and nodded.

"All right. We should have your results in soon." She picked up her supplies and left the room.

"Thank you for staying," Melanie said to me, smiling tiredly.

"It was the least I could do." The very least. God, if she only knew.

"So tell me, what have you been up to for the past couple of days? I need to hear about something normal."

I had to stop myself from laughing. Normal? My life hadn't been normal for decades. It certainly wasn't normal now. I had a brother who was hell-bent on finding the truth about his abductors, a housekeeper whose fingerprints were found at a crime scene in the main ranch house, a best friend whose father was probably a psycho child molester and murderer... Normal? Hell, I could use a little normal too.

But Melanie didn't need to hear all my baggage right now. "Talon and I took a trip to Denver, the night after..."

God, why had I started out that way?

"It's okay," she said. "You mean the night after I left your house. The night they took me."

I inhaled, bracing myself. "Yes. That night. We went to Denver to talk to that news correspondent we told you about, Wendy Madigan."

"Did you find out anything new?"

We'd found out some new information that I wasn't sure was accurate, but I didn't want to burden Melanie with any of that. "Sweetheart, that can wait. Right now, you need to get some rest if you're going to get out of here today."

"I need to go to the police station when I leave. They have my purse and my cell phone. They recovered them from my loft."

"You're not going anywhere without me by your side today," I said. "I'm going to take care of you."

"You don't have to."

"I know I don't have to. I want to."

For as long as she'd let me, before she found out the truth.

★ ★ ★

Melanie got a clean bill of health two hours later, and her release papers were signed. I wanted to take her straight home, but she insisted we go to the police station to retrieve her personals first. When we finally got to her loft—accompanied by a police officer since it was still considered a crime scene— we found her living room, kitchen, and bedroom in shambles— from the intruder or from the cops, neither of us knew.

"Oh my God," she said.

"Just take the few things you need, ma'am," the officer said. "I'll give you some time in the bedroom." He went to the living room.

I thought quickly. "Just grab a change of clothes. You're coming home with me."

"No, I can't. I don't want to impose."

"For God's sake, Melanie. You've seen the size of my house. I live alone. You're not imposing."

She gave me that soft smile. "Are you insisting?"

"I am."

"Oh, good. I know I can't stay here tonight, and I'm not sure..."

"What?"

"I'm not sure I'll ever feel safe here again."

"You don't have to worry about that for now." Forever, if

I had anything to say about it. But she wouldn't feel the same way once I told her the truth, that I'd neglected to take her phone call on purpose.

"I need to call my insurance company."

"We'll take care of that when we get to my house."

"I'll need to be here when they come..." She sat down on her bed with a sigh. "My God, Jonah, how do people function after something like this? I've helped people recover from much worse. Why am I nearly paralyzed with fear?"

I sat down next to her and took one of her bandaged hands in mine. "You know that what you're feeling is completely normal. You will get through this, Melanie. You will."

"Yes, all I need to do is *want* to do the work." She let out a tiny laugh. "How many times have I said those words to others? Others who have been through so much more than I've been through. And you know what? They don't mean anything."

"That's not true, and you know it."

"I don't know, Jonah. I just don't know how to get through this."

"The same way you tell your patients how to get through things, Melanie. One day at a time. One hour at a time. Whatever it takes."

Tears misted in her eyes, and I pulled her into an embrace.

My God, I wanted her. I wanted to take all the pain away. I wanted to find who had done this to her and pummel him into tomorrow. Why did the universe want to punish the people I loved most in the world?

CHAPTER TWELVE

M e l a n i e

We arrived at Joe's house in the early afternoon. He set me up in one of his guest rooms. I had been hoping he would put me in his room with him, but I didn't dare ask for it. Perhaps he didn't feel the same way I did.

He yawned. The poor thing probably hadn't slept very well in a chair.

"Do you have work you need to do?" I asked.

"Nothing that can't wait."

"You run this huge ranch. I know you have work to do."

"This is more important," he said. "What can I get you? What do you need?"

You. I need you, Jonah.

But I didn't voice the thought. "A shower," I said. "I haven't had one since..."

Since the night.

My heart sped up. I would have to deal with this one way or another.

Day by day, just as Jonah had said, and just as I'd told my patients on many occasions. Day by day.

I would start with a shower. I'd have to take off my bandages. I wanted to get a good look at how they were healing anyway. Some of the cuts had been deep enough to require stitches, but most of them were pretty shallow.

I went into my "room." The shower wasn't as decadent as the one in Jonah's master suite, but it was wonderful. I turned it on and began to unbandage my hands when a knock sounded on the door.

Jonah stood there. "I thought you might want this." He handed me a small bottle of lavender essential oil.

I couldn't help myself. One hand still bandaged, I launched into him and slammed my lips onto his.

He opened quickly and kissed me back.

How I'd missed this. Had it really been only three days? I felt like a lifetime had passed.

If only I could thread my fingers through his beautiful hair, but some of the cuts on my unbandaged hand were still oozing a bit.

But as ravenous as he had been on my mouth mere seconds ago, Jonah unclamped his lips from mine and pulled back. "No, you need your rest. As much as I want you, I'm not going to start something with you now."

"Why would I not want you to start something? You stayed with me all night. You brought me to your home to protect me. I want you too. Now."

He backed away from me until he ran into the chest of drawers against the wall. "You need your rest. We shouldn't be doing this."

"Jonah, please. I need to do this now. I need to feel the good in the world."

He shook his head. "I'm far from the good in the world, Melanie."

His full lips tightened, and he closed his eyes for a moment before opening them again. The muscles in his shoulders tensed. Even under his western shirt, I could tell. My God he was beautiful. Truly beautiful, just as he had always been. The streaks of silver at his temples and throughout his several days' stubble drew me. I wanted to feel that stubble against my most intimate places. I wanted to feel alive. Alive with him. The man I loved.

"You *are* everything good in the world, Jonah." I cupped his cheek with my one unbandaged hand.

He took my hand away from his cheek and kissed it. Then he opened it and looked at my wrist and my palm. "This is what happened because I wasn't there for you."

"What are you talking about?"

He stared straight into my eyes and cupped both of my cheeks. "Do you have any idea how strong you are, Melanie? Most people would have just accepted their fate, let themselves go to sleep and die in peace. But not you. You figured a way out."

Strong? I wasn't strong.

I cleared my throat. "The survival instinct is amazing in a human being. I've seen it in my patients, including your brother, and that's all that was going on with me. It had nothing to do with strength."

"How can you say that?" He shook his head, his mass of dark hair swaying. "You're so strong, so intelligent, and so... cunning. You figured a way out of an unwinnable situation. You're incredible."

"No, you don't understand. I wasn't thinking at all. I was acting. I was surviving. And my adrenaline—"

He placed his finger over my lips. "Yes, your adrenaline probably helped. It kept you conscious when you should have been passed out. I'm damned grateful for that, but *you* found the way out. Your adrenaline didn't do that. You did. You used what you found and worked the situation to your advantage." He shook his head again. "I'm not..."

"Not what?"

He swallowed visibly. "I'm not worthy of you, Dr. Carmichael."

I let my mouth drop open. I wanted him to repeat the words because I wasn't sure I heard him correctly. He didn't think he was worthy of *me?* After I had been the one who had left him hanging, sneaking out of his house like a scared teenager? He was so wrong. So, so wrong. I opened my mouth to say so, but he stopped me with a gesture.

"Take a shower, Melanie. I'm going to make you a pot of tea or something. I don't think I have any of that relaxing herbal stuff, but I'll find something." He turned away from me and walked out of the room, shutting the door behind him.

Wow. He didn't think he was good enough for me? The man was obviously delusional. I had been the one who'd let him down, not vice versa.

What was going on?

I let out a sigh and then removed the bandages from my other hand. Of course my right hand had been injured worse. I was right-handed. Not that it mattered, since I was on a three-week leave of absence from work. I wouldn't need to be writing much in the next couple weeks unless I went back to my work in progress—a book on preventing suicide in teens.

My heart wasn't in that at the moment. This whole situation had evolved because I hadn't been able to prevent the suicide of a troubled young woman.

I finished undressing, laid my clothes out on the bed, went to the bathroom, started the shower, and dropped a few drops of the lavender oil onto the shower floor. Soon the relaxing scent wafted around me. I inhaled.

I was lucky to be alive. Damned lucky to be alive.

I got into the shower, the water stinging the cuts on my hand. I washed my hair quickly, and then my body.

Lucky...

Gina hadn't been so lucky.

Why did I deserve to be so lucky?

And then it hit me with the force of a thousand marching soldiers. What I had gone through. What I had escaped. The true reality of it all.

I could be dead right now.

Dead, and no one would ever have known what had happened to me.

I slowly slid my body down the slick shower wall until I was sitting, my knees clasped in front of me.

And all those tears I'd tried to hold back finally fell.

CHAPTER THIRTEEN

J o n a h

I found a few tea bags in a cupboard and boiled some water. One was labeled chamomile, the two others Earl Grey. I had no idea which Melanie would prefer, so I chose the chamomile. Funny, how little I knew about her—other than how great she was at driving me insane in the bedroom. She liked Thai takeout. She liked red wine. She liked the scent of lavender. I smiled. She liked to wear beige cotton bras and underwear. God, how amazing she would look in that Midnight Reverie line I'd seen in the lingerie shop near her office. I had shredded a couple pairs of her cotton panties. Perhaps I'd replace them with purple lace. I smiled again, but my lips curved quickly downward.

Unfortunately, there was no future for me with Melanie. Not after I'd failed her in her moment of need.

I would never see her in deep purple lace. I would never see her wearing the diamond choker buried in my top dresser drawer either.

I'd been determined that she would surrender to my darkest, deepest desires, so determined that I had purchased the elegant piece of jewelry to give to her as a collar, to show the world that she was mine and mine alone.

That could never happen now. How could I ask her to let

me bind her? To let me handcuff her? Not after what she had just been through.

And definitely not after she found out how I had let her down in her time of greatest need.

After the chamomile had steeped for about ten minutes, I walked back to the bedroom where I had situated Melanie. I knocked on the door, but she didn't answer. Perhaps she was still in the shower. I opened the door, and sure enough, the shower was running. I set the cup of tea on the night table and turned to leave when I heard a whimpering—a soft whimpering, like a child crying.

Unable to look away, I knocked softly on the bathroom door and opened it. "Melanie?"

Through the glass doors, I could see Melanie huddled on the floor of the shower, the water still pelting her.

My heart began to beat wildly. Was she okay? Quickly I yanked the shower door open, grabbed her, soaking myself, and pulled her out of the wetness, carrying her like a baby.

"It's okay, sweetheart. I'm here. I'm here." I set her down gently on the toilet and grabbed a large towel, wrapped it around her, dried her off as best I could, and then brought her out to the bed where I laid her down. "Baby, talk to me. Are you okay?"

She sniffled against me as I held her.

"Please, tell me you're okay."

"I'm okay," she whimpered.

It was a silly question, I realized in retrospect. Of course she wasn't okay. She had been through a major ordeal. She would need some time to heal now.

I was well-versed in needing to heal.

"It's okay to cry, sweetheart."

She hiccupped. "I had to hold back the tears for so long. I couldn't let them get through. I had to keep my brain on, had to figure out how to get out of there. And then in the hospital... Everyone around... I just couldn't let myself..."

"And you don't think you're strong?" I shook my head. "Baby, you're the strongest woman I've ever met."

She burst into tears once more and rubbed her face into my shirt.

"It's okay to cry. Go ahead and cry. I'm here. I'm here."

She sobbed for only a few more minutes before she regained her composure. I reached for the box of tissues that sat on the night table, pulled one out, and handed it to her. "Here you go."

She blew her nose loudly and then reached for another tissue to wipe her eyes. "I'm sorry you had to see that."

"I'm not. I'm glad I could be here for you." I was going to be here as much as I could for her until it was time to tell her the truth. That I had failed her.

And then she would leave me.

But right now, she needed me. I would not fail her at this moment.

She pulled back from me a bit. "I know better than to break down like that."

"Baby, after what you've been through, you're entitled." I took her hands in mine. "Do you need some help bandaging these up again? We have all kinds of first aid supplies around here. Ranching work causes a lot of injuries."

She looked down at her hands. "The ones that are stitched are fine. Maybe just Band-Aids for the few that are still open."

"Stay here. I'll be right back." I returned with one of our many first aid kits. "Do you want antibiotic ointment?"

She shook her head. "There's no need. Antibiotics are severely overused in our country."

I couldn't help a small smile. She was still being a doctor, even after all she had been through. I softly pressed Band-Aids over the larger cuts and then kissed each of her hands. "Did you bring anything to change into?"

"I just grabbed some clothes out of my drawers and threw them in a duffel bag. I honestly don't even know what I brought. I just wanted to get out of there. Quickly."

"Never you mind about that. I have something that will fit you perfectly."

I got up, went to my own bedroom, and grabbed the robe she'd worn three days ago. I brought it back to her and placed it around her shoulders, removing the towel. "I think this fits you."

That got a small smile out of her. Lord, even fatigued, with her wet hair hanging in yellow strings around her face, she was the most beautiful woman I had ever seen.

I reached for the mug on the night table and handed it to her. "This is chamomile. I think it's supposed to relax you."

She nodded and took the mug, taking a shallow sip. "Thank you." She set it back down on the table.

"What else can I do for you? Let me take care of you."

"Just hold me, Jonah. Please, just hold me."

I lay down on the queen-size bed and gathered her into my arms. She fit so well against my frame, as if we were perfectly formed to fit together like puzzle pieces. Just having her in my arms like this made my cock burn. It hardened against the denim of my jeans.

Making love wasn't what she needed right now, but when she nuzzled against my neck and started kissing me there, I lost all my resolve. With a groan, I pulled her against me and took her lips with mine.

I had learned to be gentle with Melanie, to bring her into my world slowly, and now, even though I desperately wanted to turn her over and spank her bottom red until she was screaming for more, I suppressed my urges and was determined to go gently.

She opened her mouth for me instantly, but instead of forcing my tongue inside like I normally did, I went slowly, licking around the edge of her lips, nibbling on them, and then running my tongue along her gum line. Slowly and tenderly I twirled my tongue around hers.

And I was shocked when she pulled away.

"Jonah? What's the matter?"

"Nothing. We don't have to do this if you don't want to."

"I *do* want to. What kind of kiss was that? Where's your normal kiss?"

"My normal kiss?"

"Yes, your forceful, mind-bending kiss. That's what I want. That's what I want now. What I *need*."

"I was trying to be gentle, after all you've been through."

She smiled, and God she was beautiful.

"You're sweet to consider my feelings. But I need you right now. I need *you*. I need to feel alive. What better way to feel alive than to share my body with somebody I care about? Somebody I—" She stopped abruptly.

"What?"

She bit her lip. God, she was sexy.

"Someone I...*love*, Jonah."

I jerked my head back, dazed. "You *what?*"

She sat up, biting her lip again. "Someone I love."

I started to speak, but she stopped me.

"No, I have to say this. Twenty-four hours ago, I didn't know if I would live. Let me tell you, looking death in the face makes you rearrange your priorities quickly. All I could think about was that I had fallen in love with you, and I might not ever be able to tell you. I love you, Jonah. You don't have to say it back. I don't expect it. But I know I can't go one more minute without telling you."

I opened my mouth. The words "I love you too" hovered on the tip of my tongue. Because I did love her. I loved her with all my heart. But once I told her the truth, that I had purposely ignored her phone call, she would no longer want me.

She touched her fingers to my lips. "Don't say anything now. Please. Just know that I love you. That's all I need for now, for you to know that. And for you to make love to me."

I was so unworthy. She was offering her love, and her body, and I was unworthy of both. But I didn't have the strength to deny her. I would make love to her this last time, and then, I would tell her the truth.

CHAPTER FOURTEEN

Melanie

He kissed me then, the kiss I was craving. He forced his tongue between my lips and took, took all I had to give, and I gave it freely. I welcomed it. I wanted to give him all of me, everything that was left of me. If it was not meant to be for the future, I would deal with that eventually. But this was now. This was one moment—one I wanted to cherish.

Our tongues swirled together, both of our voices vibrating with hums of desire.

When we finally broke the kiss to both take much-needed breaths, he trailed his lips over to my ear, biting on my lobe and pushing his tongue inside.

"You're so beautiful, Melanie. God, I want you so much."

It wasn't a confession of love, but desire, and I would take it. It was enough for now. He kissed my neck, and then my shoulders, tiny little nips, and he finally made it down to my nipples.

He sucked them. Hard.

Just the way I liked.

I groaned, my hips moving of their own accord, undulating beneath him. I longed to reach for his hard cock and free it from his jeans, but with my injured hands, I wasn't sure if that would be a good idea.

I moaned as he continued to suck my nipples.

"Take off your clothes, Jonah. Please. I want to see your beautiful body. I want to feel your warm skin against mine."

He let my nipple drop with a soft pop. He didn't answer me, but stood and slowly began to undress. I opened my eyes to enjoy the show. He unbuttoned his fawn-colored western shirt, and with each new inch of tan skin exposed, my own skin prickled, my nipples hardened further, and I grew more slick between my legs. When his shirt finally ended up in a crumpled heap on the floor, I drank in his bronze chest, the black and silver hairs scattered over it, the dark disks and the nipples protruding from them. I gazed downward to the arrow of hair that led to the bulge beneath his jeans.

He slowly unbuckled his belt and then unsnapped and unzipped his jeans. He sat on the bed and took off his boots and socks and then stood again, lowering his jeans and boxers to the floor. His larger than large cock sprang out, and a gasp left my lips.

That was for me. That beautiful hardness. All for me. Simple, frugal Melanie Carmichael. This was what I did to him.

This was what I did to the magnificent Jonah Steel.

I let out a groan without realizing it.

His lips curved up at the corners. "My God, Melanie. My God."

"You are absolutely gorgeous, Jonah. You're perfect."

"I'm far from perfect. Very far from it. But you... My God."

He lay down next to me, the warmth of his naked body infusing through me. Tiny kisses rained over the shell of my ear.

"I'm burning for you, Melanie. I'm fucking burning."

If he was indeed burning, why was he being so gentle with me? That was normally not a problem for Jonah Steel. Of course, I knew why. He was being a gentleman in the true sense of the word. I had been through hell, and he didn't want to push too hard.

But right now I wanted him. All of him. Everything he could give to me, I wanted. I would take it without reservation. I needed to *feel*.

I turned to him and kissed him. Just like he'd kissed me before, taking everything I could from him, showing him what I wanted him to do to me.

When we both started panting, he pulled away. "You need to stop this. You don't know what you're doing to me."

I turned his cheek, forcing him to look into my eyes. "I need you. I need everything from you, Jonah. Now."

He pulled away again and sat on the edge of the bed. "No, you don't." He reached for his boxers on the floor.

"What are you doing?" I gasped. "You're not thinking of leaving, are you?"

"I have to. Because if I don't, and you ask me for that again, I might just give it to you."

"Then give it to me."

He turned and scorched me with his dark eyes. "You have no idea what I desire from you, Melanie. A little slap was just the beginning. And right now, after all you've just been through, you can't take what I want from you."

A sudden jolt of fear speared through me. This was the darkness that I had only glimpsed in Jonah before now—the darkness that burned within him, the darkness that I was not able to stay away from.

I wanted him. I wanted to give him everything I could. I

was in love with him.

He had told me once that I would surrender to him eventually. At the time I had my doubts, but no longer.

But he had a point. I had just been through a traumatic experience, and this was my way of dealing with it at this moment. I wanted sex. I wanted orgasms. I wanted to shout to the rooftops that I was alive and well and had outsmarted the man who'd tried to kill me.

But was I ready for what Jonah wanted? I couldn't even fathom what it was that he wanted. If it went beyond the occasional slap, could I truly surrender to him?

He was right.

Today was not the day to find out.

But I still needed him. Still needed him to make love to me.

I pulled him toward me. "I don't want you to leave."

"But if you ask me—"

I covered his lips up with two fingers. "I won't. I won't ask you for that. Not until I'm ready."

"I've been ready, Melanie. I want you. It's what I burn for. It's what I desire more than anything. And one day maybe you'll find out what I want. But not today."

I nodded. "Would you still stay with me for a little while longer? Feeling you beside me gives me...comfort."

He sighed then, his features softening, becoming less angular. "Yes, but I won't be able to keep my hands off of you."

"I don't want you to."

He lay back down beside me then and kissed me. Still a kiss of fire and passion, but slightly more tender this time. He was holding back. That much was obvious. But I didn't force it this time. Because, as much as I knew that I wasn't ready for what he had in mind, I had an inkling that he wasn't ready for it either. At least not with me. This was something we would both have to grow into.

We kissed for a long time, and then he moved downward, kissing my breasts, sucking on my nipples hard, while he trailed his fingers over my vulva.

"You're so wet for me, Melanie." He smoothed his fingers through my slick folds. "So fucking wet. I want you so much right now." He thrust two fingers inside my heat.

He slid down my body and softly licked my clit.

I writhed beneath his ministrations, my hips undulating, my breathing becoming rapid. As he tongued my most secret place, the convulsions started deep within my womb and radiated outward. Soon the climax overtook me, bubbling through me like hot lava.

"Jonah!" I cried out. "I'm coming. My God, I'm coming."

"That's right, baby," he said against my patch of dark blond hair. "You come for me. Come all over my face. Drench me in that sweet cream of yours."

I thrust upward into him, rubbing my pussy against his lips, his stubbly beard. I would no doubt have razor burn, but I didn't care. It felt so good, and another orgasm took me on a flight to the moon.

When I finally came down, Jonah moved his body over mine, his hard cock pushing against my slick entrance.

"I need you, Melanie. I need you so much right now."

"Then take me. Take me now."

He plunged into my body, stretching me, the depths of my pussy accommodating him. So full I was, so full and complete.

He pulled out and thrust back in. "You feel so good. So fucking good around my cock."

I had gotten used to Jonah's graphic language during sex, and now turned me on.

"I love the way you fuck me. I love the way you fuck my pussy."

The words sounded foreign from my lips, but not foreign to my ears. My nipples tightened even further, and waves of pleasure began to ripple through me again. Those words—the dirty graphic words. They made me hot.

As my third climax took me to new heights, Jonah increased the speed of his thrusts, grinding into me, fucking me with wild abandon. And I loved it. Every single fucking moment of it.

"I'm about ready, baby," he said, sweat dripping from his forehead onto my cheek. "I'm going to fill you up. Fill you all the way up. Make you mine. Mine."

Mine. I loved the sound of that. Was it possible he felt the same way about me? Did he love me back?

I didn't have time to contemplate the question because then he thrust so far into me that I thought he touched my soul. I came yet again, but it was different this time, like an explosion of warmth around my entire body, penetrating into my heart.

This was it.

This was what love felt like.

Surely he could feel it too.

He lay atop me for a few moments, and I welcomed the weight of his hard body. When he moved over to my side, I whimpered at the loss of his warmth.

"I'm sorry," he said. "I hope that wasn't too rough for you."

I shot my eyes open. "You weren't rough at all. You've been way rougher other times."

"But after what—"

"You gave me exactly what I needed, Jonah. You were right. I wasn't ready for everything from you. But for a few minutes, I just wanted to escape what happened, and you gave me that. No one but you could've given me that."

He chuckled. "I'm one of about a million men who would have been glad to fuck you."

"Fuck me? Was this just a fuck to you?" I couldn't believe he'd said the words.

He shook his head. "You've never been just a fuck to me Melanie."

Thank God. Although I didn't voice the thought. I stayed silent and snuggled up to his warm body. For a moment, I thought I felt a shudder running through him. But then it was gone.

I must have imagined it.

CHAPTER FIFTEEN

Jonah

I stopped my shaking, hopefully before Melanie had noticed. I didn't want to give her any more cause for concern. She had enough to deal with now without worrying about me.

This woman meant so much to me. I couldn't bear the thought of losing her, and I would lose her, as soon as I came clean about ignoring the phone call. But right now she needed me, and I would not let her go through this alone.

I needed to get back to Talon and talk to him about what he'd decided to do about Felicia. So many questions were still unanswered. But I couldn't leave Melanie. If she woke up and I wasn't in the house, she would freak, and rightly so.

I was exhausted, having been up all night in that uncomfortable chair. As much as I wanted to help Talon uncover the mystery of his past, right now I needed sleep. So did Melanie. Once she drifted off, I relaxed a little.

★ ★ ★

When I woke up, darkness had already fallen. I checked my watch. It was after nine p.m. I was disoriented at first and then realized I was in the guest room with Melanie. I reached next to me to touch her. But she was gone.

I got up, quickly put on my jeans, and walked out to the

kitchen. There was Melanie, in my black silk robe, looking as luscious as anything, putzing around in the kitchen. I cleared my throat.

She looked up. "Hey, sleepyhead."

"Sorry."

"Don't be sorry. I know you didn't get any sleep last night. I wasn't planning on waking you at all."

"What are you up to?"

"Just fishing around for something to eat. I can't believe I'm actually a little hungry. That's a good sign. I mean, after my"—she paused—"abduction and all."

I nodded. Undoubtedly, it was. "I'm not much use in the kitchen. I can have Marj come over and whip us up something."

"Oh, don't be silly. We'll find something. Or we can order something."

I couldn't resist a chuckle at that one. "We're over a half hour from a small town. No one delivers out here for takeout. Most places close by nine on weeknights."

Her eyes widened. And I laughed again.

"This ain't the city, honey."

She joined me in laughter. Not her normal laughter, but still a happy sound. She was something else.

She opened the refrigerator door and then turned to me, her expression aghast. "I'm so sorry. I'm being kind of presumptuous, aren't I?"

"Of course you're not. You're my guest here. I don't expect you to go hungry. What do I have in there anyway?"

She stuck her nose in the fridge. "Ha. Bacon and eggs. The perfect comfort food, and something I can actually make." She pulled the food out of the refrigerator. "Where do you keep your skillets?"

"I have no idea."

"You don't make your breakfast?"

"One of my men brings me a massive breakfast burrito in the morning, compliments of his wife."

"I see. Well, if you don't mind me being a nosy Nellie, I'll just look around until I find what I need."

"Like I said, I want you to make yourself at home."

Melanie found the skillet she was looking for, and soon my kitchen smelled like the country ranch house when we were kids. I half expected to look outside and see a beautiful orange sunrise rather than the night sky. This was how the house smelled every morning when Mama was alive, before—

Damn. No matter what happened, it always came back to that. Before Talon's abduction. Back when my mother was my mother, and we three boys were her life.

Wendy Madigan had told Talon and me that our mother had been mentally ill. Part of me didn't doubt that. Mentally fit people didn't normally kill themselves. But she had been such a good mother. Devoted to her children, to our father, to the ranch. But that was all before...

Before...

About ten minutes later, Melanie set a plate in front of me filled with scrambled eggs and three slices of bacon. "I hope you're hungry."

I wasn't sure when I had eaten last, and I found that I was famished. I gobbled up the food in short order.

I didn't want to bring up Melanie's kidnapping, but I did need to know what was going on. "Have the police contacted you again? Do they have any idea what happened?"

"No. I haven't heard anything. It hasn't been very long yet. I'm just hoping they can find the place where I was held. I gave them a detailed account—well, as detailed as I can remember, with my adrenaline freaking me out—of where I had driven from when I escaped."

"It's too late now. You won't be hearing anything more tonight."

"Oh." She stood. "Totally forgot something for us to drink. I suppose it's too late for a pot of coffee, although that's what this meal screams for."

"There's probably some orange juice in the fridge. Or we can drink water. Or make some tea."

"OJ sounds perfect." She rooted around in my kitchen again until she found two glasses.

The scene before me—Melanie in my kitchen, making herself at home—looked more than good to me.

It looked right. It *felt* right.

If only I hadn't failed her.

She set a glass of orange juice before me, and I drank it down in one gulp. When was the last time I had drunk something? The martini with Talon last night. I was clearly dehydrated.

I was restless. Being with Melanie had given me some solace, but I had no right to ask her to make love again. There was only one other thing that would give me the peace I craved—a midnight swim.

"Would you like to go for a swim with me?" I asked.

"It's dark out. And isn't it too cold?"

"You've been in my pool before. It's heated. But if you're too cold, you can get in the hot tub while I have a swim."

She looked at her palms. "I guess my hands will be all right. I'll need more Band-Aids."

"As I told you, I have tons of first aid supplies."

"I have to admit, swimming would be great for my ankle in its condition. Of course, I don't have a suit..."

I laughed aloud. "And we've been through that before too. This is my house. No one's going to interrupt us."

"That's what you said the last time."

She had me there. And that was what had led to—

I didn't want to think about it. I just wanted to get into my swimming pool and enjoy the night with the woman I loved.

"Will you be all right in here alone then? I really would like to swim."

"I'm being silly, aren't I?" She shook her head. "It's just that...when Jade and Talon showed up, and I got embarrassed, that's why I left, and then... It was all so silly, really. But this was all my fault, Jonah."

Her fault? It was *my* fault. I hadn't answered her phone call. "This is *not* your fault. That man had no right to do what he did. And if it takes me the rest of my days, I'll find out who did it and why, and I will make sure that he rues the day he ever laid a hand on you."

"I can't ask you to do that."

"Who said you were asking?"

"Jonah, your plate is so full already with running the ranch and trying to unravel Talon's history. You can't take mine on as well."

"Who says I can't? We will figure it all out, Melanie. I promise. But right now, would you please take a swim with me?"

She smiled, and her beautiful emerald eyes lit with green fire. "All right. Like I always tell my patients, if you fall off the bike, get back on." She stood and came to me, gazing down. "I can't thank you enough for letting me stay here for a while."

"Please don't worry about that. I want to help. It's the least I can do."

If she only knew.

I stood beside her, and together we walked out onto the deck and down the walkway to my swimming pool. I shed my jeans and dived in naked. The water was warm yet crisp against the night air.

I rose to the surface. Melanie was shyly touching her toes to the water.

"Go ahead and get in the hot tub if this is too cold for you. I'll join you in a while." I was aching to do a few laps and work off some of this tension.

"It actually feels good." She tentatively shed the robe and laid it on a chaise longue. Then, instead of going in slowly via the steps as I expected her to, she walked to the edge, only limping a bit, and executed a perfect swan dive into the water.

When she rose, her blond hair slicked back against her head, her breasts bobbing on the surface, I said, "I thought you said you weren't much of a swimmer."

She laughed. "I'm not. But I'm a pretty good diver."

"So I see. That was perfect."

"Not exactly perfect, but it will do." She started swimming forward.

I followed, doing several laps of the front crawl and then switching to the backstroke.

After a couple laps, Melanie rested on the side of the pool, sitting on the steps, while I continued swimming.

When I was sufficiently winded, I joined her near the side. "Ready for a dip in the hot tub?" I asked.

"Sounds heavenly." She followed me to the tub.

As we stepped into the hot water, it occurred to me that

I had never had a woman in my hot tub. I'd had women in other places in my house, but never out here. I was happy that Melanie would be the first. If only she could be the last.

She took a seat in one of the shallower seats, stretched her arms out on the railing, and inhaled. "This feels great. The only thing missing is—"

"Lavender?"

"Yes. How did you know what I was thinking?"

"Maybe I know you better than you think I do." I hoped that was true.

She closed her eyes, inhaling again. "Wow, this could relax the tension out of anyone. And boy, do I need that."

I leaned over and kissed Melanie's forehead. "Just relax all you need to, baby. No one is going to bother us."

And then a voice.

"Joe?"

CHAPTER SIXTEEN

Melanie

I popped my eyes open, covering my chest with my arms. This was seriously happening again?

Jonah stood up, stark naked. "Bryce? What the hell are you doing here?"

The man glanced at me and then quickly turned back to Jonah. "Sorry. I've been trying to call you. Since you didn't answer, I thought I'd come by."

"It's after ten."

"That didn't stop you from pounding on my door a couple weeks ago at midnight, remember?"

"Touché, bro." Jonah turned to me with an apologetic look. "This is...Melanie Carmichael."

"I'm sure sorry. I didn't know you had a woman over here." The man named Bryce smiled.

"Well..."

I wanted to sink into the water. How many times was I going to go through this? Getting caught naked at Jonah Steel's house was becoming a habit that I really wanted to break.

"Hey, look," Bryce said. "I wouldn't come over here unless it was an emergency."

"Yeah?" Joe said. "What's going on? Is Henry okay?"

"Henry's fine. He's with my mom." Bryce shielded his

eyes. "Would you please put something on?"

Jonah stepped out of the hot tub, retrieved his jeans, and donned them over his wet legs. He then grabbed a towel and the robe and brought them to me. "You don't have to get out yet if you don't want to. Just relax. You're safe out here."

I didn't feel particularly safe, although I didn't consider Bryce to be a threat. I knew he was Jonah's friend. "I'll get out, but thanks."

I tried to stay as modest as possible as I stepped out, wrapping the towel around me. I grabbed the robe and took it inside. When I got into my guest bedroom, I took a quick shower to get rid of the chlorine, and then I rooted through the duffel bag I had brought. I hit pay dirt with a pair of soft flannel lounging pants and an old white T-shirt. Perfect.

I went back into the bathroom and combed through my hair, blew it dry until it was merely damp, and then decided to go to bed.

But sleep would not come. Every time I closed my eyes, the masked man appeared.

I walked back out to the kitchen. Jonah and Bryce were sitting at the table with drinks.

"I'm sorry. I don't want to interrupt you," I said, warming.

"It's okay," Jonah said. "Do you want something? A cup of tea?"

I shook my head. "Maybe just some water."

He began to stand, but I stopped him.

"I can get it myself."

He smiled and turned back to Bryce. "So what's going on? Stop beating around the bush."

Bryce hedged. "Is it okay to talk?"

I turned around. He was looking straight at me.

I bit my lip and rubbed at the back of my neck. "I'm just leaving. Don't mind me."

"No, Melanie, I want you to stay. I know you don't want to be alone right now." He turned to his friend. "You can speak in front of her. You can trust her. Talon trusted her, and look at his outcome."

Bryce met my gaze. "It's really great to meet you, Melanie. I've heard nothing but good about you."

Nothing but good. I had helped Talon. He was one of my success stories, and I had many more. I needed to remember those things as I tried to deal with Gina's suicide and consequently what had happened to me.

I attempted a smile. "Honestly, I don't want to interrupt you guys."

"Look, I want you to stay," Jonah said.

Bryce nodded. "Yeah, really, it's okay."

Since I didn't want to go back in the bedroom by myself, I relented and sat down at the table, taking a tentative sip of my water.

Bryce rubbed his forehead. "My dad."

Jonah tensed. Someone who didn't know him might not have noticed, but his jawline and forearms became rigid.

"What about him?" Jonah asked.

"He's missing. He went to the city on business three days ago. We didn't think it was a huge deal. He called Mom each night, until last night. He didn't call her. We haven't heard from him."

"Did you call his hotel?"

"Yeah. They don't have any record of him staying there."

Jonah visibly tensed again. He knew something. I had learned to read body language well as a therapist. There was something Jonah wasn't saying.

Jonah cleared his throat, seemingly taking longer than usual to do so. "Have you called the police?"

"Yeah, this morning. But they haven't been any help so far."

"Well, he's a grown man. There's not likely much they can do."

"But he's the mayor, for God's sake. No one's seen him since Tuesday morning."

I jolted in my seat. The mayor? I had seen him—or at least someone whom the person manning the cash register called "Mayor"—on Tuesday, in the late afternoon, buying duct tape and rope at the little hardware store in town. Right before I drove home. Right before...

I opened my mouth to speak, but decided against it. I'd let them talk for a few minutes. This really didn't concern me.

"Mom is beside herself. She's convinced someone took him. I'm not sure. Maybe he ran off with someone." Bryce shook his head. "No, he couldn't have. He's never lied to her in his life, and he wouldn't start now."

More uneasiness from Jonah. It was thick in the room, and I wondered if Bryce sensed it. I certainly could.

"I'm sorry about what you and your mom are going through. But what do you think I can do?"

"I need you to help us find him, Joe. I know you guys have resources. Like those high-priced PIs who are working on your case."

"High-priced is an understatement," Jonah said.

"I don't care what it costs." Bryce pounded his fist on the table. "I need to find my dad. I need to do it for my mom. And for my son. I want Henry to know his grandpa."

And yet more ripples of stress from Jonah. He was squirming, and a few beads of sweat emerged at his hairline. I could almost see it in color—angry red radiating around him like a fiery aura.

What was going on? I opened my mouth again. "This really isn't any of my business, but you said your father was the mayor?"

Bryce turned to look at me, his gaze serious. "Yeah."

"I don't know if this is relevant or not, but while I was here on Tuesday, I drove around Snow Creek for a little bit later that afternoon. I stopped in the hardware and office supply store, and there was an older man with silver-gray hair making a purchase. When he was done, the cashier called him 'Mayor.'"

"What?" Bryce said. "That can't be right. He drove to Grand Junction that morning."

"I'm not saying it was him," I said. "All I can tell you is that he was a man of average height with silver-gray hair, and the cashier, an older man named Gus, referred to him as 'Mayor.'"

"Sounds like him, Bryce," Joe said. "He could have easily come back from Grand Junction that afternoon."

"Then why didn't he come home? He told Mom he was staying in the city for a few days."

Tension was still sliding off Jonah in waves. He gripped his glass with white knuckles, his forearms flexed. "Melanie, do you remember what he was doing in the hardware store?"

"I don't really know much of anything. I didn't talk to him. He was buying a few things. Duct tape and rope, I think."

"You must be mistaken," Bryce said. "Why would my father need duct tape and rope?"

"Duct tape and rope are pretty normal things to have around," I said.

And they were also the things the masked man had used to bind my hands and ankles. My heart thudded, and I dropped my mouth open.

"Melanie?" Jonah looked at me with concern. "What's wrong? Are you all right?"

I looked at Bryce, my knuckles tight as I clenched my glass of water. "Tell me. What color are your father's eyes?"

CHAPTER SEVENTEEN

Jonah

"They're blue," Bryce said, looking at me. "Why?"

"It's just... It's nothing, really." Melanie looked down.

"Melanie," I said. "Why did you ask that? Did you see the color of the mayor's eyes when you were in the hardware store?"

She shook her head. "His back was to me. I had a view of the counter where he was making his purchases. That's how I know what he was buying."

"Then why do you want to know the color of his eyes, sweetheart?"

I hadn't meant to call her sweetheart in front of Bryce, but I couldn't bring myself to be sorry I had. We wouldn't be a couple for much longer, once she found out the truth, but for now, it felt kind of good to have him think that we were.

"I don't know. It was a silly question." She yawned. "I think I'll take this glass of water back to my room. I'm sorry to bother you."

Melanie didn't want to go back to her room and be alone. I could see it in her eyes, her demeanor. I touched her arm as she walked by me. "You can stay."

She smiled and shook her head. "I'll be all right. Just come check on me later, okay?" She shuffled out of the kitchen and down the hallway.

I turned back to Bryce. "Before you ask, she's staying here for a few days. Her loft was...broken into."

"I'm sorry to hear that. Seems we have a rash of crime around here these days."

More than my best friend even imagined, if what I suspected about his father was true. "Bryce, I'm sure your father is fine."

I was speaking the truth. The mayor was an iceman. I didn't know where he'd gone off to, but I knew for damn sure that he had a reason for it.

"I hope you're right. But I need to find out. Can you help me?"

Talk about being between a rock and a hard place. Bryce was my oldest friend in the world, and on a normal day, I would have moved heaven and earth to help him. Today? I wasn't so sure. One thing niggled at me, though. Why had Melanie asked the question about the mayor's eyes?

I sighed. "What do you need me to do?"

"Float me a loan of a couple grand? I need to hire someone good."

That I could handle. "Sure, man. Absolutely. Consider it a gift." I stood. "My checkbook's in the office."

"No, no, I'll pay you back. Every dime."

"All right," I said. "If it'll make you feel better. I understand." And I did. Bryce was a good man. He didn't want to owe me or anyone else.

He followed me to my office, where I wrote him a check for five thousand dollars. I handed it to him. "That should get you started."

"That's more than I asked for. Thanks, Joe. I owe you

one."

"You don't owe me anything."

That was the truth. Because eventually, my best friend was going to hate me, when I told him the truth about his father.

★ ★ ★

Melanie was still awake when I checked on her. She sat up in bed when I entered.

"I'm sorry, baby. Did I wake you?"

"No. I haven't been sleeping. I'm just a little on edge."

"Perfectly understandable." I sat down on the bed and took one of her hands. "How are you doing? You need me to stay in here with you tonight?"

She nodded, biting her lip.

"All right. I'm going to take a quick shower, and then I'll be back in, okay?"

She nodded again.

"I'm going to let Lucy in for the night. I'll tell her to stay in here with you while I shower."

She smiled.

I got up, went back to the kitchen, and let Lucy in. Then I went to my bedroom and showered. When I returned to Melanie's room, I found Lucy cozy on the foot of her bed. I laughed. "She knows better than to get on the bed."

"Don't blame her. I coaxed her into it. Having her here just feels good."

"If it feels good to you, she can stay." I smiled. "I just hope there's enough room for me."

"I'll always make room for you, Jonah."

I snuggled up next to her. She was naked. I hadn't been

expecting that.

"Why do you have pajama pants on?" she asked.

"I just want you to feel safe tonight," I said.

"Safe from you?"

I let out a sigh. "You're always safe from me. I would never hurt you." Except that I already had. She just didn't know it yet. I shouldn't have said those words, even if I felt them deep in my soul. I'd rather burn in hell for eternity than harm Melanie Carmichael. Why hadn't I considered every single possibility when I saw her phone call that evening? Why?

I was so tired of failing people.

"Just take them off, Jonah. I need to feel you against me. I need to know that you're here."

Having no barrier between Melanie and me was a prescription for a hard-on. She didn't need more sex right now. She needed sleep, and so did I.

I sat up, removed my lounge pants, and then snuggled back against her, trying to ignore the throbbing in my groin. I kissed the back of her head. "Sleep now. I'm right here. I won't let anything happen to you. I promise."

She seemed restless for a few minutes, but finally settled down. When her breathing settled into a shallow rhythm, I finally joined her in sleep.

★ ★ ★

Saturday morning. Again I awoke in a strange bed, and Melanie was nowhere to be found. I got up, put on my discarded lounge pants, and walked to the kitchen. The same smell of my childhood breakfasts in the big ranch house drifted toward me.

Melanie was at the stove, cooking.

She turned when I walked into the room. "That's the end of the bacon and eggs. I think we need to go shopping."

"Okay."

"Want some coffee?"

"Yeah. I'll get it."

I sat down at the table with my cup of coffee. In a few minutes, she brought me a plate of food.

I inhaled and took a bite. "Just as good as last night."

"It's Saturday, so I wanted to let you sleep. But I suppose there are no days off for you here on the ranch."

I shook my head. "No, not really. But the three of us do tend to show up a little later on weekends. The guys know it. I won't be missed."

"Good." She sat down next to me with her own plate and cup of coffee. "I need to go to my loft today. I can't stay away from it forever."

"You think you should call your insurance company first?"

"I texted my agent yesterday. An adjuster and a cop will meet me there this afternoon. It's a crime scene, so the cop has to be there. I was wondering if..."

"I'd go with you?"

She nodded, and the lip biting began.

"Of course. I wouldn't expect you to go back there alone. What time do you need to leave?"

"My appointment is at three."

I looked down at my watch. "It's only nine now, so we have some time." I reached down and gave Lucy a pat on the head.

"So what do you normally do on Saturday?"

"I have to go to the office, see what's going on, maybe get out in the pastures. But I'll be back by one thirty or two, and you and I can then go to the city and meet the insurance guy at your loft."

She looked down.

"Will you be okay here? Alone?"

"I have to be. I can't have you missing your work for me."

"Jade is home on Saturday. I can call her and have her come and stay with you. Marj might be free too, unless either Talon or Ryan has her doing something around the ranch."

She shook her head. "It's sweet of you to offer, but I won't be a burden. I can't be. That's not...me."

"The way you react after such a trauma doesn't define who you are, Melanie. It's perfectly normal to want someone with you."

She forced a smile. "You've obviously been with a really great therapist."

"Only the best in the world."

She stood and took her plate to the sink. "I need to get groceries. Can I possibly borrow a car? I have no idea where mine is at the moment. I assume it's still parked at the loft."

"Are you sure you're ready to venture out on your own? In a car?"

"I have to. I have to get back on the horse." She laughed softly. "See, I'm speaking your language now."

"Yeah, I suppose." I wasn't a natural rider like Talon and Ryan, but I had been riding horses since I was barely able to walk. "And of course you can borrow a car. I have three."

"Okay. I'll take a shower, and then I'll drive into town and pick up some groceries for you."

"You mean for us."

"I didn't want to be presumptuous."

"Melanie, you can stay here as long as you need to. Take this day by day. Right now, getting into a car and going to town for groceries is a big step. Are you sure you don't want me to go with you?"

"I hate taking you away from your work," she said. "I can do this, Jonah. I need to do this."

★ ★ ★

I finished my work at the ranch, texted Melanie to see if she was okay, and upon her response, I decided to go and see Talon at the main ranch house, since I still had an hour before Melanie and I had to leave to meet the insurance agent at her loft in Grand Junction. I needed to talk to Talon about Felicia. He and Jade had given her the weekend off, so I didn't risk running into her. I wouldn't know what to say to her.

I got to the main house and knocked. Talon's mutt, Roger, came to the door, peering at me through the window, panting with a doggy smile on his face.

When no one answered the door, I let myself in. "Hey there, guy." I knelt down and gave Roger a pet on his head. "Where is everybody?"

"Who's there?" A woman's voice came from the family room.

I walked through the foyer, through the kitchen, and down a few steps into the large family area. Jade's mother, Brooke Bailey, sat on the sofa, her legs propped up. She wore a brace on one knee. She had shattered her knee in the car accident that had nearly taken her life.

"I didn't mean to frighten you," I said. "I'm just looking for Talon."

"He and Jade went off somewhere," Brooke said.

"Is Marj around?"

"No, she's in town for her cooking class."

Right. I had forgotten. Marjorie was now taking classes in the city. She left on Friday afternoons for an evening class, stayed for classes all day Saturday, and then drove home. She'd be home tonight.

"Anything I can do for you?" Brooke asked.

"No, thank you. Can I get you anything while I'm here? It must be hard for you to get around."

She smiled. Brooke Bailey was still beautiful. I had nursed a major hard-on for her when I was a teen. Funny that she would turn out to be Jade's mother. Her hair was still dark honey blond but now was cut short in a pixie style, rather than the silken locks flowing over her shoulders that she had worn during her modeling days.

"It's a little easier now that I'm healing," Brooke said. "But I would love a glass of iced tea if there's any in the refrigerator."

"Sure, I'll look."

"Get yourself a glass too," she said. "I'd love some company for a while."

I checked my watch. I still had plenty of time to pick up Melanie to go to the loft, and I was a little parched. I poured two glasses of iced tea, went back to the family room, and handed one to Brooke.

"Thank you." She took a sip.

I moved toward one of Talon's leather recliners, but she patted the sofa beside her.

"Sit here. Let's talk."

I couldn't imagine what Brooke thought we were going to talk about, but I didn't want to be rude. She was Jade's mother.

"So, Jonah," she said. "I hear you used to have my best-selling poster hanging in your bedroom."

My cheeks warmed. Not too many things embarrassed me at this late stage in my life, but Brooke Bailey had just succeeded in doing so.

I cleared my throat. "That was a long time ago, ma'am."

She chuckled. "Ma'am? As I understand it, I'm only five years older than you are, Jonah Steel."

Jonah Steel? I wasn't exactly sure why she was using my full name, but I got the distinct feeling she was trying to flirt with me. I squirmed in discomfort.

"I suppose that's true." I took a sip of my iced tea.

"When you get to be our age, a few years here and there certainly don't matter, do they?"

"No, I suppose they don't." Another drink of the tea. I desperately wanted to stand and get out of there. But she was Jade's mother, and I couldn't be rude.

"It's lonely here, you know. I'm alone here all day while Jade's at work and Talon is out at the ranch. Marjorie comes and goes, working at the ranch or running errands in town. I'm by myself most of the day."

"Doesn't your nurse come every day?"

She nodded. "Oh, yes. Jade and Talon have been very good about seeing that I'm looked after. But it's not the same as having a...*friend* to talk to."

"I suppose not." I set my glass of tea down on the coffee table. "I really do need to be going."

She grabbed my arm just as I was about to stand. "Please, don't go. I'd really like to get to know you better, Jonah."

Made perfect sense to me, and not in a good way. I looked into her blue eyes, so like Jade's. No doubt, she was still a beautiful woman. One of her eyes was a little misshapen due to the accident a couple months ago, and lacerations had left her with a few facial scars, but it didn't detract from her beauty and glow. She still had a model's body, and she had one hell of a rack. Not quite as big as Jade's, but more than Melanie had.

Melanie's weren't small, but they weren't huge either. They were pretty damned perfect in my opinion.

"You must know how handsome you are," Brooke said. "Your brothers are handsome too, but you... You're rugged handsome. Dark handsome. Something in you longs to be set free. I can sense it."

I tugged on the collar of my shirt. I didn't like how she was presuming to read me. This wasn't going anywhere good. I wished I could run like hell out of Talon's house.

"I'm dying to know more about you."

I tensed, picking up my tea and gripping the glass. "What do you want to know?"

"I'd like to know if you've ever kissed an older woman."

I jerked out of my seat. Up until the last several weeks, that answer would've been no. I had never been with a woman who was older than I was. But Melanie was two years older. Not that she looked a day over thirty. Then again, neither did Brooke.

"Are you going to answer me?"

"This conversation is heading into an area where I'm not comfortable," I said.

"There had to be a time when you dreamed of kissing me." She grabbed my arm and pulled me back down onto the couch. "Now is your chance, Jonah Steel."

CHAPTER EIGHTEEN

M e l a n i e

Spending a few hours in the town of Snow Creek shopping for groceries wasn't as scary as I'd thought it would be. However, I did feel a little like a fish out of water. Everyone knew each other in this town. Two people walked by and called each other by name. People in the store stopped to chat.

But no one knew me. I got a lot of strange looks from the Snow Creek residents. In a small town, any new face probably raised questions.

It was a cool fall day, so after I picked up several bags full of groceries to replenish Jonah's kitchen, I stored them in the car he'd lent me. I still had some time, so I walked around town like I had several days earlier. I forced myself to relive that day, to retrace that path. Waiting any longer would just have made it more difficult. I walked by the little eatery and the little antique shop where I'd seen a phoenix figurine, to the little hardware store that doubled as an office supply place. Where I had bought...

I still couldn't bring myself to formulate the words in my mind.

The package still sat in my loft, next to my filing cabinet.

This was where I'd seen the mayor. Perhaps Gus and I were the last to see Bryce's father. I walked into the store, a little bell on the door tinkling.

Gus looked up from the book he was reading behind the counter. "Afternoon, ma'am. Can I help you with anything?"

"Maybe. I was in here several days ago."

"Of course. I should have remembered such a pretty lady. What can I do for you?"

"I believe the mayor was also in that day, purchasing some rope and duct tape?"

Gus frowned for a moment. "You may be right. I haven't seen him in here since, though."

I didn't know whether I was at liberty to say that the mayor was missing. Perhaps Bryce wanted to keep that fact quiet, so until I knew for sure, I didn't want to divulge the information. But I could ask some questions about the purchase.

"Do you have any idea why he was buying those things?"

"Are you a detective or something?"

I shook my head. "No, I'm a psychotherapist, actually. I'm a friend of the Steel family. I was just wondering why the mayor would be buying rope and duct tape."

"Everyone needs duct tape," Gus said. "That and WD-40. Two things no household should be without."

"What do you mean?"

"If it's stuck together but isn't supposed to be, you use WD-40. If it's not stuck together but it's supposed to be, use duct tape." He smiled. He was missing one of his lateral incisors.

"That's funny." I chuckled a bit. "Tell me, how long have you lived here in Snow Creek?"

"All my life. This used to be my daddy's store. I don't have a son or daughter to give it to, so when I go, it'll close, or maybe someone will buy it from my estate."

A little more information than I'd wanted. "What about the rope?" I tried to replay the mayor's purchase over in my mind's eye. Was it the same kind of rope the masked man had used to bind my ankles? It was white rope, of a normal thickness. It could've easily been the same rope, or it could've easily been different.

"Maybe Evelyn wanted to hang up some laundry. I have no idea."

"Evelyn?"

"Yeah, she's the mayor's wife."

I nodded. This wasn't getting me very far. "Do a lot of people come in here to buy rope and duct tape?"

"Rope and duct tape are two of my biggest sellers. Everybody has need of one or the other at some point. What's with all the questions?"

"Nothing. I was just curious."

Of course everyone had need of rope or duct tape sometime in his life. A world-class detective I was not.

"It was nice seeing you again, Gus."

"I didn't get your name, ma'am."

I left the store without answering.

CHAPTER NINETEEN

Jonah

"Look, I—"

Brooke pulled me in against her and smashed her lips to mine.

This would've been a dream come true for me...if I'd been fifteen. But I was thirty-eight and in love with another woman. I unclamped from her as quickly as I could.

"Don't you find me attractive, Jonah?"

"Of course I do. But you're Jade's mother. And you're in the middle of recovering from a terrible accident."

"I'm so lonely. My fiancé hasn't contacted me in...I don't know how long now."

Nico Kostas. Brooke's fiancé, and the man Talon had convinced himself was one of his abductors.

"I'm sorry you're lonely. But I'm not going to do this."

"You want me. I can see it in your eyes. You spent many nights dreaming about having me in your bed."

"I won't deny that. But I can assure you that was long ago, and I haven't had a dream about you in the last twenty years."

"Please. I need to know that I'm still attractive. I need to feel a man against me. And you're so..." She eyed me up and down. "You're perfect—rugged, dark, and perfect. This is your chance to fulfill an adolescent fantasy."

An adolescent fantasy? I was so long past adolescence. I'd been forced to grow up at thirteen. As for Brooke? I wasn't even tempted. Bryce would get a good laugh out of this. When he first found out Brooke was staying at the main house with Talon and Jade, he'd advised me to go for it. Brooke was indeed beautiful, but she was a mess inside. She had been a terrible mother to Jade, had basically abandoned her child for her modeling career, and had fallen in love first with a man who stole her fortune, and second with Nico Kostas, who had probably tried to kill her and was now nowhere to be found.

I removed her hands from my arm and stood, walking away from the couch this time. She wouldn't be able to get up and follow me, at least not quickly.

"I'm sorry. You're Jade's mother, and it would be wrong for me to take advantage."

Her blue eyes were heavy-lidded. "I'm giving you the advantage."

Clearly, she was. And if I weren't in love with Melanie, I might've given it a thought. But only a thought. She was Jade's mother first, and she also wasn't a very good person from what I knew.

"It wouldn't be right. Can I get you anything before I go?"

She shook her head. "You know what I want from you."

"Please tell Talon I stopped by. I'll call him later." I walked as swiftly as I could without running to the door.

★ ★ ★

Melanie clutched at my hand as we got off the elevator on the fourth floor of her building. Her neighbor, Lisa, who I'd met a few days earlier, was just coming out of her door with a small dog on a leash. She lit up when she saw me.

"Why hello there," she said.

"Hello," Melanie replied.

"Melanie, what's going on? The police have been around." Lisa arched her brows. "And here they are again."

Melanie bit her lip as a uniformed officer stepped off the elevator.

"I'm afraid that's...classified at the moment," I said to Lisa. I hurriedly ushered Melanie to her loft, the officer following us.

The door was still roped off with police tape. The policeman unlocked it, and we walked into the loft.

"I'm Officer Loring," the man said. "Look around. If you need to take anything with you, check with me first."

Everything was the same. It was in shambles, most likely made to look like a failed robbery.

"I know this is hard for you," I said, "but you have to figure out if anything is missing. Your insurance guy is going to need to know your losses."

"I know. I hardly looked at anything when we were here before. I just threw some clothes into my duffel as fast as I could. You're right. I have to do this."

"Do you have anything that's worth a lot? Sterling silverware maybe, or some jewelry?"

She shook her head. "Nothing like that. I have a few pieces of gold jewelry, but they're nothing."

"Let's make sure nothing is missing."

I followed Melanie into her bedroom. It wasn't in as bad of shape as the living area, although a few of her dresser drawers had been upended. She found her jewelry box and confirmed that nothing was gone.

"I guess this will be easy," she said. "The only thing insurance needs to worry about is replacing the ruined furniture and the door lock. At least nothing was stolen."

Except Melanie's sense of security. But I didn't voice those words. She was doing well, better than I could've expected. She'd roamed around town today alone, and now she was walking around her loft. I could tell she was frightened, the way she held on to my hand, the way she incessantly gnawed on her lower lip. But she was doing it, and I was so proud of her. Melanie Carmichael was the strongest woman I'd ever met.

The insurance adjuster arrived, and I stayed by Melanie's side as she answered his questions and he, along with the officer, looked around the apartment, making notes and taking photos.

When the adjuster finally left, she fell against me.

I kissed the top of her head. "You okay?"

She nodded against my shirt. "Just...exhausted. And I suppose a little overdramatic."

"Is there anything you need? Gather some stuff, and then let's go home."

"Home?"

"Well, my home." But that wasn't what I'd meant when I said home. I had meant *our* home. Melanie's and mine. How I wished that could be. But once she was strong enough, I would have to tell her the truth.

"All right." She unclamped herself from me and walked about the apartment, gathering things.

She went into her bedroom for a few moments, and I sat down on what was left of the couch. Her book was on the floor. I picked it up and gasped. The word "bitch" had been scrawled on the front cover in black permanent marker. Melanie didn't need to see this. I shoved the book under a cushion. The officer, seated in a chair across from me, eyed me.

I quickly put the book back, hoping Melanie wouldn't notice it.

"Jonah!"

I jerked upward, running into her bedroom. "Melanie? What's wrong?"

I found her in her walk-in closet, sitting on the floor, holding a towel and shoe.

"This is the towel I was wearing when... And the shoe I tried to..."

I pulled her up and took the items from her. "We'll throw them away. Or we'll burn them if you want. Anything to cleanse this place of his evil."

She chuckled nervously at that. "Now who's being overdramatic?"

"I'll take them to the dumpster downstairs. We don't need to burn them. Will you be okay here for a few minutes?"

"Sorry," Officer Loring said. "Those are evidence. They need to stay here."

Melanie nodded. "Of course. I understand. I'll be fine. I didn't want to go in the closet, but most of my clothing is here. When we were here before, I just grabbed clothes out of my drawers so I wouldn't have to come in here."

"Look around, Melanie," I said. "No one's here. This is *your* closet. He had no right to be here, but you do."

"I know." She began pulling things off of the rack. "I'm okay now."

"You need help?" the officer asked.

"No. Please, just take the towel and shoe"—she stooped down and grabbed the other of the pair—"*shoes* out of here."

He took them from her and left the bedroom. Why they hadn't been removed before now was a mystery to me.

"You okay?" I asked.

"Yeah. I just need a minute in here. Alone."

I nodded and walked out to join Loring. A few minutes later, my cell phone buzzed in my back pocket. A text from a number I didn't recognize.

I read the words, and then read them again.

I will have you.

CHAPTER TWENTY

Melanie

I was pacing around my bedroom when Jonah returned.

"Everything okay?" he asked.

"I'm okay. It's just... I don't think I can live here anymore, you know? Even if I did live here, I'd have to get all new stuff. But I really don't feel safe here."

I stopped before clamping my hand to my mouth. I hoped he didn't think I was inviting myself to stay at his home indefinitely.

"You don't have to decide that right now. Who knows when the police will release the area, and it will take a few weeks for your insurance company to settle your loss anyway. But you do need to take some time to pick out all the stuff you want."

"I don't know if I have it in me to do that today." I wasn't lying. Just being in the loft made my skin crawl, and seeing the towel and shoe had almost sent me into hysteria. I was having symptoms of post-traumatic stress disorder, perfectly normal in my case. I did need to get out of here.

"That's fine. Just find anything of value to take today, to keep it safe."

I had very little of any value. I kept all my important documents in a safe deposit box at my bank, along with some jewelry from my grandmother. The few pieces of gold jewelry I kept here weren't worth much. Pretty much everything I had was replaceable. That didn't say very much for my life up to this point. Forty years, and what did I have to show for my life? No husband, no children, though I'd never thought I had it in me to be a mother. Sure, I'd helped some people but not all of them. One was haunting me still.

I covered my eyes with my hands.

"Melanie?" Jonah's hands were warm on my shoulder.

"I'm all right," I choked out, opening my eyes. "Give me about five minutes to gather up what I need."

Jonah nodded. "Just tell me what you need. I'll take it all down to the truck."

I eyed my file cabinet in the corner of my bedroom. Gina's file was in there, as well as encrypted on my computer and on the cloud. I turned to Jonah. "Just that," I said, gesturing. "I'll grab what clothes I want. Everything else can stay. I'll follow you to your place in my car. That way, I'll have it with me."

I had some money saved up. I needed a change. I'd buy some new clothes. Some new furniture. And once this loft got back in shape after I got the insurance payment, it was going on the market. Would anyone buy a loft where a woman had been abducted?

Just what I didn't need. Another loss.

★ ★ ★

When we returned to the ranch, Jonah carried the file cabinet into my bedroom as well as a couple of suitcases I'd filled with clothes and other things I wanted, which wasn't much. It was nearing dinnertime, but I wasn't very hungry, so I decided to go to bed.

He promised not to leave the house.

I washed up in my private bathroom and then found some sweats—clean this time—and put them on. I climbed into bed, wishing for Jonah or even Lucy and her warmth against me. But I had to be strong to get through this. I was safe in the house. I had watched Jonah lock the doors.

I lay in bed for a few minutes, my heart beating in my ears. *Thump. Thump. Thump.*

It grew louder.

Thump. Thump. Thump.

★ ★ ★

"I could feel his heartbeat," Gina said. "I could feel his heartbeat thumping as he held me."

"And how did that make you feel?" I asked.

"Warm, at first. Secure in someone's arms."

"What else do you remember?"

"I remember the...hardness in his lap. I didn't know what it was, and I didn't want to be rude and ask. I didn't want to anger him because I needed the closeness, and I didn't want it to go away."

"I understand."

"Do you?"

"Yes."

"Is it true that some victims of childhood abuse don't remember the abuse?"

"In some cases."

She sighed and closed her eyes. "I think they are the lucky ones."

I could not fault her observation, but I did have a response. "Whether you think so now or not, Gina, it is better that you remember. Blocking out painful memories comes with its own problems."

"What kind of problems? It seems to me that ignorance would be bliss."

"That's the problem. Ignorance is not bliss. Perhaps a victim doesn't consciously remember these things, but they are still inside, and they can manifest a thousand different ways, sometimes as personality disorders, sometimes other mental illnesses. Sometimes the victim goes on to abuse another. In the worst cases, the victim might take his own life."

She shook her head. "I can't imagine that. I would never do such a thing. He's not worth dying for."

"I know you won't, and I'm very glad of that. But believe me, it's better that you remember. Even if it's painful. Then you can get through it. People have gotten through worse."

"I can't imagine that anyone ever had any worse," she said.

"They have, but that's not what you need to focus on. You need to focus on you. Your life. You're here now, getting the help you need. It's a rocky road, I know. But I'm here with you every step of the way."

"I have trouble sleeping. For a long time, I didn't. For a long time, I tried to just convince myself I was okay. Sometimes I was successful, others not as much. But now... It all seems so real, and I can't escape it at night."

"I can prescribe medication to help you sleep. Everything is easier to deal with when you're well rested."

"I...don't like the idea of medication."

"Sleep aids on the market today are nonaddictive," I assured her. "Think of your inability to sleep as a symptom that

needs to be relieved. If you have a headache, you take aspirin or ibuprofen, right?"

She nodded.

"So why not take something to relieve the symptom of insomnia?"

"I'll think about it," she said. "I don't want to be scared. I don't need to be scared anymore. My uncle's dead."

"I'm sure that's a comfort to you. How did he die?"

"I don't know. My parents just told me he was dead."

"They didn't tell you how? Was he ill? In an accident?"

"They just said he was dead."

"Gina, would it be okay if I talked to your parents?"

"Why would you do that?" She visibly tensed.

"I certainly won't, if you don't want me to. But sometimes it helps me get a feel for the situation, to understand why this happened, why they allowed it to happen."

"Because they didn't care. They were never home. They left me with him."

"Did you tell them?"

She shook her head. "Part of me wanted to. Part of me..."

"Did your uncle threaten you? Did he say he would hurt you if you told anyone?"

"No. He was already hurting me. He did say that this was a secret between us, that I was special to him, and that it was special to have a secret like ours."

I nodded. She was a classic case. She longed for attention and affection, and when she couldn't get it from the people she wanted it from, her parents, she took it from wherever she could. The attention from her uncle, though painful, was at least attention.

"So you didn't tell your parents. Can you tell me why?"

"Like I said, part of me wanted to, but...part of me liked having a secret from them. Part of me... Oh my God, was this all my fault? Could I have stopped it if I had told them?"

I stood and walked over to her so she could feel my closeness. I gently touched her on the forearm. "No, no, never think that. None of this is your fault. But it was attention, even if it was unwanted attention. And I understand what you mean. You were a young child, and this was something that was yours."

"Yes. That's exactly it. Oh my God, was there a part of me that actually wanted it?"

"Maybe," I said. "But not the sexual part. The close part. The being important to someone part."

She swallowed visibly, nodding.

"At least he's dead, and you're safe now."

"It's funny. I know he's dead, but I get phone calls sometimes. Someone calls and hangs up. On my caller ID, it just says 'number not available.'"

My hackles rose. "Gina, I need you to do something for me."

"What?"

"I want you to ask your parents how your uncle died."

"I don't want to talk to my parents about this. They never really took me seriously."

"I understand. But it's important that we know what happened to your uncle."

"Do you think there's a possibility that he's not dead?"

I shook my head, knowing full well I was lying. "I doubt that's a possibility. But the more knowledge you have, the more you can be certain inside."

"All right. I'll ask them."

★ ★ ★

I shot straight up in bed.

At our next session, I'd asked Gina what her parents had said. She told me she had forgotten to ask about how her uncle had died. When she had forgotten again at the next session, I stopped asking.

Why had she not been able to ask her parents? And why wouldn't her parents have told her how he had died?

Maybe because it had never happened.

Gina's uncle, whoever he was, was *alive*.

Why hadn't this possibility occurred to me before now?

I got up and turned on my light. I went to my file cabinet, unlocked it, and shuffled through the files until I found hers. I pulled out the suicide letter she'd written me.

He's not worth dying for.

Words alone weren't proof positive that a patient wasn't suicidal, but they were a damned good indicator. What if Gina *hadn't* written this note? What if someone had locked her in a garage with a running car, just as the masked man had done to me?

I was a good therapist, goddamnit. Some of my patients had been suicidal in the past, and I had always known. I had referred them for hospitalization in most cases. So how could I have missed that Gina was suicidal?

Perhaps because she *wasn't*.

And had she truly been in love with me? I'd had patients fall for me before. It was a common phenomenon, and I'd always recognized it and taken care of it before it went too far. Perhaps I hadn't noticed it with Gina because I hadn't expected a woman to fall in love with me.

Or...perhaps I hadn't noticed it with Gina because *it wasn't true.*

Was it possible that the letter was a forgery?

And why a letter? Why hadn't she e-mailed me? Nearly no one sent letters through the mail anymore...

An e-mail would be traceable. But an old-fashioned letter...

The hair on the back of my neck stood up. I shuffled through the file again, looking for something, anything, with Gina's handwriting on it. She had never sent me a check. Her therapy had been covered by her insurance.

Where could I find her handwriting?

I glanced at the letter again. Some words were blurred, and I honestly didn't know if the wetness had come from my tears or Gina's. The writing was shaky, though I hadn't thought anything about that at the time.

But now, looking at the penmanship, I could see that she'd been trembling. Anyone about to commit suicide could have been trembling. But something else might have made her tremble as she wrote.

Fear.

CHAPTER TWENTY-ONE

Jonah

I will have you.

I read the text again.

I had run the phone number through a simple search and come up empty-handed.

Clearly, the text had come from Brooke Bailey. The area code was from Iowa, where her fiancé, Nico Kostas, had told her he was an Iowa senator, although there was no record of him in either the United States Senate or the Iowa Senate.

Had Brooke been living in Iowa?

I decided to ignore the text. She was simply a needy woman, a model past her prime, who had stared death in the face and made it through. On top of that, her so-called fiancé had bailed on her and had probably tried to have her killed, although she didn't know the latter, and unfortunately we couldn't prove it anyway.

My stomach growled. It was getting close to dinnertime, but I didn't want to wake Melanie. God knew she needed her rest. I shuffled into the kitchen and took a look in the cupboards. Melanie had laid in quite a few staples. I opened the refrigerator and took out an apple, biting into the crisp fruit. That would hold me over until I figured out what I was doing for dinner.

My phone buzzed again in my pocket. This time it was a text from Talon.

Marj came home from cooking class with a vat of spaghetti and meatballs. Come help us eat it. Ryan is coming over with a couple bottles of wine.

My stomach growled again. Spaghetti and meatballs sounded great, but I didn't really want to run into Brooke again. Still, having my meal made for me would be a godsend. I would just have to wake up Melanie and tell her we were going.

I hadn't yet told Talon what had happened to Melanie. I couldn't leave her home alone. I'd have to wake her up and tell her we were going to Talon's for dinner. She might not want to.

I texted Talon that I'd have to pass.

Are you sure? We need to discuss what to do about Felicia. I asked her to come over tomorrow morning for a talk with us.

Crap. My brother needed me, but so did Melanie. I had failed them both.

I sighed. It wouldn't hurt to try. Maybe Melanie was hankering for spaghetti and meatballs, and she would want to go.

When I walked up to her door, I heard footsteps. Good, she was already awake. I knocked gently.

"Is that you, Jonah?"

"Yeah."

"Come on in."

I walked in, and she was taking a file out of her cabinet. She sat down on the floor and opened it.

"What are you doing?"

"I'm just looking through some files."

"Is everything okay?"

"Yes. I have this strange feeling..."

"What is it?"

She looked at me, her green eyes glimmering. "What if Gina *didn't* commit suicide? What if she was tied up, pushed into a garage, and left to die—like I was?"

The skin on the back of my neck began to burn. "Did you remember something?"

"She always told me the uncle who raped her was dead, but she could never tell me how he had died. I told her to ask her parents, but every time I asked her what they said, she said she had forgotten to ask."

"I suppose it's possible she just didn't want to talk about her uncle to her parents."

"Yes, that is definitely possible." She bit her lip. "But Jonah, I know a lot about suicide. I'm writing a book about preventing suicide in teens. If someone was suicidal, I'd see the signs. I didn't see them in Gina."

Melanie was grasping at straws, clearly. Trying to convince herself. I didn't know what to say to her.

"You don't believe me, do you?"

"We can look into it," I said. "I'll pay for the best investigators if you want."

"Oh, no, I'm not after your money."

I chuckled. "I know you're not after my money, sweetheart. But I have money in abundance, and I want to help you through this. Right now, though, I'm starving. How about you?"

A smile pulled at her lips. "You know, for the first time in days, I am actually famished. Not just hungry, but I want to eat something good."

That was an excellent sign. "It's your lucky day then. We're invited to Talon's house. Marj brought home a ton of spaghetti and meatballs for all of us."

Her smile fell. "I don't know..."

"Melanie, I haven't told Talon or anyone else what happened to you. We don't have to talk about that. They already know there's something between us. It could be that you're just visiting me today, and I invited you along."

"Will they mind?"

"You saved my brother's life. No one will mind. We would all happily buy your meals for the rest of your life." I smiled, giving her my hand.

She took it, and I pulled her up so she was standing next to me.

"Text them first, and make sure they don't mind."

"That's not necessary, but I will. In the meantime, do you want to change into some jeans or something?"

She nodded. I left the room and texted Talon quickly, and of course he was thrilled to have Melanie come along. In ten minutes, she came out in a pair of jeans, ankle boots, and a pullover top that accentuated her breasts beautifully. Her lips were painted a soft burgundy.

She looked fresh and beautiful. I wanted to grab her and kiss her senseless, but if I did that, we might never get out of here. As much as I wanted her, I couldn't let Talon down.

I did give her a quick kiss on her burgundy lips. "You look beautiful," I whispered in her ear.

She clamped up against me, wrapping her arms around my neck. "Can't we just stay here?"

"You know as well as I do that you can't stay in a hole forever. I will be with you. You know my brother would take a bullet for you, and so would I. We will be perfectly safe in his house."

She relented, and soon we were on our way. As we got into

the car, my phone buzzed again.

Another text from the unknown number.

CHAPTER TWENTY-TWO

Melanie

Something was bothering Jonah. He was a little tense, though not nearly as tense as he'd been the previous night with Bryce. I had never been to Talon's home. As large as Jonah's house was, the main house seemed twice as big.

My skin warmed as we walked through the foyer, past the grand living room, and into the gourmet kitchen—again, twice as big as Jonah's, which was bigger than I'd ever seen. The last time I'd seen Talon and Jade I'd been naked, sitting on the side of Jonah's pool. That had been the day I sneaked out of Jonah's house, explored downtown Snow Creek, and then traveled home, only to be...

Everything seemed to come back to that. But I had a new lease on life at the moment, something new to explore in Gina's alleged suicide. Perhaps she had been the victim of the same type of kidnapping that I had been.

And...had I not been a victim myself, would I have even thought to explore the issue further? Most likely not. I hoped I wasn't exploring in vain.

"Looks like they're out on the deck," Jonah said.

I took in a deep breath and followed him outside. I hadn't bothered to put my boot back on, and I limped a little, but my ankle was quite a bit better.

Jade and Talon I recognized, and two of the others weren't difficult to pick out. The tall woman with long dark hair was a feminine version of her three brothers, and the other man was...*wow*. Talon had once told me that Ryan was considered the best-looking and most jovial of all three Steel brothers. He was indeed gorgeous—perfect features, perfect hair, perfect searing brown eyes. And he did have a smile on his face. But I looked toward Jonah. Nothing could compare with his rugged darkness.

Talon smiled as we walked out. "Hey, Joe. Hey, Doc."

Jonah grabbed my hand. "Melanie, you know Jade and Talon. This is Marjorie, and this is Ryan." He pointed out his brother and sister, and then he gestured to an older woman sitting at the end of the table, her legs boosted up on another chair. "And this is Jade's mother, Brooke Bailey."

Marjorie came up to me first, holding out her hand. "It's so nice to finally meet you. I can't thank you enough for... everything."

I attempted a smile. "Nice to meet you as well."

Then Ryan came forward. "So you're this amazing doctor I've heard so much about." He took my hand. "So great to meet you."

"You too." Then words failed me. I didn't really know what to say.

"I hope you'll pardon me if I don't get up," Brooke Bailey said.

"Oh, of course not." I walked over and shook her hand. "I hope you're feeling well."

"I take it one day at a time, dear."

Her use of the word "dear" took me aback. I knew from talking to Jonah that she was only three years older than I was.

Marjorie took charge. "Sit down, everyone. We've been doing Italian in cooking class for the past couple weeks. Tonight was good old-fashioned spaghetti and meatballs. For some reason, no one could stick around to eat tonight, so I got to take everything home. We have enough to feed a small army."

"And I brought my Italian blend. A perfect mélange of Sangiovese, Syrah, and Merlot," Ryan said, bowing.

"You're a goofball," Marjorie told him and then turned to me. "His wine is awesome. Just pardon his humility."

I laughed. "It smells wonderful. Thank you so much for inviting me." And then I felt kind of stupid, because I hadn't actually been invited. They had invited Jonah, and he had told them I was coming along.

But Marjorie touched my forearm. "No problem at all. We should be thanking you for everything you've done for our family."

I was no doubt crimson by now, but there was nothing I could do about it.

Ryan picked up a bottle of wine. "Do you like wine, Doc?"

I attempted another smile. "I do."

"Yeah." Jonah grinned at me. "She's a red wine aficionado."

"I don't know about aficionado, but I do like a nice red wine."

"You'll love this, then," Talon said. "Ryan's a genius."

"Aw, shucks, Tal." Ryan let out a boisterous laugh. "You'll make me blush."

"As if anything could make you blush," Talon said.

Then everyone laughed as Ryan filled the two empty glasses at the table and invited Jonah and me to sit down.

I inhaled. "It smells wonderful."

Stupid again. I'd already said that.

Marjorie started to sit down but then popped back up. "Silly me. The garlic bread is still in the oven. Excuse me for a minute."

"And I whipped up a salad," Jade said. "One of the few things I'm capable of. It's in the fridge, so please excuse me."

Marjorie and Jade returned with the bread and salad, and the family began passing items around the table. I took modest amounts, even though I was starving for the first time in days. I didn't want to appear too...what? When the garlic bread came around, I took two big slices.

The food was delicious, and I didn't talk much, but I didn't need to. The family was happy and jovial, talking a lot among themselves. A few times a question was directed at me, and I answered succinctly. Jonah took part in the family conversation, though he still seemed a little rigid. I wasn't sure why.

After we finished dinner, Jade helped Brooke up from the table and came back about fifteen minutes later.

"My mother sends her apologies," she said. "She needs to lie down now and rest."

"That's perfectly understandable," I said. "It was so nice to meet her."

Jonah placed his hand over mine, in full view of everyone still seated at the table. His hand was warm and felt nice, gave me comfort. And he seemed visibly less tense. Maybe the glass of wine had done him good.

"Now that Brooke is going to bed, I need to talk to all of you," Talon said. "About Felicia."

I felt conspicuous. What was he talking about?

Jonah squeezed my hand as if to offer me reassurance. "I

haven't told Melanie a lot of what's going on."

"I can certainly leave if it will make everyone more comfortable," I said. It would certainly make me more comfortable.

"Of course not, Doc. I would've told you all of this by now anyway if we were having sessions."

I warmed. We weren't having sessions because I had been required to take a three-week leave of absence. Gina Cates's parents had filed a complaint against me with the medical board. If her parents were behind the attack on me, their complaint would have no bearing. However, I would first have to prove they were behind it, and I wasn't sure I would be able to. Only Jonah and the police knew what had happened at this point, and tonight was not the time to divulge the information. Talon clearly had something else on his mind.

Talon continued, "Felicia is our housekeeper, as you know. Has Jonah told you about the business card belonging to Jade's ex-fiancé that we found lodged underneath the carpet in her bedroom?"

I nodded.

"There are three sets of fingerprints on it. We identified one set as Larry Wade's. Jade matched them against the attorney database. One set we have yet to identify, although we are assuming they belong to Colin himself. The third set belongs to our housekeeper, Felicia Diaz."

"And Felicia is the nicest person in the world," Jade piped in.

"Yes," Marj agreed. "None of us for a minute think she could be behind any of this."

"How did you get her fingerprints?" I asked.

"We all had our fingerprints taken after the card was

found," Talon said. "We wanted to make sure that we could rule out anyone in the house."

"I see," I said.

"Anyway," Talon said, "She's coming here to talk to us tomorrow morning at ten. Joe, I really need you to be here."

"Of course I will," Jonah said.

"And Doc, feel free to join us as well."

I shook my head. "I've never met Felicia, and I'm sure it would be more comfortable for her if she didn't have a strange person there."

"Come anyway," Jade said. "You can keep my mother company. She'd love that."

I wasn't sure I wanted to spend the morning making chitchat with the former supermodel, but it would save me from being alone in Jonah's house. "Maybe I will. I'm sure your mother is a lovely woman."

I wasn't speaking the truth, of course. I had heard the stories about how Brooke had abandoned Jade for her modeling career.

"Anyway, we need to talk about how to handle this," Talon said. "Felicia's been with us for a long time."

"Yeah," Jade said, "and she didn't seem to get upset when you asked her to have her fingerprints taken."

"True," Talon said, "but the only reason I gave her was that I was installing the new security system that would be fingerprint identified."

"I see," Jonah said. "So she had no idea why we were really asking."

"No," Talon said.

"I think we should just be upfront with her," Ryan said. "None of us really think she could've had anything to do with this."

"But then how did her fingerprints get on the card?" Jonah asked.

"We're all kind of stumped about that," Marjorie said.

"Are you sure we should all be here, Tal?" Ryan asked. "She might feel like we're ganging up on her."

Talon rubbed his forehead. "I don't know. Maybe you have a point."

"I can definitely sit this one out," Jade said. "I haven't known Felicia for as long as the rest of you. I think the four of you siblings can handle things without me."

"I don't know," Marjorie said. "Ryan may be right. Maybe just you, Talon."

"No, I need some backup." He looked to Jonah. "I need my big brother."

Jonah nodded. He would do anything for Talon. The guilt that he carried ensured that. But even if he didn't carry so much guilt, I was sure he would do anything his brother needed. That was the kind of man he was.

"All right. I'll be here," Jonah said. "And there's one thing you haven't mentioned."

"What's that?" Talon asked.

"We'll need her to get a DNA test. If her fingerprints are on the card, that blood sample might be hers as well."

"He's right, Tal," Ryan said.

"Jesus." Talon rubbed the back of his neck. "How the hell am I supposed to ask for her blood on top of everything else?"

"We'll just do it," Jonah said. "We'll tell her it's necessary."

I gazed at the man I loved. My God, his strength humbled me. He had everything under control, and he'd take care of it. All that guilt that ate him up inside hadn't changed his core.

He was more than robust and able-bodied. More than strong, both physically and mentally. Jonah Steel was potent. Powerful. *Dominant.*

"It will work out," he was saying. "I'll be here, and I'll bring Melanie to babysit Brooke." He smiled.

"Actually, if Jade and Marjorie are going to be here, you probably don't need me to come and spend time with Brooke."

"Oh, no, feel free to come," Jade said. "We'd like to have you."

"In fact, I think I'll make myself scarce," Marjorie said. "This whole thing is just so...surreal. I can't imagine that Felicia is involved."

"You and I have been talking about taking a hike," Jade said. "Why don't we do it tomorrow morning?"

That was that. I would be babysitting Brooke Bailey tomorrow morning.

Jonah squeezed my hand. For some strange reason, I got the feeling he was trying to tell me something.

CHAPTER TWENTY-THREE

Jonah

The thought of Melanie spending time with Brooke Bailey didn't sit well with me, but I couldn't do anything about it at the moment. I could hardly tell Jade her mother had come on to me, or that I was pretty sure she was stalking me via my phone. All I could do was give Melanie's hand a squeeze, let her know I was there.

Jade and Talon cleared the dishes, while Marj brought out a decadent flourless chocolate torte garnished with fresh fig cream cheese for dessert.

"I made this three days ago," she said. "It contains brandy, and letting it sit in the fridge for a few days really softens the flavors."

It was of course delicious, as was everything Marj ever made. I had two servings and a cup of coffee. Finally, I stood. "We should get going."

Melanie followed my lead, standing as well. "I can't thank you enough for including me tonight. Everything was delicious."

Marj walked to her and gave her a hug. Melanie looked a little uncomfortable but returned the affection.

"It is so great to meet you. I hope to see a lot more of you out here."

"Yes, please come around more often." Jade rose and also hugged Melanie.

"Thank you," Melanie said, biting her lip.

I was burning for Melanie. I wanted to get her back to my house and fuck her senseless. But I knew I needed to go slowly, just as I had before.

Still, just to see her naked, in my bed—that would help ease my desire.

Or make it burn stronger.

Most likely the latter.

We left the house.

I drove home quickly.

★ ★ ★

Lucy ran to greet us when we got home. Melanie looked tired, and I imagined she was. It had been a tough day for her. I knew I had to leave her alone. Let her go to bed and rest, despite the hard-on raging beneath my jeans.

She knelt down and gave Lucy a pet and a hug, and then she stood and let out a big yawn.

Yeah, I needed to leave her alone.

"Is there anything you need?" I asked.

She smiled, and though her eyes were tired, the green sparkled with gold flecks. "Only you."

My pulse started beating rapidly, and my groin tightened even further.

She put her arms around my neck and looked into my eyes. "I feel better today than I have in a while, Jonah, and I'm not just talking about after being kidnapped. I mean I feel better than... I don't know. Better than I have since Gina died."

I smiled down at her. She'd used the words "since Gina died," not "since Gina committed suicide." I wanted to believe in her new theory, but I also feared she was seeing things that might not be there, hoping that perhaps Gina hadn't killed herself and that she, Melanie, hadn't missed the signs.

"I'm glad you're feeling better, but—"

She touched her fingers to my cheek. "I know what you're going to say. But I don't want to hear it right now, Jonah. I just want to bask in the fact that I'm feeling better. I'm looking at this whole situation from a different angle. I may be wrong, and I'll deal with that if it turns out to be the case. But right now, let me feel good."

"I want you to feel good. Can I help you with anything?"

She smiled again. "You can take me to your bed."

No sweeter words... I picked her up in my arms and carried her like a child, not to her guest room, but to my bedroom. Yes, she did need her rest, but I was not strong enough to deny her when she was asking for me.

When we reached my bedroom, I walked through my small sitting area straight to my king-size bed. We had made love in this bed the day she had been taken. Again, unease crept up my spine. Was she ready for this?

But again, she was asking for it. For me. She would tell me to stop if it got to be too much. I would be gentle with her, as I had been, no matter what my libido wanted.

She wasn't ready to experience me fully. But one day...

I had once believed she would succumb to my darkness.

What if she never could? Could I spend my life without giving in to my most base desires in the arms of the woman I loved?

And I did love her. I hadn't yet said the words, even

though she had said them to me. I was afraid. Afraid to divulge my full feelings and let myself become vulnerable...because eventually, when I told her the truth, she would leave me.

But would she?

Maybe she wouldn't. Maybe she would understand.

Whatever the eventual outcome, I didn't need to think about it tonight. Tonight she needed me, wanted me. I would not disappoint her.

I set her gently on the bed. "You show me what you want tonight, Melanie. I want to go at your pace. I want to give you what you need."

She smiled once more and touched my cheek, fingering my stubble. "I just want you. I want to feel you. I want to be with the man I love."

Her words lit a fire within me. I could hold back my deeper carnal desires, but I could no longer hold back my feelings. I took her hand from my cheek and pressed my lips against her palm.

"I love you too, Melanie. My God, I love you so much."

Her smiling lips trembled, and her eyes became glassy, with tears emerging in the corners. "You don't know how happy it makes me to hear you say those words."

I looked deep into her green eyes. "I hope you know that they're not just words to me. I don't say them lightly, and I'm not saying them just because you said them to me."

She bit her lip. She was adorable.

"I know that. You would never say anything you didn't mean. And I love you too. With all my heart."

"My God..." I crushed my lips against hers, lifting her forward and laying her flat on her back. I covered her with my body, kissing her, swirling my tongue with hers, my breath becoming rapid. My dick was hard, and I pressed against her thigh, wanting so much to grind into her.

But I would go slowly.

Every deep dark part of my soul raged within me, ordered me to tear every shred of clothing off of her, to tie her beautiful hands to my bed posts, blindfold her, spank her beautiful ass until it was bright pink and she was begging for me to fuck her senseless.

How I wanted her. I wanted to show her the pleasures my darkness could give her.

But not today.

When I ripped my mouth from hers to take in a gasping breath, she grabbed both of my cheeks and pierced me with her green-eyed gaze.

"Tell me what you want tonight, Jonah. Anything, and it's yours."

I groaned, and my cock grew even larger. "You have no idea what you're asking for."

"But I do. I know there's a shadow surrounding you, a dark side that wants to come out when we're together. You once told me that I would surrender to you eventually."

"I meant that when I said it, but the situation is different now."

"Why is it different? Because of what I've been through? Trust me when I say this to you again. I am truly feeling better now than I ever have since Gina's death."

I believed her. I did. But I still didn't think she was ready to experience everything I wanted. In fact, I knew she wasn't. But I could start. I could initiate her slowly. "All right," I said. "Get up off the bed. Strip for me, Melanie. Take off your clothes for me and present your body to me."

She smiled. And then she got up. "Will you strip for me after I'm done?" she asked quietly.

Clearly she didn't understand who was the master in the bedroom. But she would learn. And if it would please her today, I would strip for her. "We'll see," was all I said.

She fumbled a bit, pulling her shirt over her head, trying to be sexy. She was sexy, always, no matter what she did.

When she unclasped her bra and let her breasts fall free, she bit her lip. "I wish they were bigger."

I stood, my hard cock pulsing against my jeans. I went to her and cupped her perfect tits in my palms. "I don't ever want to hear you say that again. Your breasts are perfect. Your body is perfect. I love every inch of it. You are beautiful. So fucking beautiful."

She closed her eyes and let out a tiny choke. Then she opened them. "No one has ever made me feel as beautiful as you do."

"We haven't talked a lot about our past relationships, and we don't need to start now," I said. "Suffice it to say, whomever you were with didn't deserve you."

"I love you, Jonah."

"And I love you." I kissed her cheek, and then I sat back down on the bed. "But you still need to strip for me."

She bent down, unzipped her ankle boots, and kicked them off. "I wish I knew how to be sexy for you."

"All I want is you, sweetheart. Just strip for me. Show me that you're mine."

She unzipped her jeans and shimmied out of them until she stood before me only in her ankle socks and beige cotton panties.

I pulled her toward me then, sticking my face in her

covered vulva and inhaling. "I can smell your scent, Melanie. You're wet. I can smell that you want me."

"Oh my God."

"You want to please me? Stop wearing cotton panties. I want to see that beautiful ass and beautiful pussy in silk and lace. In a thong riding up those ass cheeks."

"Oh my God," she said again.

I inhaled once more. She was ripe. So ripe for me. I couldn't help myself. I twisted those panties and ripped them right off of her.

She gasped.

I slid my tongue between her legs, tasting a drop of her sweetness. I savored her, every ounce of her. She was everything to me. I had never known a feeling like this. She couldn't leave me. She just couldn't. I would not allow it. I wouldn't survive.

I forced the thoughts from my mind and slid my tongue through her slick folds once more. "Your pussy tastes so good, baby. Do you have any idea what you do to me?"

She sighed, the melodic sounds drifting to my ears.

"Tell me, baby. Tell me you know what you do to me. Tell me you know how I hunger for you."

Another sigh. Then, "I know. I know what I do to you."

I nipped at her clit, and she jerked against me.

"You like that, sweetheart?" I asked.

"Yes. God, yes."

I had to taste more of her, every crevice of her.

I grabbed her hips and turned her around, laying her on the bed. I disposed of her socks quickly and spread her thighs, diving in. I sucked at her, ate at her, drinking every ounce of sweet cream out of her beautiful pussy. And then I flipped her over.

"You have a beautiful ass, sweetheart. So gorgeous." I caressed her soft globes, longing to give her just a little smack, to make her ass the slightest shade of pink. I held myself in check. I would bring her in slowly. I slid my fingers through her slick folds, and then upward, over her puckered hole. This would probably be new to her, and it might be a good way to start. It wouldn't involve bondage or spanking.

I nudged her pink opening. She gasped, but didn't tell me to stop.

"Such a pretty little asshole, baby. I'm going to lick you here now, okay?"

She nodded.

I stuck my nose between her gorgeous cheeks, giving her pussy a slick lick, all the way up over her tight little hole. My cock was straining against my jeans. I was tempted to stop and undress, but not yet. Right now I was going to give her the rimming of her life, most likely her first. And it would be one she would never forget.

"Has anyone ever licked your ass before, baby?"

"No," she whimpered.

"That's because it's mine—your virgin ass." My lips and tongue burned with the first touch. With one hand, I unbuckled, unsnapped, and unzipped my jeans, freeing my aching cock. Then I spread her cheeks farther apart and sucked on her cute little hole.

She mewled into the comforter, her hips undulating.

Yes, she liked it.

When I thrust two fingers into her wet pussy, she bucked beneath me, moaning.

"Oh my God, Jonah! Oh my God!"

I massaged her G-spot as I continued to lick her sweet

ass. When she clamped down on my fingers, I knew she was about to climax.

"I'm coming! Jonah. I'm coming."

This time I didn't hold back. I gave one cheek of her butt a light smack. "That's right, baby. Come. Come for me."

When I saw the rosy flush on her ass, my cock pulsated. I was damned near a climax, and I hadn't even touched myself.

I continued probing her asshole, finger-fucking her pussy as I milked the last drops of her orgasm from her. Then I took some of her wetness, slid it upward, over her hole.

"I want to put my finger in your ass, sweetheart."

She trembled a bit.

"Okay? May I?"

"I... Yes... God..."

I got her asshole good and lubed up with my saliva and her wetness and then slowly breached the tight ring of muscle.

A swift intake of breath.

"It will be good. Just relax."

When her trembling stopped, and the muscles around my finger relaxed, I thrust in farther.

She let out a soft sigh.

"You're so hot, Melanie. God, I want to fuck you right here. One day. One day I will."

She tensed for a few seconds.

I pushed two fingers back into the wet heat of her pussy. "I'm going to make you come now, with my fingers in your pussy and your ass. I want you to scream my name when you come, Melanie. I want you to fucking scream my name."

She whimpered.

"Do you understand? You understand that you're going to scream my name?"

"Yes. Yes, I understand."

I began fucking her with my fingers both in her pussy and her ass, using reverse rhythmic strokes. Her little ass got red, flushing from the intensity of the heat I was invoking from her body. My hard cock throbbed between my legs. I ached to shove it into her pussy, her ass, her mouth—everywhere. But this was for her. A big step for her. I was going to see that she enjoyed it.

She writhed beneath me, bucking her hips, until I felt the familiar clamping of her muscles on my hand.

"You're going to come now, baby. You're going to come when I tell you to."

"Yes. Want to come..."

"Come. Now," I said through clenched teeth.

She clamped around me, spasming.

"Jonah! Jonah! I'm coming for you!"

"That's it, sweetheart. That's it. Scream my name." I thrust and thrust into both holes, slowing down as the spasms subsided. I itched to bring her to one more climax, but this was her first time with anal play, and I didn't force it.

When I withdrew from her, she flattened on the bed onto her belly and whimpered.

I worried for a moment that I had worn her out. But she turned over, her eyes blazing with green flame.

She spread her legs. "I need you now, inside me. Please, Jonah."

I couldn't help the big grin that split my face. "Since you said please." I thrust inside that burning hot pussy.

"Ahh," I groaned.

She held me tightly in the paradise between her legs. Nothing like it. But still I wanted more, needed to be deeper inside her. I pushed her thighs forward, maneuvering her calves so her ankles were over my shoulders. And I thrust into her—balls deep within that hot pussy.

Already my whole groin was tightening, getting ready to spill. I didn't want to come yet, wanted to hang on, but—

"Baby..." I released into her, pounding her deeply—harder, harder, harder—until the last drop had squeezed from my cock.

Always so much more with Melanie, so much more than the normal release. A deliverance. A pilgrimage to a higher plane. A fucking salvation.

I moved to the side of her so as not to crush her with my body weight.

She didn't move to cuddle with me right away. Had I taken it too far tonight?

But before I could voice my thought, she turned toward me.

"Thank you," she said.

"Thank you? Whatever for?"

"For showing me a little bit of who you are. For not being afraid to let me see that part of you."

I opened my mouth to speak, but she shushed me.

"I'm not naïve, Jonah. I know this is only the beginning. I won't say I'm ready for everything. Thank you. I love you, and I want to know you. This is part of who you are. And for the record, I enjoyed it very much." She smiled.

A warm glow permeated me. I turned and met her gaze. "I love you too, and thank you for letting me share this with you."

I thought about the diamond choker in my top dresser drawer that I had originally intended to offer to her as a collar, to bind her to me as my submissive—at least in the bedroom. And even though I knew she might leave me once I told her the truth about that fateful night when I had neglected to take her phone call, I still wanted her to have it.

It was hers. It had been since the moment I'd seen it in the glass case at the jewelry shop in Grand Junction. No one else would ever be able to wear it.

It was hers. Only hers.

CHAPTER TWENTY-FOUR

Melanie

Without saying anything, Jonah rose from the bed and walked over to his chest of drawers. I couldn't help smiling to myself. He had done things to me tonight that I'd never imagined. Yes, I knew they were only the beginning. Despite my reservations, I had enjoyed myself. I wanted to know him. I wanted to know his deepest most secret parts. And I wanted to please him.

I had seen some of his depth tonight. That thought made me very happy.

He came back, holding a velvet jeweler's case. I gasped.

"I saw this a few weeks ago," he said. "It was made for you. I knew it as soon as I saw it. I love you. I want you to have this."

I trembled as I opened the case. A choker of diamonds set in white gold. Or it could be platinum for all I knew. "Jonah...I can't..."

"You can. And you will."

"But the cost..."

"The money means nothing to me. You know that. You don't owe me anything for this, Melanie. It's a small payment for everything you've done for my family."

"Payment? I've been paid."

He shook his head vehemently. "That came out all wrong. I didn't mean it that way. It's not any kind of payment. I just want you to understand the cost means nothing to me. When I saw this necklace in the window, I knew you had to have it. It was made for you. Here, let me."

He took the box from me and removed the beautiful piece of jewelry. He gently clasped it around my neck. "You look like a Scandinavian princess, Melanie. You're absolutely stunning."

I gently fingered the piece. I couldn't even begin to guess how much it had cost. I had been revolted by a seven-hundred-dollar nightgown. I was no doubt wearing a luxury car around my neck.

"Before you start complaining about the cost, you are worth every penny. You're worth every penny of my fortune. And you're worth even more than that. You're priceless to me, Melanie. I love you. And I don't want to be without you."

I hurled myself into his arms. "I don't want to be without you either, Jonah." And I didn't. Not ever.

I hoped I could be enough for him. That I could satisfy all his desires. Because I would not ask him to change. Not ever. He likely enjoyed things I had never even thought about and couldn't comprehend. But I would please him. And God bless him, he was willing to go slowly with me.

He gently laid me down on the bed. "Please, Melanie. I want to feel you next to me. I want to know that you're mine."

I sighed against his shoulder, snuggling into him. "I'm yours. For as long as you want me."

He went rigid for a moment.

"Is anything wrong?"

"I'll always want you," he said. "Always."

★ ★ ★

Lucy woke us up with tickles and licks Sunday morning. It was early, only a little after six, and Jonah had to check on some things at the ranch. He kissed me on the forehead. "Are you sure you'll be okay?"

I still felt good. Better than I had in so long. I trembled a bit at the thought of staying alone for a couple of hours, but he wouldn't be long. He had to get back and shower, because we needed to be at Talon's house by ten.

"I'll be fine. Just hurry back, okay?"

This time he kissed my lips. "I will." He winked. "And don't shower until I get back."

I chuckled as he left. I lay in bed for a few moments, after urging Lucy to join me. I might have dozed off a bit, but then I got up about an hour later. I put on Jonah's robe, went to the kitchen, and let Lucy out. He had left a pot of coffee on, so I poured myself a cup and then looked around the kitchen until I found the dog food. I made sure Lucy had food and water and then sat down to drink my coffee. I had taken only a few sips when I walked to my guest room.

My folders and papers were still scattered over the floor. I hadn't heard anything from Officer Lee or anyone from the police department in Grand Junction. Had they questioned Dr. Cates? As far as I knew, Erica Cates was still in the hospital. I decided to call the hospital and check. A quick phone call confirmed that she was still an inpatient in the mental health unit.

If my new theory had merit, perhaps Dr. Cates was not behind the attack on me. After all, if Gina did not commit suicide, but instead had been murdered, the same person who murdered her had probably attacked me.

I doubted that Dr. and Mrs. Cates had killed their own daughter. They might have been neglectful parents, but they didn't strike me as murderers. Of course, they still could have been behind the attack on me because they still thought their daughter had committed suicide on my watch.

Again, though, they didn't strike me as murderers. They might hate me, but did they have the ability to kill me?

I didn't think so.

But her uncle? The uncle who was supposedly dead? Granted, just because he was a child molester didn't mean he was capable of murder. But it made it a whole lot more likely.

Dr. Cates had told me that a friend of Gina's—and I couldn't remember the name he used—had told him Gina had been in love. At the time, I'd thought Dr. Cates was referring to Gina being in love with me, but now I wasn't so sure. Just as Gina had given me no indication that she was suicidal or that she had feelings for me, she had also given me no indication that she might be bisexual or gay. Had she been in love with a man? Or had her friend been exaggerating?

I needed to get the name of the friend, and I needed to talk to her.

Dr. and Mrs. Cates would not talk to me. I felt certain of that. So maybe I would take Jonah up on his offer to hire some private investigators to look into this. And maybe one day I would be able to repay him for it. I had gone through life so far without taking anything from anyone, and I didn't plan to start now.

I didn't think about my own parents much. They were a lot like Gina's, truth be told. They had both been professionals and probably should've never had a child. They gave me the necessities of life, and I never wanted for anything...except their love and affection.

Funny that they should pop into my mind right now. I hadn't seen them in nearly ten years, and we rarely communicated. I had put myself through college with scholarships and student loans. My master's in psychotherapy had been fully funded with a teaching assistantship stipend. I had paid my student loans off quickly and then saved up money for a down payment on my loft. My parents could've helped me, but I hadn't wanted their money.

That was one of the reasons why I had wanted to help Gina so badly. I had come from a home like hers, but of course, I had been much luckier than she had been. While the mental abuse and neglect from my parents had taken its toll, at least I was never physically or sexually abused by anyone.

I walked into my bathroom and shut the door, looking in the full-length mirror. I dropped Jonah's robe around my shoulders into a puddle of silk on the floor, and then I forced myself to look at my naked body. My ankle was still bruised but wasn't giving me much trouble as long as I didn't push it, and my hands were still scratched up but were healing nicely. However, those things were not what drew my gaze.

I had never thought of my body as special. It was a normal size six, sometimes an eight. Boobs that were not too small but also not big, a lean build, not very many curves. My eyes were a nice green, but that green eliminated a lot of colors from my wardrobe, including the purple I wanted to wear. My hair was thick and light honey blond. It had some delicate waves and fell right below my shoulders.

My parents hadn't thought I was special enough to pay attention to, and as a child, I'd spent most of my life with my nose in a book.

I stared at my body, and I tried to see myself through Jonah's eyes.

Jonah Steel, the most magnificent man I had ever laid eyes on, loved me.

This reflection in the mirror was beautiful to him, beautiful to a man with more strength, more intelligence, and more love to give than anyone I'd ever known. This man was devoted to his brother, to his whole family. And now he appeared to be devoted to me.

I smiled at my reflection. My body wasn't perfect by a long shot, but it was mine. And that's why Jonah loved it. Because he loved *me*.

I had never thought myself worthy of such love since my parents hadn't given it to me. But Jonah thought I was worthy. Jonah knew what I was going through. I hadn't told him the whole story, but he knew enough.

From now on, Melanie, you will stop thinking of yourself as average. You are smart, determined, hard-working, and you are a damned good therapist. Your body and your mind are beautiful.

I smiled when I heard the thud of cowboy boots outside in the hallway. I left Jonah's robe lying on the floor and turned on the shower.

★ ★ ★

Talon met us at the door of his house, the little mutt panting at his feet. I reached down to pet Roger.

"Felicia isn't here yet. I figured we'd talk to her in the kitchen." Talon turned to me. "Brooke is out on the deck.

There's a carafe of coffee out there, and some fruit and croissants."

"Okay," I said. "I'm really not sure what I'm supposed to talk to her about."

"Look, Doc, no one thinks you have anything in common with an aging supermodel. But she's just a lonely woman, and she would like someone to talk to. Jade and Marj left early this morning for their hike. The two of them really do need a break from her."

Jonah looked at me. "If this is uncomfortable for you, you don't have to do it. You can stay in here with us."

I shook my head. "No, I don't think that would be appropriate since I've never met Felicia. I'll make do. I'm sure Brooke and I will be fine."

"Well," Talon said, "she's nice enough. She and Jade have a rather fragile relationship at the moment, but they're working on it."

"You're not asking me to give her free therapy, are you?" I smiled.

Talon laughed. "No, God. I wouldn't wish that on you, Doc."

I walked slowly toward the door that led from the kitchen out onto the deck. Jonah hadn't told Talon what I'd been through, at my request. He had enough on his mind without having to worry about me.

I walked toward the table where Brooke was sitting and helped myself to a plate. I placed a croissant on it, a pat of butter, and then a few slices of pineapple, kiwi, and some strawberries. "I guess Palisade peach season is over," I said.

Brooke looked up at me. "Oh, hello. You're Talon's therapist, aren't you?"

She had just met me the previous evening, but I wasn't about to bring that up. "I am. And you're Jade's mother."

"Guilty," she said. "What are you doing over here this morning?"

"Jonah had some business with Talon, so I tagged along."

"You're just fresh as a daisy," Brooke said, "with gorgeous bone structure. I'd love to do a makeover for you. You'd be stunning."

I groaned inwardly. "How nice of you to offer. I'll give it some thought."

Her smile seemed forced. "My goodness, that's a lovely bauble around your neck."

I nervously fingered the diamond necklace and said a simple, "Thank you."

"A gift?"

I nodded.

"You and Jonah seem...close."

"I'd say we're close. We're in love with each other."

Was I allowed to say that? Jonah had only just professed his love for me last night. Maybe he wasn't ready for Talon and everyone else to know. I bit my lip. I hoped I hadn't just committed a major faux pas.

I set my plate down, poured myself a cup of coffee, and sat down next to Brooke. I took in the scenery. The yard was huge and beautiful. Roger had followed me out and was frolicking around, chasing a squirrel. The pool here was bigger than the pool at Jonah's, at least as far as I could see. It was several hundred feet away from the house. This was how Jonah and his brothers had grown up, in luxury.

But luxury didn't matter, not after Talon was taken. So much was more important than luxury.

From what Talon had told me, his parents had been stern but loving before his abduction. Afterward, his mother couldn't cope and killed herself within two years. And his father? I really didn't know much about him. I still didn't understand why he had buried the whole situation under the rug.

Talon was hell-bent on figuring it out, and for the first time, I felt like I really understood his passion for uncovering the truth. I had that same passion now. I needed to know the truth about what had happened to Gina. Something about the situation didn't add up.

Brooke had been talking, and I hadn't heard a word she said. "I'm so sorry. I zoned out for a moment. What were you saying?"

"I asked if you and Jonah are serious."

Serious? Hadn't I just said we were in love? That meant serious to me, although perhaps not to her. "I'd like to think we are."

"I see." She took a bite of a croissant. "He's very good-looking, isn't he?"

"Yes, he is."

"He would've made a gorgeous male model in his day," Brooke said. "When I was modeling, all the top models couldn't have held a candle to him."

I couldn't argue with that. Jonah was indeed gorgeous. I wasn't exactly sure what to say to her, though. It didn't matter because she kept talking.

"Jade and Talon said Jonah had a huge crush on me. He had my posters plastered all over his bedroom wall."

I wasn't much younger than Brooke herself, and I remembered her posters well, specifically one of her in a blue bathing suit. It had been one of the best-selling posters of all time. I had spent many hours staring at that poster in the local Kmart, wishing I had a body like hers.

She was still a very pretty woman. Her blond hair was short now, and one of her eyes was slightly squinty—from the accident, Jonah had told me. She had light silvery-blue eyes much like Jade's. And although she was wrapped in a terrycloth robe, I figured her body was still way above average.

For a moment, self-doubt crept into me. I was no Brooke Bailey.

But Jonah loved me. Hadn't I just promised myself to stop thinking of myself as average?

First step. Do not let Brooke Bailey intimidate you.

So I laughed nonchalantly. "I'm sure he did. I'm sure most adolescent males worshiped you from afar."

"Oh, yes. You should've seen the fan mail I got. I wouldn't be surprised if I got a letter from Jonah himself."

I smiled. No reason in the world existed for me to envy this woman. She was living in the past, unable to accept that her modeling days were over. Clearly, she was lusting after Jonah. Could I blame her? The man was magnificent.

But he loved *me*. I didn't need to throw that in her face. It was enough that I knew.

She returned my smile, pulling a smartphone out of the pocket of her robe. "Would you excuse me? I need to send a quick text."

CHAPTER TWENTY-FIVE

Jonah

Felicia had arrived, and Talon was bringing her to the kitchen when my phone buzzed in my pocket. Another text from the strange number. I would have to have words with Brooke at some point, but obviously not now.

I stood when Felicia entered the kitchen. "Thank you for coming over on a Sunday," I said.

"Mr. Jonah, I'm confused. I thought I was meeting with Mr. Talon and Miss Jade."

"Jade and Marjorie had some plans," Talon said. "So I asked Joe to come over."

"Is something wrong? Are you not happy with my work?"

I cleared my throat and looked to Talon. It was up to him to take the lead here. Felicia worked here, at his house, although technically the house belonged to all of us.

"Your work is fine," Talon said. "We've always been very pleased with you. You know that."

"Oh, good." Felicia rubbed her hands together nervously. "Is there any coffee?"

I stood. "Of course. I'll get it."

Felicia stopped me. "No, I'll get it. I know my way around this kitchen better than any of you." She smiled.

She came back with a mug of coffee and sat down.

I looked at Talon again.

This time he cleared his throat. "Felicia, this isn't easy."

Her eyes widened. "Are you letting me go?"

"I don't want to, but something has come to our attention that we need to discuss."

"Oh, no..." Tears formed in her eyes.

"What is it?"

"It's my parents... They're so sick and old... And I..."

"Felicia, don't worry about your parents. We will make sure they're taken care of."

"No, that's not what I mean."

"What do you mean?"

"I've been feeling so guilty."

"About what?"

"I..." Tears misted in her eyes. "I'm afraid."

"Look, there's no reason to be afraid," I said. "Let us tell you why we called you here, and we'll go from there."

She nodded, trembling.

Talon cleared his throat. "We found a business card in Jade's old room. It has three sets of fingerprints on it. One of them is yours."

"I'm so sorry," Felicia said.

"You don't seem surprised," I said.

She shook her head. "I'm so sorry," she said again.

"Time to come clean, Felicia." Talon rubbed at his temple, the muscles in his forearms strained. "This family has been through a lot, and we need the truth from you. Now."

Felicia swallowed audibly and nodded. "A couple months ago, a man came to my house. He was dressed all in black, even a black mask."

At the words "black mask," my brother visibly stiffened.

"He said if I didn't do what he said, he would kill my parents. They are old and weak, and they could never fight back. I didn't know what to do."

"Felicia," Talon said through gritted teeth. "What did he ask you to do?"

"He gave me a red rose and told me to put it on Miss Jade's pillow. And then he gave me a business card that belonged to her old boyfriend, Colin Morse. He told me to drop it somewhere in Miss Jade's bedroom."

"And did you?"

"Yes. I put the rose on her pillow one morning while she was in the shower. The business card, I didn't just drop it. I... put it under the carpeting. When those private investigators came to the house and pulled everything out of Miss Jade's room, and then no one said anything to me, I figured they just threw the business card away."

"No, we didn't throw it away. We had it analyzed for fingerprints. That's how we found yours."

"I suppose I should've worn gloves. But I wasn't thinking straight, Mr. Talon. I was so scared."

"Felicia, we're glad you didn't wear gloves," I said. "Otherwise we wouldn't know what happened."

"You do believe me, don't you? You know I would never hurt any of you. I love your family. You've given me so much."

"Why didn't you come to us?" I asked. "We trust you to come into our home. We trust you with our security codes. Why would you not trust us with this?"

She trembled, clenching her coffee cup. "I was scared. I was so afraid he would hurt my parents."

"Felicia," Talon said. "I want you to think hard. Can you tell us anything else about the man?"

"Just he was all in black."

"How tall was he?"

"I don't know. Average I guess."

"His build? His eyes?"

She widened her eyes. "Blue. He had blue eyes. Cold blue eyes."

"Could the man in the mask have been Colin Morse?" I asked.

Felicia trembled. "I... I don't think so. I only met Mr. Morse once, but he was taller than this man. I don't remember the color of his eyes, but I don't think they were blue."

I had only met him once myself, and I couldn't remember the color of his eyes. "Do you remember his eye color, Tal?"

He nodded. "Not blue. They're greenish brown. You sure this guy had blue eyes, Felicia?"

Felicia gulped. "Yes, I'm sure. I'll never forget him."

"Did he tell you why he wanted you to do this? Was he trying to frame someone?"

She shook her head vehemently. "No. He didn't tell me why, and I didn't ask. I didn't think to. He had a knife to my throat, Mr. Talon." Felicia burst into tears.

Talon clearly wasn't in the mood to coddle Felicia, so I went to her and placed my hand on her forearm. "Calm down. You're safe here. We just wish you had told us when this happened. We could've installed a security system in your home, to make sure your parents were safe while you were gone."

"I could never ask you for such a favor," she sobbed.

"I don't know how we would have handled it at the time," I said, "but we would have believed you, and we would have helped you."

"I know that. I was just so"—she hiccupped—"frightened."

I looked at Talon. "We need to get a system installed at her home. Pronto."

"Agreed," he said.

"Then you're not going to let me go?"

Talon shook his head. "No. But we are going to ask you a lot more questions about this. Can you deal with that?"

She hiccupped again as she nodded.

"I have some private investigators working on this. I'm going to have them question you. Perhaps the police also. This is important, Felicia. Do you understand that?"

She nodded, still sobbing. I got up and grabbed the box of tissues from the counter and set it down in front of her. She took three and blew her nose.

"Do you understand?" Talon said again.

"Tal..." I began.

"Joe, look, this is serious. She might have information that can lead us to the perpetrator."

"Yes, she might, but right now, hounding her isn't going to get you anywhere. She's not in any condition for it." I secretly hoped he wouldn't bring up the DNA test right now. I wasn't sure Felicia could handle it.

My phone buzzed again. Goddamnit, another fucking text from Brooke. Just what I didn't need at the moment. She was supposed to be out there talking to Melanie, and she's fucking texting? I set my phone down harshly on the table.

"Anything wrong?" Talon asked.

"No." I turned to Felicia. "You need to get hold of yourself. Pull yourself together. We're not going to let you go, but if anything like this ever happens again, you need to come to us."

"Yes, of course. But he threatened me and my parents.

Said if I said a word to you—"

I stopped her with a gesture. "We know what he said. But you need to trust us if something like this ever happens again. You need to trust us to protect you. We *will* protect you."

And for the first time in twenty-five years, I actually felt like I could protect someone I cared about.

"If you'll excuse me," I said, pocketing my phone, "I need to have a word with the ladies outside."

CHAPTER TWENTY-SIX

Melanie

Conversation with Brooke had grown stale. The only thing she wanted to talk about was her glory days of modeling, so I let her talk. I had nothing to say to her anyway.

I breathed a sigh of relief when Jonah walked out the sliding doors onto the deck. Thank God. I hoped they were done with Felicia and that we could go home. I smiled to myself. I was thinking of Jonah's home as my home.

When I looked up at him, his facial features were tense, his gorgeous full lips set in a line.

"Jonah?" I said tentatively.

He softened. "Hey, sweetheart. Have you two had a nice"—he cleared his throat—"talk?" His gaze riveted to Brooke's phone sitting on the table.

"Oh, yes," Brooke said, gushing. "Melanie here is a wonderful conversationalist."

Ha! I'd hardly said two words. But I smiled. "Yes, we've been just fine."

"Let's go home," he said, holding his hand out to me.

I took it and didn't look back at Brooke as we walked to the kitchen. Felicia was nowhere to be found. Just as well.

I said a quick good-bye to Talon, and then we were on our way home.

★ ★ ★

Once we walked in the house, I turned to Jonah, taking his hand. "Can you come with me? I want to show you something."

"Of course." He followed me to the guest room where my folders were still splayed on the floor.

I was about to do something I had never done. I was going to show someone else the suicide letter from Gina. I had never put it in her official file since it was private correspondence between her and me and had nothing to do with our sessions. I had no idea if she'd left any other notes. Her parents never mentioned any to me, but they hadn't talked to me much except to accuse me of not recognizing that she was suicidal and then to file a charge against me with the medical board.

If what I suspected was true, Gina did not leave any other suicide notes.

Because she had not committed suicide.

"Jonah, I'm going to trust you with something. Something big."

"You can trust me with anything."

I cupped his cheek, his stubble rough against my still-sore fingers. "Thank you. Thank you so much for that."

"I love you, and I trust you. I want you to know that you can trust me with anything."

I combed through the files until I found the letter, which had been in the back of Gina's file. I handed the piece of pink stationery to him.

As he read, I went over the letter in my mind. I had long since memorized its contents.

Dear Dr. Carmichael,

I can no longer go on.

This isn't your fault. You did your best to try to help me, but I'll never be able to forget what my uncle did to me when I was so young. I tried, and I prayed that I could heal, but it's just not in the cards for me.

There's something else I need to tell you. This isn't easy for me, and I wish with all my soul that I had the courage to tell you in person.

I love you.

And no, I don't mean I love you as a friend or as a therapist. I mean I'm in love with you. I'm truly in love with you.

I don't normally fall in love with women, at least I never have before. The feelings I have for you are so strong that I'm not sure I've ever felt anything close to them for anyone, male or female. I dream of kissing your red lips, taking you into my bed and making love. I dream of you holding me in your arms, chasing the beasts away.

I don't expect you to return my feelings. I know you could never be interested in someone as horribly defective as I am. But before I leave this earth forever, I want you to know how I feel.

Please don't blame yourself. I know you did your best for me. No one on this earth could have helped me. I'm too damaged. I wanted to be whole, but I know now that I never will be. I'm not good enough for you or anyone else. You deserve so much better.

That's why I must leave. Please don't worry about me. I've chosen a painless and cowardly way to die. For that's what I am, a coward. I don't have anything more to give to this life.

I will love you forever, even beyond the grave.

Yours,

Gina

When he finished, he sat down on the bed. "Wow."

I sat down next to him, caressing his forearm. "I hope you don't think less of me because I didn't tell you about the letter. In truth, I haven't told anyone. It was personal correspondence to me and not part of her official record. I know I should've turned it over to her family when I received it, but I...couldn't."

"I don't think it would have been a bad thing to show it to them," he said. "But I also don't think it changes anything. If nothing in your sessions indicated that she was suicidal, you're still in the clear. After all, the deed was done by the time you got the letter."

I nodded. "This letter was the bane of my existence for many months, Jonah. I never thought to question its validity. But after having been kidnapped myself and thrown into a garage with a running car, I began to wonder. Could the same thing have happened to Gina?"

"It's probably a long shot, baby."

"It could be. Probably no one thought to look at her wrists or ankles for signs that she might have been bound, that she could've been killed the same way my attacker tried to kill me. And if my theory is correct, when the killer went back later, he simply unbound her, put her in her car, and made it look like she had committed suicide. The letter to me served as further proof."

"No one knows about that letter."

"Precisely. It only serves as further proof to me. If her parents found her unbound in the garage with the car running, they wouldn't have thought twice about suicide. It was apparent. But as a therapist, I would require more proof because nothing in my sessions with her indicated that she was suicidal."

"So you think the letter is a forgery."

"Yes, I think it might be. She may well have written it, but what if she was forced to do so? And the killer added the part about her being in love with me to further throw me off track?"

He furrowed his brow. "Wow."

"It's funny. I've been thinking more clearly since I was attacked. It's like I stepped outside the box and started looking at the situation from a different angle. It made me question Gina's suicide. So then I started thinking about the letter. I've had patients develop feelings for me before. It's very common in therapy. Granted, they were all men, but I saw the signs right away and nipped them in the bud before they could go too far. It seems I would've seen the signs if Gina had been in love with me. And I've had suicidal patients before. I'm well-versed in suicide. I know the signs, Jonah. I've spent the last several months going over and over her sessions in my mind, and I can't find any indication that she was suicidal, other than a remark she made when she was flashing back to the first time her uncle raped her. She said 'I'd rather die.' But she was talking to her uncle at that specific time, not saying it in real time. In fact, she had told me earlier that her uncle wasn't worth her life.

"It finally dawned on me, after I was attacked, after I was left to die the way Gina died... Maybe I missed those signs because they weren't there." I took the letter from him. "And something else never dawned on me either. Why would she send me a letter? I haven't gotten a handwritten letter in ages. Why wouldn't she have sent me an e-mail?"

"Maybe because an e-mail is delivered instantaneously, and she didn't want you to try to stop the suicide."

"But she could have put the e-mail in her out-box and programmed it to be sent later."

He nodded. "That's true."

"I realize I could be wrong, but I have to know for sure. She always said the uncle who had abused her was dead, but she could never tell me how he died. I asked her several times to ask her parents about it, but she kept saying she forgot, or that she didn't want to talk to them about the situation. Even though I stressed to her how important it was that she understand how he died and that he was gone, she wouldn't take that step."

"Do you think maybe the uncle isn't dead?"

I nodded. "It's a leap, yes. But it rings true for me. Maybe, Jonah, just maybe, I didn't make a mistake here. Maybe I didn't miss the sign that she was suicidal. Maybe she wasn't, and maybe that uncle, whoever he may be, found out she was in therapy and thought she might go to the police, so he took care of her."

"But why would he do the same to you?"

"Because I knew the truth about him. She could have told me his name, for all he knows."

Jonah rubbed his chin, looking thoughtful. "Like I said, we'll put some private investigators on this. And we'll need to talk to her parents. As far as I'm concerned, they are still prime suspects in your attack."

"Yes, I understand that they are. I haven't heard from the police. I'm going to give Officer Lee a call tomorrow."

"You've raised some good points, sweetheart, but why didn't any of this occur to you before?"

"I think I just didn't believe in myself enough. I didn't..." I sighed. "I was programmed from a young age to think of myself as average, no matter my successes. Average body, average mind. In fact, when I first awoke after being taken, I decided to let the chips fall where they may because maybe I deserved it for letting Gina die. But now... I don't know. Once I was actually in that garage with that running car, things changed. *I* changed. For the first time, I truly understood the human instinct for survival. I got out of that horrible, frightening mess, Jonah. I got out of it alive by using my wits. Granted, a little bit of luck helped too, but I was determined, and do you know why I was so determined?"

He smiled. "Because you realized you're brilliant, and you knew you had a good life?"

I laughed, shaking my head. "No. I was determined to get back to you. I had fallen in love with you, and it killed me that I might not ever be able to tell you."

"Oh, baby." He pulled me to him and kissed my forehead. "You have no idea how glad I am that you got out of that situation alive. If anything had happened to you..."

I edged back a little. "Nothing happened to me. I'm here, safe, with the man I love. Sure, I have a few scars, and it's taken a toll on my mental health, but I'll recover. I know I will now."

"You're the strongest woman I've ever met." He kissed me on the forehead again. "Every day you amaze me more."

"I never thought of myself as strong. I never thought of myself as anything other than average in every way."

"Baby, you are so much more than average."

I smiled. "I see a little of that now. Don't worry. I'm not going to get a big head or anything. I won't be turning into Brooke Bailey anytime soon."

"Oh, God. Please."

"That woman has such a big head. I don't know how she got through Talon's door. All she talked about today were her glory days of modeling. Oh, and she talked a little bit about you."

"Me?" Jonah squirmed.

"Does that make you uneasy?"

"No. But she..." He raked his fingers through his hair. "I'm not quite sure how to tell you this."

"You can tell me anything."

"I know that. It's just... Brooke came on to me yesterday."

I shot up from the bed. "What?"

"Don't worry. I'm not interested in her."

"She can keep her mitts off of my man!" And then I laughed in spite of myself. "I can't believe those words just came out of my mouth."

He laughed. "You know, you're cute when you're jealous."

"Jealous of that has-been?" Then I frowned. "I didn't mean that. She's kind of...sad, really."

"Brooke Bailey was given the gift of beauty," Jonah said, "but so were you, Melanie. And you were given so much more than she was. Now that her modeling career is over, all she has left is her vanity. Her past successes. She's the one who's jealous of *you*."

"Why in the world would she be jealous of me?"

He guffawed. "Because you have me."

CHAPTER TWENTY-SEVEN

Jonah

She looked at me and burst out laughing.

"Not exactly the reaction I was hoping for." I smiled.

"Oh, no, it's just the way you said it. Poor Brooke."

"Poor Brooke? How about poor me? She's been stalking me over my phone."

Melanie dropped her mouth into an oval. "What?"

"She's been sending me texts. Saying stuff like she will have me. She wants me. That kind of crap."

"She can stop that right now," Melanie said.

"She sent me two this morning while I was sitting in Talon's kitchen. Didn't you notice her using her phone?"

Melanie scratched her nose. "I remember her using it once. Honestly, though, she could've used it more than once. I stopped paying attention to her after a while."

"I came out to confront her about it and tell her to stop, but you looked so relieved to see me, I decided to just get you out of there."

"Yeah, I was certainly ready to leave."

"I'm sorry to drag you through that."

"It was my decision. I didn't want to stay here alone. I'm going to have to be okay with that from now on. I know you can't be here all the time. You have a ranch to run."

"Yes, and unfortunately I have to be in the north quadrant at the crack of dawn tomorrow."

She turned to me, cupping my cheeks. "Look, I really am feeling better. Believe it or not, I think the attack on me jarred me a little. Yes, in a bad way, but also a good way. I was forced to use my brain, to think about things that I normally wouldn't think about. And it opened my mind to these new things, to look at Gina's situation and her letter in a different way. To see that maybe Gina wasn't suicidal." She shook her head and chuckled. "To think, I almost destroyed that letter."

"What?"

"I walked into the hardware store in Snow Creek the day I was taken. I bought a document shredder." She closed her eyes. "That's the first time I've even allowed myself to think the words 'document shredder.' I was so freaked that I had bought it, that I was thinking about destroying the letter."

"Wow."

"I know. My head was a little screwy that day. It has been since Gina's death. But no more. I'm going to figure this out."

"But what if..." I couldn't finish.

"I'm wrong?" She bit her lip. "I might be. And I'll deal with that. Every doctor loses patients. It's a chance you take when you're a healer." She sighed. "We'd all like to be able to heal everyone. Every doctor out there. But no one can."

I wanted to be supportive of Melanie. She was so strong. So we would investigate this theory of hers. I just hoped that it didn't turn out to be nothing. I wanted as much as she did for her to be able to put this behind her.

Melanie's phone rang. "Do you mind?"

"No, go ahead and take it."

I left the room for a moment, looking through the kitchen

to see what we could whip up for lunch. I was hungry. My freezer was full of frozen meals that my personal chef had made up for me. I pulled out two, not even looking at the labels, and threw them in the microwave to heat up.

I poured two glasses of iced tea and returned to the guest room.

Melanie was just ending her phone call.

"What was that about?" I asked.

"It was Officer Lee. They found the place where I was held."

My heart stopped. "Yeah?"

"It's in a rural area, about two hours from here. It's owned by some corporation. No names of individuals are on record except for the registered agent, an attorney in Grand Junction. His name is Frederick Jolly."

I couldn't help a laugh. "Jolly?"

Melanie smiled. "Yeah, I know. Funny name."

"Have they arrested Dr. Cates?"

"No, they haven't."

"Why the hell not?"

"They questioned him, but he has an ironclad alibi. He was with his wife at the hospital pretty much nonstop during the entire time I was gone."

"That doesn't mean shit. He could have hired it out."

"I agree, but they don't have any probable cause. Plus, he reported the Eldorado as stolen. A couple days before I was taken."

"That could all be part of the ploy."

"I know that, and so do the police. They're putting some detectives on the case."

"Well, there's no reason why *we* can't question him."

Melanie shook her head. "Nope. In fact, he's rented a small townhome in Grand Junction."

"Then it's settled. I have a big day around here tomorrow, but we can go to the city on Tuesday. First, we'll visit this Mr. Jolly and get some information from him, and then we'll go and see the esteemed Dr. Cates."

Melanie smiled and took a sip of the iced tea I'd handed to her. "What do we do in the meantime then?"

I smiled. "I'm sure we can think of something, and I think it might begin in my swimming pool. Right after lunch."

★ ★ ★

Melanie insisted on wearing her bathing suit for our afternoon swim.

"Each time I've been in your pool, you promised me we would be alone. And each time, someone has shown up and embarrassed the heck out of me. Not this time."

I simply smiled at her and humored her by wearing trunks myself. What she didn't know was that the suit would be long gone thirty seconds after she got into the pool.

The morning with Felicia had me antsy, so I dived in and swam several laps before worrying about divesting Melanie of her suit.

When I finally took a break, she still hadn't entered the water. She was lying on a chaise longue, her eyes closed. Her suit was an emerald-green one-piece that perfectly matched her eyes. She looked gorgeous, but Melanie had the body for a bikini.

A purple bikini.

Better than that, purple lace lingerie.

I smiled as I walked to her chaise and stood over her, dripping.

She opened her eyes and jerked upward. "What are you doing?"

"Getting you wet." I grinned. "And then I'm going to get you *wet*."

I picked her up from the chair, walked to the pool, and unceremoniously dumped her in.

She bobbed to the surface, laughing. "That's the second time you've done that to me."

"And it was fun both times, so don't think I'll be giving it up any time soon."

She laughed again. "Did you do your laps?"

"Yup, and now I'm ready for a soak in the hot tub. Join me?"

She pulled herself up on the edge of the pool and then stood. "Sure."

"But Melanie, first the suit comes off."

"I don't know. Every time—"

I stopped her with a kiss. She opened for me instantly, twirling her soft tongue around mine. It had been a while since I'd simply kissed her. Kissed my woman. And I had missed it. I had missed it a lot.

Her nipples hardened under her suit, grazing against my wet chest. My cock grew in my trunks. I needed a fuck—a good old-fashioned fuck in the hot tub with this beautiful woman. I edged her across the concrete toward the tub, still kissing her. When I broke the kiss and inhaled, she sighed against my neck.

Slowly I caressed the straps of her suit over her shoulders until I had exposed her breasts. Her nipples were turgid and beautiful, and I bent to take one between my lips. Hard. Just the way she liked it.

She inhaled sharply. "Jonah..."

"Relax, baby. No one will interrupt us this time. You have my word." I continued to suck on her hard nub. Such gorgeous nipples. Fuck, she made me hot.

"Jonah... Oh, God."

"Mmm, your nipples taste good, baby, but I want to taste something else." I smoothed the suit over her hips until it lay on the hard concrete beneath us. "Spread your legs."

She did, kicking the suit a few feet away. I knelt between her legs and slithered my tongue over her slick pussy. God, she tasted so sweet. And she was wet. So fucking wet.

"Mmm," I said against her vulva. "I could eat you forever."

She moaned above me. "Feels so good..."

I swirled my tongue over her clit, and she jerked. I stood, moving us over to some soft grass. And then I knelt again as she stood above me, and I continued to suck her sweet cunt. I wanted to make her come. I wanted her to gush all over my face. If I could bottle her scent... Take it with me everywhere...

I continued licking her, flicking her clit. She grabbed my head, threading her fingers through my hair, yanking me toward her. She began grinding on my face. My hard cock throbbed between my legs. I longed to thrust it into her, but I wanted her to come all over my face first.

"Oh!" Her pussy throbbed against my mouth. "I'm coming, Jonah. Oh my God!"

I lapped at her, sucking every last drop of cream from that pussy. I couldn't wait any longer to have her. I pulled her down and laid her on the grass. I quickly pushed my trunks over my hips and plunged inside her.

Sweet wet heat. She gripped me like a vise, so tight.

As much as I wanted to bring her to another climax, that would have to wait. My balls tightened, and those tiny convulsions started at the base of my cock and radiated outward, through every cell in my body, until my skin tingled all over and I poured myself into her.

"My God, I love you." I plunged once more, emptying my essence into her body.

I lay atop her for a moment and then turned on my side. I had a straight shot view of my sliding glass door in the distance. It was closing, and a tall figure who looked suspiciously like Talon was walking backward into the kitchen.

I shook my head. "Are you fucking kidding me?"

CHAPTER TWENTY-EIGHT

Melanie

"What is it?" I asked.

Jonah stood and pulled his trunks, which were still around his knees, over his hips. "It's nothing, baby. But you may want to put your suit back on."

Warmth infused my already heat-laden body. "What?"

"I think Talon is here."

"Oh, for God's sake." I stood, scanning the area for my suit. I spied it on the concrete by the pool and ran to it, pulling the wet fabric onto my slick body as quickly as I could. "This is the very last time we have sex near your pool. The very fucking last time."

"I'm so sorry, sweetheart. I'll see what he wants, and I'll get rid of him."

"I may as well come with you," I said. "I certainly don't need to be modest around him now. Or your friend Bryce, for that matter."

Jonah's dark eyes gleamed with amusement.

I swatted him lightly. "You think this is funny?"

"Baby, it *is* a bit amusing. It's kind of like a bad cartoon."

"Then you may be surprised to know that I never really wanted your brother or your best friend to see me naked."

"Honey, never be ashamed of that beautiful body of yours.

In fact, I'm thinking maybe we should plan a trip to a nude beach."

My mouth fell open. "Please be kidding."

"Oh, no, I'm not kidding. In fact, a nude beach should be nothing to you now." He let out a peal of laughter.

I swatted him again. "You're a big pain in the ass."

"Yes, but I'm *your* pain in the ass." He smiled, his gorgeous laugh lines crinkling, his beautiful dimples dimpling, his perfect teeth sparkling. The man was magnificent. And more than that, he was beautiful on the inside—darkly beautiful. And tortured. In a different way from his brother, but tortured nonetheless.

"You know, I might just take you up on that nude beach." Oddly, I wasn't lying. The idea of a nude beach with Jonah was starting to appeal to me.

"I won't forget that, Melanie. Now, do you want to go inside and see what Talon wants, or do you want to hide out here?"

I let out a sigh. "I think hiding is kind of moot now, isn't it?"

He smiled at me, and I melted into a big puddle of butter.

"Come on," he said. "Talon has no secrets from you."

I walked with Jonah back to the deck and then into the kitchen, Lucy following at our heels.

Talon was sitting at the kitchen table. He cleared his throat. "I'm really...sorry..."

"Ever think of calling first, bro?" Jonah asked.

"I did. No answer."

"Did you ever think that maybe that means I'm busy and don't want to be disturbed?"

"You weren't in your office, and Dolores didn't know

where you were. I figured you might be here, and maybe your phone died."

Jonah's facial features softened. He was relenting. He would never ignore a call from Talon. If there was ever a man who was devoted to his brother, it was Jonah Steel.

"Hey, Doc," Talon said, not meeting my gaze.

I chuckled, remembering how embarrassed I had been the first time Talon and Jade walked in on Jonah and me when we were naked in the pool. It didn't bother me nearly as much now. Something in me had changed since my attack. I was still scared of things going bump in the night, but something burned inside me, a new confidence.

"Hey to you too," I said. "If the two of you will excuse me, I want to go dry off and put on something decent."

"That suit is decent, Melanie," Jonah said. "You look amazing."

I smiled and turned and walked out of there.

"Come back after you change," Talon said. "I want you to hear this too."

"Okay," I said over my shoulder.

I took a quick shower to rinse the chlorine out of my hair and then put on a pair of sweats and a tank top. I gave my ankle a once-over. Still a lot of bruising, but the pain had subsided quite a bit, as long as I didn't try to run any marathons. I walked back out to the kitchen, and Jonah had poured everybody a glass of iced tea. I sat down in front of the extra glass and took a sip, quickly followed by another. I was parched.

"I was telling Joe," Talon said, "that the only thing Felicia can tell us about the guy who threatened her is that he had blue eyes. Larry Wade has blue eyes."

"I see." I took another drink of iced tea. "Larry Wade isn't the only person around here with blue eyes, though."

"I know that, Doc, but he's the most likely suspect. Who else would want to screw around with me and Jade?"

"Are you ready to go talk to Larry, Talon?" Jonah asked.

Talon threaded his fingers through his wavy dark hair. "I don't know, man. Some days I think I'm ready, and other days the idea just freaks the hell out of me. Seeing him, being in the same room with him, talking to him... I don't want to go back to that dark place."

"Talon, you've left that dark place behind," I said. "But you're right about one thing. Any kind of healing involves removing the negative influences from your life. Larry Wade is definitely a negative. You don't have to see him."

"I'll think about it," he said.

"What does Jade think?" Jonah asked.

"She says it's up to me, that she'll support whatever decision I make. But she feels the same way as you do." He glanced at me. "She doesn't want me put in harm's way."

"She's a smart woman," I said.

"Here's the problem though," Talon said. "We've determined that the third set of prints on the business card *doesn't* belong to Larry."

"What?" Jonah stood and started pacing around the kitchen. "How did you find out?"

"It was pretty easy. Larry was fingerprinted when he was arrested. Mills and Johnson hacked into the database and retrieved them and then checked them against the set Jade found in the attorney database."

"So how do we know which ones are Larry's real fingerprints?"

"We can assume the more recent set, from when he

was arrested. His fingerprints in the attorney database were obviously tampered with, and probably recently, to make it look like he'd had his hands on that business card."

"This is fucking crazy." Jonah continued pacing, his body tense.

"What is it?" I asked.

He shook his head, pursing his lips. "Nothing. Nothing at all."

I didn't believe him for a minute, but I wasn't about to push it with Talon there. Talon was upset enough as it was.

Talon stood. "Jade will be home from work soon. I should get back to the house. I like being home when she gets home."

I smiled. "That's sweet. You and she are lucky to have each other."

He nodded. "That's the truth, for sure."

"Sorry to interrupt your pool time again, Joe."

"Don't worry about it." Jonah patted him on the back. "You know I'm always here for you."

Warmth coursed through me at the love and devotion Jonah had for his brother. He was a man of honor and integrity.

After Talon left, Jonah began pacing around the kitchen again.

I touched his arm. "What's eating at you?"

"I have to tell you something. I can't keep it inside any longer, but I need you to keep it to yourself. I haven't told Bryce yet, and I can't tell Talon until I tell Bryce, but I think I know who one of the abductors is."

My heart nearly stopped. "Who?"

"The mayor. Bryce's father."

"The same mayor who— Oh my God!" I clamped my hand over my mouth. The same mayor who I had seen buying duct

tape and rope the day I was attacked.
  And he had blue eyes.

CHAPTER TWENTY-NINE

Jonah

I could almost see the clockworks in Melanie's mind. She was putting two and two together, and it didn't take her long.

I told her the whole story about Tom Simpson and his birthmark.

"You have to tell Talon," Melanie said. "You can't keep this from him."

"I know it." I grabbed a handful of my hair. "But I have to tell Bryce first. It's his father, for God's sake, and he's my best friend. Bryce has to know who his father is."

"But Talon is your brother," Melanie said. "That trumps best friend."

She had a point. "All right. I will. I've tried a couple times to tell Bryce, but we've always gotten interrupted. But you're right. Talon is my brother, and he suffered at this man's hand. But all I have as proof is the birthmark, which I haven't even seen."

"Then how do you know it's in the right place?"

"Marjorie saw him at the gym. She said it was right there on his right upper arm, under his armpit."

Melanie's peachy cheeks went pale. "Oh my God."

"I know. There are so many loose ends in this situation, and they just become more and more unraveled the deeper we dig." I thought back to the words that Larry Wade had said to Bryce and me the last time we saw him.

The truth is overrated. Once you open the door to that dark room, getting out is damn near impossible.

The man was a lying psychopath, but maybe he had a point. We were all healing now. Was it really necessary to open all the doors? So far, every door we had opened had led to more doors. Answers had only posed more questions. We seemed further away from the truth now than we had been when we'd started this journey.

"Jonah, the mayor bought duct tape and rope. The day I was taken." Her lower lip trembled.

"I know. You told me."

"I was bound with duct tape and rope later that evening. By a man with blue eyes."

I tensed, running my fingers through my hair. "You don't think..."

"I don't know, honestly. But it's possible. If the mayor is the psychopath you say he is, he would be capable of anything."

Could there be a connection between Melanie's abduction and our situation? My God, if that crazed lunatic had not only molested my brother but had also abducted my woman...

Couldn't go there yet. Too farfetched.

I needed a break from Tom Simpson and what he'd done to Talon. I stopped pacing and took Melanie in my arms. "Sweetheart, it's possible. Anything is possible when dealing with a psychopathic criminal."

"It just seems a little too coincidental, don't you think?"

I nodded. "It does. But he could have been buying those things for any number of reasons."

"You're right." She sighed. "It is definitely a long shot. And lots of people have blue eyes. If I could have seen the mayor's eyes that day, I could tell you better. The guy who attacked me had really cold blue eyes. Icy cold. Almost unreal looking."

Tom Simpson's eyes were definitely cold. But had I noticed how cold they were before I knew what he was? I wasn't sure.

"I'll tell you what. Let's go see Dr. Cates tomorrow and get some information on Gina's uncle. I need to focus on something other than Steel family drama for a little while."

She snuggled her head into my shoulder. "I do think it would be a good idea for you to take a step back for a day or two. But don't feel like you have to dive headfirst into my ashes."

"Melanie, I want to help you. And I will not let you go see that man alone."

"Good," she said, "because I don't want to go alone."

She wouldn't go alone. I would do all I could to help her, to protect her, while I had the chance. Because as soon as I told her the truth about the evening she was attacked, she would leave me.

My brother had left me that day twenty-five years ago.

Just like my mother had left me two years later.

Just like every woman I had been involved with—and there weren't many—had left me because they couldn't deal with what I truly was...or was not.

I buried my nose in her blond hair, still damp from her shower, and inhaled the coconut scent. "I love you so much, Melanie. So fucking much."

I felt her smile against my shoulder. "I love you too."

I only hoped her love for me was enough to survive what was coming.

* * *

I took Melanie to lunch at her favorite sushi place in Grand Junction. The raw fish was actually starting to grow on me. After that, we headed toward the office building that housed the law firm of Decker and Jolly. Melanie had thought we should call Frederick Jolly first and not just barge in, but I thought it might be better not to let him know we were coming. I had a strange feeling that he might disappear.

We took the elevator up to the fifth floor of the building and entered the firm.

"May I help you?" a gum-popping receptionist asked.

"We're here to see Frederick Jolly," I said.

"Do you have an appointment?"

I shook my head. "Just tell him that Jonah Steel is here with Melanie Carmichael. We want to talk to him about the Fleming Corporation."

"Fred doesn't usually see people without appointments," she said, "but I'll see if he's in. Go ahead and take a seat." She gestured to some chairs and couches. "Help yourself to a cup of coffee or a doughnut if you want one."

We sat down, ignoring the coffee and doughnuts after our huge sushi lunch.

A few minutes later, the receptionist said, "I'm afraid Mr. Jolly can't see you. Why don't you call and make an appointment?"

I walked up to the receptionist, leaving Melanie sitting in the waiting area. "Look, we're seeing Mr. Jolly today," I told her in a calm voice. "Tell him that I'm Jonah Steel, of Steel Acres Ranch, and I'm here with Dr. Melanie Carmichael, who was recently held captive on a property owned by the Fleming

Corporation."

The receptionist widened her eyes and gulped as she got back on the phone.

I sat back down next to Melanie. Within a few moments, a somber-looking man in a blue pinstripe suit with black hair slicked back from his face walked into the reception area.

"Mr. Steel?"

I stood.

"I'm Fred Jolly."

I almost burst out laughing. He certainly didn't look like a man named Jolly. I held out my hand, but he didn't take it.

"Thank you for seeing us without an appointment. This is Dr. Melanie Carmichael."

Melanie stood. "Nice to meet you," she said.

"If the two of you would come back to my office, please."

We followed him down the hallway, passing secretaries and assistants working in their cubicles, to a lush corner office. Nice digs. Well, his name *was* on the letterhead.

He ushered us into his office, shutting the door behind him. "Have a seat, both of you." He gestured to the leather chairs in front of his desk and then sat down behind his desk. "What can I do for you?"

CHAPTER THIRTY

Melanie

Jonah cleared his throat. "You can tell us the names of the individuals behind Fleming Corporation."

"I'm afraid I'm under no legal obligation to do so."

"We've checked with the Secretary of State, and no directors or officers are listed. The only name listed is yours, as the registered agent."

"And as the registered agent, I am not bound to disclose anything to you."

I spoke up then. "Look, Mr. Jolly, we understand your situation. Being a doctor, I understand the concept of client confidentiality."

"I never said Fleming Corporation was my client," he said.

"Well, then, that makes your job a little easier," I said. "The privilege doesn't apply."

"That's neither here nor there." Jolly cleared his throat. "I have no obligation to tell you anything."

Jonah stood, his eyes dark and serious, his nostrils flaring. "Let's cut to the chase here. Dr. Carmichael was held captive last week on a property owned by Fleming Corporation."

"Ma'am, I'm sorry for any hardship you've endured, but I don't know anything about that."

"That's because I was able to keep it off the news,"

Jonah said. "For Dr. Carmichael's privacy. She's a renowned psychotherapist here in Grand Junction."

"Look," I said. "We're just trying to figure out who did this to me. You're our only lead."

Mr. Jolly stood and came from behind his desk. "Then I'm afraid your only lead is a dead end. I'm going to have to ask you to leave now."

Jonah tensed, and for a moment, I feared he was going to do something he might regret. But he stood and smiled. "Thank you very much for your time. We will be in touch."

We walked quickly out of his office, down the hallway, through the reception area, and out the door. Jonah said nothing during the elevator ride, and I waited until we were clear of the building before I spoke.

"He's hiding something," I said. "I have to be good at reading people in my business, and I usually know a liar when I see one."

"Agreed," Jonah said. "If the corporation isn't a client, he's not bound by any ethical obligation not to disclose the information we want. The fact that he won't means he's either part of the corporation or he's being well paid to keep quiet."

"I guess it's on to see Dr. Cates," I said.

"We're not done with this Jolly fellow yet. We just have to figure out how to approach the situation. If he's being paid to keep quiet, I can pay him to talk."

I swallowed. "Jonah, I don't want you to spend all your money trying to figure this out."

"Melanie, my love, I couldn't spend all my money in three lifetimes. You don't need to worry about that."

I shook my head and smiled. "You are some kind of wonderful, you know that?"

"I'm far from wonderful," he said. "But trust me when I say I would do absolutely anything for you." He threaded his fingers through mine as we walked to his car.

CHAPTER THIRTY-ONE

Jonah

Melanie wanted to go to the hospital and check on Mrs. Cates, so we headed there first. We were in and out quickly, Melanie getting an update from the nurse on duty. Dr. Cates wasn't there, so we drove to the address of the townhome he had rented in the city.

On the way, something occurred to me. "You don't suppose they would've brought Gina's old Eldorado out here to Grand Junction from their home in Denver, do you?"

"Good point. I wouldn't think so. So that means—"

"How did they know it was stolen?" I finished. "The police said Dr. Cates had reported it stolen a few days prior to your escape, right?"

"As I understand it, yes."

I pulled up into the parking lot in front of the townhome. Melanie sat still, staring straight ahead.

"Are you okay?" I asked her.

She nodded. "Just a little...nervous, I guess. I'm about to face the man who probably was my attacker."

"Something to keep in mind, Melanie."

"What?"

"If your theory is correct, and Gina didn't kill herself, it's just as likely that whoever did kill her also attacked you. And that most likely was not Dr. Cates."

"Or perhaps her parents murdered her. Who knows? From what she told me, they were very distant parents. Not affectionate at all. Of course, that doesn't mean they're killers."

"No, it doesn't," I agreed.

"Besides," Melanie said, "the guy who took me basically told me he was a hired assassin. I believe the words he used were 'I wouldn't stay in business for long if I weaseled out of a job for more money. No one would trust me.'"

"So that could mean one of two things," I said. "Either he was a hired killer, or he was lying to you. And I'm thinking that when someone kills for a living or for sport, he's already thrown caution to the wind and would have no problem lying."

That got a small smile out of her. "You're right."

I gripped her shoulders, turning her toward me. "You don't have to be afraid. I will be with you, and I will not let him harm you. I will never, ever let anyone harm you again. Do you hear me?"

She nodded, biting her lip.

"All right. Are you ready?"

She nodded again. "As ready as I'll ever be."

We got out of the car, and Melanie held on to my arm as we walked to the door of his townhome. He was on the end of a triplex, which was good. A neighbor on only one side.

I knocked on the door loudly.

We heard some shuffling behind the door, but no one opened it.

I tried the doorbell next, pressing it twice.

Still no response.

No screen door separated me from the wooden door, so I pounded with all my might on the wooden door.

He was there. I could feel it in my bones.

Melanie shivered beside me. Damn it, we had come all this way. He was going to talk to us.

"Hey!" I shouted. "Open this goddamned door, or I swear to God I'll kick it in!"

No response again.

"I fucking warned you!"

Melanie tugged on my arm. "Jonah…"

"Don't worry," I said to her. Then, "I meant it. I'm going to kick down this fucking door!"

I stepped back, focused, let out a scream, and aimed a sidekick at the door. It didn't budge.

I closed my eyes, breathing deep, visualized myself kicking that door off its hinges, and then let out another cry and side-kicked the door once again.

The wood cracked.

As I readied to kick once more, the door flew open. A man, who I assumed was Dr. Cates, stood there, a look of fear and indignation across his face.

"Are you insane?" he said to me.

"Just a hair short of it." I pushed him out of the way and walked into the townhome, Melanie holding on to my arm again. "I'm Jonah Steel. And you know Dr. Carmichael."

"What the hell are *you* doing here? I was perfectly within my rights to file a complaint with the medical board against you."

Melanie opened her mouth, but I gestured for her to be quiet.

"As much as I'd love to interrogate you about that, that's not why we're here."

"Then why are you here? I've already told the police I had

nothing to do with your kidnapping, Dr. Carmichael."

"I don't believe that either," I said, "but that's still not why we're here."

"Then what the hell do you want? And you're going to pay for that door, by the way."

"Yeah, I'll pay for it. And don't even think about calling the cops on me. I'll make your life hell."

He opened his mouth, but I raised my fist at him.

"I'm doing the talking now. I'll let you know when it's your turn. We need some information. Information that Dr. Carmichael was never able to get from your daughter while she was alive."

"I don't see what—"

"You don't listen very well. I told you I would let you know when to talk. Now shut the fuck up. I want to know the name of your brother-in-law. The one who assaulted and raped your daughter. You remember? The reason she needed therapy?"

"Doesn't matter. He's dead."

"How did he die?"

"Uh...cancer."

"What kind of cancer?"

"Lung cancer."

"Was he a smoker?" I asked Melanie. "Did Gina ever say her uncle smoked?"

Melanie shook her head, biting her lip.

"Seems like something Gina might have mentioned."

Cates fidgeted nervously. "You don't have to smoke to get lung cancer."

"True. But most lung cancer cases result from smoking. If your brother-in-law didn't smoke, it's unlikely he had lung cancer. I think you're lying, Dr. Cates. And you know something else? I don't think he's dead."

His face turned red. "He's dead."

"Let me see the death certificate."

"I don't have it."

"Then give me his name. I'll go to the records office and get one myself."

His face turned ruddier. "I don't have to tell you anything."

I lunged at him, grabbing him by the collar and pushing him up against the wall. "That's where you're wrong. We're not leaving until we get the information we came for."

"I'll call the cops on you."

"Go right ahead. I'm sure they'll be interested in the information I want from you too."

Melanie stepped forward. "Dr. Cates, please. Gina would never give me this information. I don't know why, but I have my hunches."

"Your hunches aren't worth anything," he said. "You let my daughter die."

"What if I didn't?" she asked. "What if your daughter was murdered?"

Cates's face reddened. "That's not true. She committed suicide. We found her dead in the garage in that damned Eldorado."

"But what if someone put her there? Like someone tried to do to me?"

He said nothing.

"Look," I said. "I want the name of your brother-in-law. I want his date and cause of death. And I'm not leaving here without those pieces of information."

"While you're at it," Melanie said, "we also need the name and phone number of Gina's friend. The one who told you she was in love."

"I don't have to give you anything."

I pushed him harder into the wall, grasping his collar in my fists. "Listen," I said through clenched teeth, "you see what I did to your door. What do you think I could do to *you?* I could grind you into a fine powder. Then you would call the cops on me, and they would take me away in handcuffs." I laughed. "You know something? I don't fucking care. My attorneys would have me out on bail in twenty-four hours. They would get me off on some technicality and expose every dirty little secret you're hiding to discredit you. That's the kind of money I have. So give us the information we want, or I will beat you into a finely mashed pulp and to hell with the consequences."

He closed his eyes. Two tears squeezed out of the corners. "All right, all right. Just don't hurt me."

I loosened my grip. "Your brother-in-law—is he dead?"

Cates shook his head. "No, he's not."

"That's what we thought. Did you tell Gina he was dead? Or did you tell her to tell everyone else he was dead?"

"We told her he was dead. We never told her how or why. She asked a few times, and we changed the subject."

"You know, there are some people in the world who should never have children, Cates. I put you in that category."

"Jonah..." Melanie touched my arm.

"For God's sake, Melanie. I'm right, and you know it."

She sighed. "Yes, I do believe you're right."

"How dare the two of you judge me?" He looked to Melanie.

I tightened my grip on his collar again. "First, you don't talk to her. Ever. Don't even look at her. You don't deserve to. Second. What the fuck is the name of your brother-in-law?"

"I don't know."

"Are you fucking kidding me? You don't know his name?"

"I only know his birth name. He goes by a lot of other names. I don't know what he's going by now."

I let Cates go, and he fell to the floor.

"He uses aliases?" I said.

Cates nodded. "He's got...issues."

"You think? Really? A man who rapes his niece has issues?" I shook my head. "You disgust me. A guy who cuts in line has issues. Your brother-in-law is a goddamned psychopath. Now, what's his fucking birth name?"

"Theodore. Theodore Mathias."

"Any middle name?"

"I...don't know."

"And you know some of his aliases?"

"There are several, and I'm sure I don't know them all. John Smith. Nicholas Castle. Milo Sanchez. I can't think of any more right now. I know I'm forgetting some of them."

My blood ran cold. "You get a piece of paper, and you write all those names down. Got it?"

He stood, brushing off his scholarly tweed jacket. He walked into the kitchen, and I followed at his heels. He took a pad of paper and a pen out of a drawer and wrote.

"Do you know his birth date?"

"I don't. Erica might know it. She's his younger sister. Her full name is Erica Helene Mathias Cates."

"Jonah"—Melanie touched my arm—"I really don't want to bother her. She's in a fragile mental state at the moment."

I turned to her. What a wonderful woman. Even now, she was thinking of others, always helping people. After all she'd been through, she was still Melanie. A good soul.

"You're lucky that Dr. Carmichael is so forgiving," I said. "I, however, am not." I took the piece of paper he handed me and handed it right back to him. "You forgot the name and number of Gina's friend. The one who said she was in love with someone."

"Oh." He hurriedly wrote down another name and handed the paper back to me. "Marie Cooke, with an e."

I took my wallet out of my back pocket. I folded the paper and placed it in my wallet, and then threw a couple thousand dollars in Franklins on the floor. "That should cover the damage to the door, and then some." I turned to Melanie. "We don't have any more use for this guy. Let's go."

CHAPTER THIRTY-TWO

Melanie

I wasn't sure what to say to Jonah as we drove back to the ranch. He had arranged for us to have dinner with Jade and Talon at the main house. He wanted me to tell Talon what had happened to me. And he was right. It was time. None of it had been my fault, and I needed to talk about it. I knew as well as Jonah that sweeping something under the rug didn't help at all.

Brooke's nurse had taken her into Grand Junction overnight for physical and occupational therapy, so she wouldn't be around. Marjorie was there though, which I didn't mind.

Talon had given Felicia a few weeks off, with pay, to deal with the new developments. So Marjorie was the resident cook. She made a delicious dinner of shrimp scampi.

Ryan was noticeably absent. I was fine with that because he and I hardly knew each other.

"He'd like to be here," Jade said, "but he's got so much work at the vineyards."

"It's okay."

After I told them my sob story, Talon went rigid.

"Besides Jade and Marj here, you're the most important woman in my life, Doc. I'd like to strangle anyone who tries to harm you."

"You have to get in line behind me, bro," Jonah said.

"I'm fine. My ankle is almost all the way healed. I only had to wear the boot for a few days. And my hands." I held them up. "I suppose there will be some scarring, but otherwise, they still work. I guess it's a good thing I went into psychotherapy and not surgery."

"This isn't any time for joking, Doc," Talon said.

"Honestly, I'm fine. I...don't even know how to explain it, but after this experience, I'm looking at things through a different lens. I'm kind of stepping out of the box, you know?"

"Do you have any idea who could have done this to you?"

"We have a few ideas." This was the part I was truly dreading—telling them all about Gina. I had already told Talon during one of our sessions that I had lost a patient to suicide, and I'd also told him I had made my peace with it, which had been a bold-faced lie.

But I was beginning to make my peace with it now. Before I did, though, I had to find out if she had actually committed suicide.

I teared up a bit as I told them the story of Gina...including the letter.

"We saw her father today," Jonah said. "He denies having anything to do with Melanie's attack, of course, and apparently he has an ironclad alibi because the police questioned him and then let him go."

"Well, that doesn't mean anything," Talon said.

"Right now, I just want to find out if Gina did indeed kill herself. So many things don't add up. Like her being in love with me. I never got any kind of vibe like that. And I'm good at recognizing signs if a person was suicidal. She didn't have any. You were in worse shape when you came to see me, Talon." I clamped my hand over my mouth. "I'm sorry. Doctor-patient confidentiality."

Talon laughed. "Everyone here knows exactly the kind of shape I was in when I went to see you."

"Well, I'm still sorry. My point is, you were in worse shape than she was, and you weren't suicidal."

"No, I was never suicidal. Many times I'd wished I were dead, but somehow, my will to live always surfaced at the right time."

Jade smiled. "All of us here are really glad it did."

I nodded, choking up. I had grown fond of Talon.

"Anyway, she always told me that the uncle who abused her was dead, but she could never tell me how or when. So today, we went to talk to her father. It turns out the uncle is not only alive but has been known to use a lot of aliases."

"Why would anyone use aliases?" Marj asked.

"Most likely because he was doing something he shouldn't have been doing," Jonah said. "His name was Theodore Mathias. He went by several aliases, and Cates couldn't remember all of them." Jonah pulled his wallet out, taking out the piece of paper Dr. Cates had given him. "John Smith. Nicholas Castle. Milo Sanchez."

Talon jolted. "What? Read those again."

"John Smith. Nicholas Castle. Milo Sanchez."

"Milo Sanchez. Where have I heard that name before?"

I shrugged. "I've never heard it before."

Marjorie and Jade shook their heads as well.

"Okay, now that's bugging me." Talon got up from the table and began to pace.

These Steel men loved to pace.

And then he shot from the kitchen.

I looked at Jonah, who shrugged.

"Talon?" Jade rose.

Before she could leave the kitchen, though, Talon came back, carrying a file folder. "It's all in here," he said.

"What?" Jonah asked.

"Remember when I told you that Biker Bob had found the records of the guys he did the phoenix tattoo on between twenty-five and thirty years ago?"

Jonah nodded.

Talon pulled out a piece of paper and set it in front of Jonah. "Read it and weep."

He scanned the document. "Christopher Headley. Declan Stevens." He cleared his throat. "And Milo Sanchez."

Ice filled my veins as I suppressed a shudder. "Could it be possible?"

"Doc, did Gina ever mention to you that her uncle had a tattoo?"

I thought back through our sessions. "No, she never mentioned it."

"How old was Gina?"

"Early twenties," I said.

"Her abuse was well after mine." Talon paced around the kitchen and threaded his fingers through his hair. "I can't fucking believe it."

"This is Colorado," Jade said. "Hispanic surnames are common here. This doesn't necessarily mean anything with regard to your case, Talon."

Jonah rose. "This whole thing is just too close for comfort. What if Gina's uncle and one of Talon's abductors are the same man? It's not that big of a stretch really. They're both child molesters. Psychopaths. Killers."

"Amazing," I said, shaking my head. "When I first started thinking about this new theory—that maybe Gina didn't kill herself but had been murdered instead—there was still part of me that didn't believe it was possible. But now..." Now I was the one to rise, pacing around the large kitchen. "Jonah is right. All of this is too close for comfort."

"But Gina died before you met Talon," Jade said.

"True." But there had to be more to this. There just had to be. I sat back down. "You mind if I look at this file?" I asked Talon.

"Of course not. Look at anything you want."

I grabbed the file and riffled through the papers. Just dates that fit the time frame and names. The tattoo had been done on the left forearm in each case. And there was a photograph of the tattoo.

My eyes were drawn to the colorful illustration. This was the actual image that had been both hell and heaven to Talon during his time in captivity. The image that had taunted him, was a menace to him but was also his liberation, on whose wings he flew up in smoke, escaping his brutal reality.

I stared at it. It was hauntingly beautiful, with colors of orange, blue, fuchsia, red, yellow.

"I don't suppose this Biker Bob would remember what any of these men looked like, would he?" I asked.

Talon shook his head. "Believe me, I've interrogated him on everything. It took him months and lots of incentive, if you know what I mean, to find this."

"Have you considered the possibility that this has been fabricated?"

"I have. But Bob seems like a pretty good guy, although I think he spends most of his life stoned."

"If only he could tell us whether the man had brown eyes," Jade said. "That's the only thing you remember about the tattoo guy, right, Talon?"

"Yeah. Unfortunately, I don't remember what color eyes the one with the birthmark had."

Blue. I said the word inside my head while looking to Jonah. He shook his head slightly at me. He didn't have to. I would never have broken his confidence.

But he and I would be talking later. He had to tell his brother what he knew about Tom Simpson. And soon. I turned to Talon.

"We could always go back into guided hypnosis," I said. "Maybe you can remember something else. Of course, I'm not supposed to be practicing at the moment."

"Doc, I don't care. I want you to take me back there."

"Honestly, Talon, I shouldn't do it. While my license isn't technically suspended, I have been asked nicely to take a leave of absence from my practice for three weeks. Gina's parents have filed a complaint against me with the medical board."

"Hell, Doc, I'd trust you to hypnotize me even if you didn't have a license. Besides, you said your license is still valid, right?"

"Yes, it is."

"Then I want you to do it. I need to find out more. Maybe I can remember something they said while they were talking. Maybe something I saw. There has to be something."

"Talon," Jade said, "are you sure you want to go back there again?"

"I'm sure I *don't* want to, blue eyes. But I'm sure I have to. I don't think I'll ever sleep quite right until I know I've done everything I can to bring those fuckers to justice."

"I understand," she said. "It's just so hard on you."

"I think you need to take what Jade is saying into consideration," I said. "I'm happy to do the therapy with you if you want me to do it, but remember, as I've told you before, your healing is not dependent on finding these guys or bringing them to justice. Your healing has to be something you control. And unfortunately, finding these men and making sure they get what's coming to them isn't within your control."

Jonah smiled and took my hand. "She is brilliant as well as beautiful."

I warmed. And then it occurred to me that I had said an awful lot about Talon's healing in front of Jade and Marjorie. But he didn't seem to mind.

"I honestly do understand what all of you are saying, but this is important. If they're still out there, they can prey on other children. If I can do something to make sure that doesn't happen, I want to do it."

"All right. I can't use my office right now because technically I'm on a leave of absence. But we can do a guided hypnosis anywhere you're comfortable. Here, or Jonah's house. Whatever works for you."

"You mind if we use your place, Joe? With Brooke here all the time, I just don't feel comfortable."

"Of course," Jonah said. "Anything for you. You know that."

"Okay," I said. "Obviously, my schedule is flexible at the moment. And I know you're always busy. So just let me know when and where, and we'll make it work."

"Thanks, Doc. You're the best."

Jonah squeezed my hand and whispered to me, "He's right about that."

His phone started vibrating on the table, and he picked it up. "Damn."

He must've gotten another text from Brooke.

"I don't know quite how to tell you this, Jade," Jonah said, "but I think your mother has been sending me texts."

"What?"

"This is kind of embarrassing. She came on to me the other day."

"What?" Jade said again.

"Look, I've got nothing against her. I understand where she's coming from. Her modeling days are over, and she wants to make sure she's still desirable. I told her I wasn't interested, and I thought she got the message."

"Shit, Joe, this might be my fault," Talon said. "I kind of told her you used to worship her when you were a kid."

"Yes." Jonah rolled his eyes. "She mentioned that. Anyway, she's been texting me. Not anything creepy. Just stuff like 'I want you.' 'You're so hot.' This last one says 'We are meant to be together.'"

"Jonah, I'm really sorry," Jade said. "I'll put a stop to this right away."

"I'd appreciate it. I figured it was her because the number has an Iowa area code."

"Iowa?" Jade raised her eyebrows. "The number I have for my mom has a New York area code. She's had it for years."

"Really? I just assumed, because she was dating that man who said he was a senator from Iowa."

"She didn't identify herself as my mother?"

"No, not by name, but the messages started after she came on to me."

"You mind if I look at the number?"

"Not at all." He handed Jade his phone.

"That's not her number, Joe. At least not one that I know of."

CHAPTER THIRTY-THREE

Jonah

Then who the fuck had been sending me texts? It had never occurred to me to actually call the number because I thought it was Brooke. I certainly didn't want to lead her on. I was still hesitant to call. Now this was getting kind of creepy.

"Who the hell could have an area code in Iowa?" I asked.

"It's possible my mom has another phone," Jade said. "But I've only ever seen her use one."

"Maybe she has a phone hidden somewhere," Marj said.

"With my mother, anything is possible. I'll search her things."

"You don't have to do that," I said. "I don't want you to violate her privacy or anything."

"All right, if you're sure you don't want me to," Jade said.

"Let me please call this number first. I've never tried it because I just assumed it was Brooke and I didn't want to lead her on at all." I left the kitchen and walked out to the living room, sitting down on the satin brocade couch. I dialed the number and put the phone to my ear.

It rang. A ringback tone. Classic rock.

But no answer and no voice mail message.

I went back into the kitchen and told them what had happened. "When I researched the number online, all I could find was that it was an Iowa area code."

"We could put Mills and Johnson on it," Talon suggested.

I shook my head. "No. I want them concentrating on what they're doing for you and for Melanie. Those are much larger issues. Once all that is settled, maybe I'll have them try to uncover the identity of my phone stalker." I let out a laugh. I wasn't nervous, exactly, just slightly on edge. If Brooke Bailey wasn't my phone stalker, who could it be?

Melanie yawned. "Jonah, we should probably get going." She turned to Talon and Jade. "Was there anything else you guys needed?"

"No, I think we're good," Talon said.

"Thanks so much for dinner," Melanie said, looking at Marj. "It was delicious."

"No problem," Marj said. "You're welcome here at our table anytime. I hope you know that."

Melanie blushed adorably. "That's nice of you to say."

"After what you've done for our family?" Marj came forward and gave her a hug. "Seriously. Anytime."

I smiled at my sister. I was so grateful to her for welcoming Melanie to the house. Talon and Jade already had, but this was Marjorie's house too.

"And Jonah," Jade added, "I'm really sorry about my mother. I'll tell her that you're involved with someone."

"No, don't embarrass her. Besides, I think she knows."

Melanie was still blushing. She was so beautiful. But right now she was embarrassed, so I needed to get her out of there.

"To echo Melanie," I said. "Thanks to all of you for dinner."

"Good night, Doc. I'll give you a call about the session."

She nodded.

I took her hand, and we left.

★ ★ ★

Once we got back to my house, I let Lucy out and then turned to Melanie. "I don't suppose you want to go for a dip in the hot tub?"

She blushed again. "I don't think so. Somehow I just know someone will interrupt us."

I laughed. "All right. Then, would you come to my bedroom with me?"

She cupped my cheeks and drew me down for a soft kiss. "I will always come to your room with you. Always."

I fingered the diamond choker around her neck. "Someday, I hope I can tell you why I gave this to you."

"Why not tell me now?"

I grinned. "Because you're not quite ready to hear it yet."

"Okay. Then you'll tell me later."

"Like I said, I hope I get that chance."

"Why would you not get that chance? I'm not going anywhere."

I looked into her beautiful green eyes curtained with thick brown lashes and framed with sculpted mahogany brows. She had an oval face, a perfect shape, high cheekbones tinted the slightest peach. She wasn't wearing any makeup. She didn't need it. Her lips were always a natural ruby red, probably from biting them so much. I smiled. If only what she said could be true. But once I told her that I had neglected to take her phone call that horrible evening, chances were good that she would leave me. Especially since I'd now waited so long to tell her. I should've come clean at the beginning. Fuck.

For now, I let go of the choker and stroked her neck. "You're so beautiful."

Her hands were still on my cheeks. "And so are you. Maybe that's not the right thing to say to a man, but you *are* beautiful. Every part of you. And not just in the physical sense."

My heart thumped. So much she didn't know. So much darkness that she hadn't seen...and might never see. I was not beautiful. But for now, for this one moment, I let her words sink under my skin. For her, tonight, I would be a beautiful person.

"Come to bed with me," I said.

I took her hand and led her to my bedroom. This time I didn't ask her to strip for me. I removed her clothes myself, slowly, deliberately, relishing each new inch of skin I exposed. I trailed my lips over every inch of naked skin, raining tiny kisses onto her succulent flesh.

I removed her shirt and bra, letting those beautiful peachy breasts fall gently against her chest. Her red-brown nipples were erect already, beckoning for my mouth. I licked one gently, rolling the other one between my thumb and forefinger.

She sighed beneath my touch.

"You like that, baby?" I said against her rosy breast.

"You know I do."

I continued to lick, teasing her nipples, until she finally took my head and pushed it into her breasts.

Then I sucked harder, just the way she liked. She moaned.

I set her down gently on the bed, removed her shoes and socks, and then slid her jeans and panties—still beige cotton— over her slim hips.

I knelt next to the bed and spread her legs. "Lie back, baby."

She did, her lovely nipples still hard.

"I want to taste you." I started by flicking my tongue

lightly over her clit.

She trembled. I kissed her inner thighs, all the way down to her knees, and then went back the other way, to her pussy. Another quick flick of my tongue over her clit, and then down the other thigh. Her skin tasted of salt and dreams. And then, when I got back to her pussy...

Fragrant and delicious.

This woman was everything. Everything to me.

How could I bear to let her go?

No. Not going to think of that now. I slid my tongue between her wet folds, and my already hard cock throbbed.

Here she was, naked on my bed, and I was still fully clothed.

I wanted to make tonight about her. About what she liked. Not about me trying to introduce her to what *I* liked. I would be gentle. For now. I smiled against her sweet pussy. Making slow, sweet love to her would be no hardship.

As much as I loved taking the dominant role, with Melanie, I could go either way. Making love had never been so perfect as it was with her.

And the fact was, I might never get the chance to introduce her into my private world of pain and pleasure. So while I had the privilege of having her in my bed, I would please *her*. I would do what she liked.

I slid my tongue over her wet slit once more, determined to bypass her asshole this time. But to my surprise, she lifted her thighs, pulling them upward, baring herself to me. Did she want me to lick her ass?

I looked up. "Melanie, tell me what you want."

She bent her neck, meeting my gaze. "Lick me...*there*. Please."

I smiled. She was so cute. She couldn't even say "asshole." Adorable.

I had been determined to make this about her, but hey, if this was what she wanted. I slid my tongue over her puckered hole.

She sighed.

I took that to mean that she liked it. I lubed her up well with my saliva, forced my tongue into a point, and began to probe the tight hole.

"Oh..." she groaned.

I continued tongue-fucking her asshole until I couldn't take it any longer. I needed to taste her again. I slid my tongue up her slick slit. I sucked at her, eating all that cream out of her pussy, until I had the urge to kiss her mouth. I leaned forward, still fully clothed, and brushed my lips against hers.

"Kiss me, Melanie. I want you to taste your juice on my tongue."

She opened for me, and I delved in, swirling my tongue with her warm silky one.

The taste of her sugary mouth mingled with the taste of her pussy. Was there any sweeter nectar? Her kisses intoxicated me. I had never been the kind of man who could make out with a woman for hours, but with Melanie, I felt like I could kiss her forever. My cock was straining against my jeans, but still, I didn't want to move my mouth from hers and get undressed.

We kissed and we kissed, for a long, long time.

Until I realized I hadn't yet brought her to climax. I tore my mouth from hers and trailed my lips down her sleek neck, over her shoulders, down her arms to each finger. Up again to her other shoulder and down. I gave her breasts some deserved attention, nibbling on her nipples as she arched beneath me.

Then I rained kisses over her smooth abdomen, to her triangle of blond curls, to that beautiful red pussy.

I licked her clit, and then I forced my whole tongue inside of her wet heat. She was so wet and gushing for me. I wanted her to come all over my face. I continued tongue-fucking her, alternating with sucking on her clit. She writhed beneath me, fisting her hands in my hair and pushing me farther into her heat.

I lapped her up, savoring every drop of her juices, and then, when she started to clamp down a bit, I shoved two fingers deep inside her, pushing up against the anterior wall, her G-spot.

And she shattered, coming all over my face and fingers.

I sucked at her relentlessly, and when her orgasm started to subside, I gave her clit a little nip, and she soared again.

"Oh my God, Jonah. So good. So good."

I flipped her over onto her hands and knees and buried my face between her gorgeous ass cheeks. I couldn't wait any longer to have her. I stood back, unbuckled my jeans, and forced them over my hips. And I plunged inside that hotness.

So complete. I had never felt this way with anyone. Every moment I entered her was amazing, made me feel so whole, like we were truly one being.

I had never had sex like this.

And I never would again.

I fucked her hard, pounding into her, because I knew it wouldn't take long for me to reach climax.

When my balls tightened, I gritted my teeth and rammed as hard as I could into that sweet heat.

As I exploded inside her, I closed my eyes. "Melanie, goddamnit, I love you."

When my orgasm finally started to subside, I withdrew, still in my boots, my jeans and boxers around my thighs. My beautiful woman was naked, glistening with a sheen of perspiration. And I hadn't even bothered to take off my clothes.

Would it always be like this with Melanie? I couldn't wait to take two minutes to disrobe before I had to fuck her?

We'd been together for weeks now, but my passion and desire increased every time we were together.

I longed to show more of the darker side of my desires.

But not now.

As long as I could have her, I would turn away from my baser instincts.

Because I might not have her for much longer.

CHAPTER THIRTY-FOUR

Melanie

I rolled over onto my back and looked at Jonah. He was gorgeous, his finely sculpted face shining with sweat, his wavy hair plastered against his forehead, his black-and-gray stubble glistening.

I smiled. "Maybe you should get undressed."

He returned my smile and sat down on the bed, pulling his boots and socks off. He made quick work of the rest of his clothes and then lay down beside me. I looked into his dark eyes, alive with fire.

"Would you tell me about...what you like?"

He closed his eyes and let out a groan. "I like what we just did together. It's wonderful with you."

"I believe you. I see it in your eyes and I can feel it when you want me. And believe me when I say it's exactly the same for me. Absolutely wonderful. But I know there's a side of you that you haven't shown me. I want to know all of you."

He sighed and then turned on his side to face me. "Sweetheart, I love you. I've never said that to a woman and meant it like I do with you. Hell, I've only said it to one other woman in my life, when I was young. During a summer fling after high school."

"You've never dated anybody seriously?"

He shook his head. "I've had my share of conquests, and I've had a few girlfriends over the years. But I didn't fall for any of them, and they eventually left me. Sex was fun. Dating was sort of fun, but nothing like what I feel for you."

I looked at him seriously. "Did any of them do...those things you like to do?"

He smiled. "Most of them did, yes. But I was never serious about any of them. I never collared anyone."

"Collared?"

He cleared his throat. "Bound them to me formally. As my submissive."

I swallowed. *Submissive.* I knew the term. And I knew what it meant. Sort of. "Where did you meet them?" I wasn't sure I really wanted to hear the answer to that question.

"Here and there."

"That's not an answer. Did you meet them online?"

"Oh, hell, no. I would never do online dating."

I wouldn't either, although I had considered it. The truth was, I hadn't had anyone serious in my life for a while either. Same as Jonah, I'd dated here and there, but nothing ever came of any of it, and truth be told, I'd never said "I love you" to any of them.

"So where did you meet them then?" I prodded.

"There's...a club. A club in the city where the leather community hangs out."

I gasped, and then felt really stupid for doing so. I wasn't so naïve that I thought there were no such things as sex clubs. I knew better. But I had lived in Grand Junction for the last fifteen years. I knew it like the back of my hand. Where the hell was the sex club?

"Do you still go there?" I asked.

He shook his head. "I've outgrown a lot of that—the scenes in public kind of thing. It's not my thing anymore. Never really was something I did regularly. If I was dating someone at the time who enjoyed it, we would go."

I bit my lip. "What kind of things did you do there?"

"Look, Melanie, I will never take you there. I haven't been there myself in five years or so."

"Still, I'm asking. What kind of things did you do there?"

"Those clubs aren't for the faint of heart, sweetheart. I didn't do anything wrong, and everything I did was fully consensual on both sides, but someone like you..."

"What do you mean, 'someone like me'? I'm a psychotherapist, for God's sake. You think I haven't heard about kink?"

I hadn't had any patients who were into kink, but I wasn't ignorant to its existence.

"All right. Sometimes my s— er, lady and I would do a scene."

"What do you mean by a scene?"

He let out another sigh. "The thing you need to understand about clubs like these, is they have a certain amount of members who are voyeurs. People who like to watch."

I nodded.

"And then there are people who like to *be* watched."

"And were you one of those?"

"Not overly. Sometimes I would do a scene with my woman in public. Most often I would do it in one of the private rooms. Except for when I was with..."

"Who?"

He closed his eyes. "Are you sure you want to go there?"

"I love you. I need to know about you."

"I'm not into the club scene anymore, Melanie."

"That doesn't matter. It was a part of your life, and I want to know about it."

He opened his eyes. "All right. But if you go running and screaming out of here, I'll never forgive myself."

"I won't. I promise."

"Good, because if you do, I will catch you. And bring you right back into my bed." His eyes heated me from the inside out.

"So tell me."

"I was dating—hell, dating isn't the right word. I was sleeping with this woman named Kerry. She was a true submissive. In fact, she wanted to be my slave."

"Slave?"

"Yes. She wanted to be my live-in house slave, at my beck and call. She wanted me to rule over her not only in the bedroom but also in everyday life."

I was shocked. A submissive I could understand, but a slave? "You mean there are people who do that?"

He nodded. "Lots of people enjoy it, men and women alike. I knew a couple at the club who were these everyday people. The woman was the master—or mistress, as a female is called—and the man was a high-powered orthopedic surgeon by day. At home, he was kept on a leash."

"Wow..."

"I assure you I wasn't into anything like that, Melanie. I have nothing against people who do it. If it works for them, more power to them. Anything consensual is okay in my book, as long as others don't get hurt. But I promise you I never even thought about taking Kerry as my slave. I do like a submissive woman in the bedroom, but I don't want a slave at home. I want a partner."

"I see."

"One thing I love about you, Melanie, is your brilliance, your intelligence. You know your own mind. I could never ask you—or anyone, for that matter—to be a slave."

"That's good. I can tell you right now I would never be a slave. But like you said, if that works for some people, I suppose it's a good thing."

"It is, for some people. But anyway, that's what Kerry wanted. And once I found out that was what she wanted, and I told her I couldn't do it, she ended the relationship. But before, when she was simply my submissive, we would often do public scenes in the club."

"Because you wanted to?"

"No. Because *she* wanted to. She loved to be watched."

"That's so foreign to me. I was so embarrassed when Talon and Jade, and then Bryce, and then Talon again, caught us naked in your pool."

"That's a little different. That was my family and my friend. It's different at the club. There, everyone is in the lifestyle. Those who like to watch get to watch. Those who like to play get to play. Those who like to be watched are watched. Everyone is there for a specific reason."

"So what did you do with Kerry at the club? And where is this so-called club anyway? I'm very familiar with the city. I live there, remember?"

He smiled. "You'd be surprised what can be found in the seamy underground side of the city. But to answer your first question... Are you sure you want to know?"

I nodded.

"Kerry liked to be tied up and spanked. Which I like as

well. She liked other things too, things I had never tried before, and some of which I probably won't do again."

"Like what?"

"She liked needles."

"Needles?" I gasped.

"Yes. I was always very careful not to break her skin, even when she begged me to. But she loved sharp points and needles. She also liked candle and wax play."

"What...exactly do you do with candles and wax?"

"You can do a lot of things. She liked me to hold a taper over her breasts and let the hot wax drip on her nipples. She also liked me to penetrate her with a lit candle."

I gasped again, my hands over my mouth.

He smiled. "Not the end that was lit."

God, I felt stupid. "Of course. I knew that."

"Is this overwhelming for you? Are you sorry you asked?"

"No, I need to know."

"I promise you that candles and needles aren't my thing."

Something snapped in me. So candles weren't his thing. But...what would that feel like? To have hot wax dripping down my breasts, over my nipples? Did I want to know?

Before I could ponder any further, Jonah went on.

"Kerry liked them, and because I was her Dominant and I wanted to please her, I did them. And she liked being watched, so I did them in front of other people."

"But you were the Dominant. Wasn't it her job to please you?"

"It's not like that, baby. It's a two-way street. We please each other. It's all about pleasure for both the Dom and the sub."

This was all a lot to digest. "Did you...enjoy those things?

The candles and the needles?"

"Even though they're not really my thing, I did, but only because she enjoyed them. You have to understand the Dominant personality. Yes, I like to be in charge, but it's never my desire to hurt anyone. I want to ultimately bring pleasure, not pain. Sometimes, though, pain is pleasure."

"I don't know if I'll ever understand that."

"You may not. I've often wondered myself why this is the type of play that appeals to me. You're a therapist, so you tell me. Why do you suppose I like that?"

Nothing like being put on the spot. "Honestly, the type of sex a person likes has very little to do with other parts of his life. But if I had to make a guess, I'd say you need to be in control."

"Why would I need to be in control? I mean, I used to go to skid row and deliberately get beat up, just so I could punish myself for not being there for Talon."

I nearly snapped my neck with a double take. "You did? You did that on purpose?"

"Aw, hell... I never told you that, did I? Fuck."

My heart went out to him. "You can tell me anything. You know that. Nothing will change the way I feel about you."

"I'm not sure that's true..."

"Of course it's true. How could you doubt my love for you?"

He didn't respond.

"You don't go out looking for trouble anymore, do you?"

"No. I haven't had a desire to. But wouldn't it make more sense if I wanted to take a submissive role in the bedroom?"

"No. Not at all. You're a heterosexual male, so you have sex with women. Women didn't abuse Talon. Men did. So you were trying to be punished by men because you felt it should have been you instead of Talon. But in your relationships with women, you like to exert control, and that could be because of any number of things. There could be no bigger explanation for them than that you're the owner of a very successful ranch. Your whole life is about control."

"You think?"

I smiled. "Jonah, it takes months of therapy to uncover things like this. That's just my best guess at this point."

"I see. I hope you're not sorry I told you these things."

I touched his face. "Not at all. It helps me understand you a little bit better to be honest. But truthfully...I don't think I want to go to your club."

"It's not *my* club. I told you, I haven't been there in over five years, and I have no desire to go there anymore. I've grown out of a lot of that stuff. Whether that's good or bad, I don't know. Some people live their whole lives in that lifestyle. Others just experiment. Everyone is different."

"Are you saying you were experimenting?"

"With Kerry, because she was into some stuff that I wasn't. And with the others...some yes and some no."

"I think... I think I've heard enough for now."

"At least you're not running out of here."

"No. I won't leave you. I love you. And your past is part of who you are today. But I need to go slowly."

"I understand. Today I was determined just to make slow, sweet love to you, Melanie. I wanted to do what you wanted, what you deserved. Because that's how much I love you. I want to please you more than I want to please myself. I wasn't even going to lick you...down there." He smiled. "But when you asked me to, I couldn't help myself."

I smiled. "I never thought I would enjoy anal play. I had no idea that part of me was so sensitive."

"It's pretty amazing."

"It is." I somehow felt very daring. "So turn over. Let's see how you like it."

CHAPTER THIRTY-FIVE

Jonah

"Melanie," I said. "I think you're forgetting that I like to take a dominant role."

"And you're forgetting that I love you. I want to show you the pleasure that you show me."

I laughed out loud. "I can't fault your reasoning."

"And I assure you," she said, "I will never ever think of you as anything but a truly dominant male. You are the epitome of a man's man. Broad shoulders, amazing muscles in your arms and legs. And the way you stood up to Dr. Cates... Wow. I know you will protect me with life and limb if you have to."

I turned to her and cupped her cheeks, staring at her beautiful green eyes. "Absolutely, Melanie. I would do anything for you. I'd take a bullet for you if I had to."

Guilt rushed over me. I hadn't been there when she needed me. If only I had taken that phone call... I had been over this in my mind time and time again. Even if I had taken the phone call, I might not have been able to get there in time. Talon and I were already on our way out of town. And I didn't know how long she was in her loft before they left. But I could've at least gotten the police involved. Yes, she had said 9-1-1 had rung busy. But I would've stayed on the fucking phone until I got a goddamned answer. I would have turned the world on its side to keep her safe.

Why hadn't I answered that phone?

"Well, since you say you'd do anything for me, get on your hands and knees, Mr. Steel. I'm going to lick your ass." She burst into giggles. "I can't believe those words just came out of my mouth."

I joined her in laughter. I couldn't believe those words had come from her mouth either. But I loved the fact that she wanted to give me the pleasure that I gave her, and I had no doubt that she saw me as strong and dominant. So I obeyed her and got on my hands and knees.

"Now let's see what you can do with that mouth," I said.

She was tentative, at first, exploring the cheeks of my ass with her hand, and I could feel her hesitance.

"It's okay, Melanie. Touch me. I crave your touch. Everywhere."

"I don't want to disappoint you. I don't want to do it wrong."

"You could never disappoint me. And there is no right or wrong. This is just pleasure. Pure pleasure."

The touching stopped for a moment, and even with my back to her, I knew she was biting her lip.

And then, a tiny prickle of warmth slithered between the cheeks of my ass.

My pulse raced. I had licked many assholes in my day, but this was the first time anyone had licked mine. Now I could see why women liked the practice so much. The flesh was way more sensitive than I would've thought, although I should've known that, given how women had responded to me over the years.

It was a new sensation. My thighs began to tingle beneath

me, and my cock hardened.

She became bolder, stroking her tongue up my entire crack, back down, and then focusing on the hole. She swirled her tongue around it, poked at it, prodded at it. My rim of muscle was too tightened up for the tip of her tongue to go in, but the prodding... Fuck. My cock was throbbing between my legs.

She moved away from my asshole for a few moments, kissing the cheeks of my butt, the tops of my thighs. Goose bumps erupted on my flesh, and the tingling sensation continued. I desperately wanted her to go back to my ass, but I didn't feel comfortable asking her to. This whole thing was probably way out of her comfort zone.

Luckily, I didn't have too long to wait for more tongue in the ass. My God, it was sensational.

"So good, baby," I groaned. "That feels amazing."

She licked faster then, my words perhaps spurring her on. Soon I felt saliva river down my perineum and my balls.

And goddamnit, I had to have her.

How I longed to shove my cock in her tight little asshole, but that would have to wait.

The next time she removed her mouth, I flipped over quickly, my erection huge and standing straight.

She bit her lip—that beautiful red lower lip.

"Sit on my cock, baby. I need to be inside you."

She gnawed more on that lower lip. "Did you like it?"

I closed my eyes and groaned. "My God, sweetheart. Look at this fucking hard-on I have for you because of what you were doing."

She smiled and sank down on my cock.

Sweet fucking Jesus. I had come home.

"Now fuck me, baby," I said. "Ride my cock. Ride me all the way home."

She lifted off of me and plunged back down. My skin tingled, my nerves sizzled, every cell in my body prepared for an orgasm.

"That's right. Fuck me, baby. Fuck me hard."

Her beautiful tits bounced as she fucked me, and I reached for them, thumbing her erect nipples. She sighed beneath my hands. Still fucked me hard.

She was an angel above me, her blond hair falling in waves over her soft shoulders. Her green eyes were closed.

She bit that luscious lower lip of hers, always ruby red and ready to be kissed.

"God, baby. You're so beautiful."

She fucked me harder, and then...one of her arms slithered down to her abdomen, and she began stroking.

I nearly exploded into her then. So beautiful, watching her touch herself. I groaned. "Baby, I can't believe how gorgeous you are."

Her fingers slowly padded over her folds and her opening, which was slick with juices. She rubbed herself while continuing to fuck me.

I hoped she would come soon because I was nearly there. I gritted my teeth, trying to hold back, not wanting it to end because her gyrating hips pushing up and down on my dick felt so good.

And then—

"Oh!" She forced her beautiful pussy down on my cock.

That was the end for me. I spewed up into her, releasing everything into her, my heart, my body, my soul. All into this beautiful woman.

Melanie. My Melanie.

I closed my eyes, thrusting my hips up into her, milking every last drop from my cock.

"Melanie." I opened my eyes.

Her long hair was plastered in damp strips to her creamy body.

"I love you," I ground out.

Her orgasm was still reeling, her eyes still closed, her body still shuddering above mine. God, she was beautiful. Her body was covered in a shiny coat of dew.

So perfect.

She pulled herself off me, and immediately I felt that sense of loss. But soon she was snuggling in my arms, her head tucked into my shoulder. I wrapped my arms around her.

How perfectly she fit against my body, like we'd been created to slide together. No one had ever felt so good against me, as if she were cut perfectly to fit my mold.

And in my heart, my soul, the deepest marrow of my bones, I knew no one ever would again.

* * *

A few days later, Melanie arranged to meet Talon at the house to do a therapy session including hypnosis. I had finished my work for the day, so I decided it would be a good day to drive into the city and have a chat with Larry Wade. Bryce had gone with me the last time, but this time I needed to see Larry alone. There were questions I needed to ask—questions I couldn't ask in front of my best friend. I couldn't ask Talon to go with me either. He wasn't ready to face one of the men who had abused him so horrifically. Plus, I had every intention of asking Larry point blank about Tom Simpson and where he might be hiding. I needed to be armed with the most accurate information possible when I told Talon and Bryce my suspicions.

And while I was at it, I'd ask about Milo Sanchez, and if there was any connection to Nico Kostas or Gina's abusive uncle.

Would he answer? Probably not. So I'd have to be on guard. I'd have to try to get him to slip up.

I sat at the table looking through the glass, waiting for Larry to come and talk to me on the phone. Because it was only me this time, a guard didn't need to escort Larry to the visitor's area. For violent offenders like Larry, even though he hadn't been convicted of anything yet, the guards really didn't like to use the open area.

I was slightly disappointed. I wanted to look my uncle straight in the eye and ask questions. Granted, the glass was clear, but it still created a barrier—a barrier I didn't want right now.

Finally, a guard escorted Larry down the walkway to the desk in front of me. We were separated only by the glass. I picked up the phone.

Larry picked up the phone as well. "What the fuck do you want now?"

"Nice to see you too, Uncle Larry."

Again, Larry looked like he had aged. His face had healed, but had lost weight, and his forearms were bruised and battered. Clearly, he was still getting into some trouble behind bars.

"Just here to ask you some questions," I said. "I hope you're feeling more talkative today."

"Can't say that I am."

"The offer still stands. You tell me what I want to know, and I'll hire the best lawyer in Colorado to represent you."

He said nothing.

"So...I'm going to ask you again about Nico Kostas. Does that name ring a bell?"

"Nope."

"How about Milo Sanchez?"

One of his brows lifted. Nearly microscopically, but I noticed. I again cursed the glass between us. If only I could get a look straight into his face, with no barrier, not even a clear one.

"Recognize the name?"

Larry cleared his throat. "No."

"Theodore Mathias."

Again his brow lifted, just slightly.

"Nicholas Castle?"

Nothing.

"John Smith?"

Nothing again. Either he had trained his eyebrows to stay down, or he didn't recognize the names.

"Is it possible that all those men—Nico Kostas, Milo Sanchez, and the other three—are all the same person?"

"I have no idea what you're talking about," Larry said.

"Some of them even sound similar. Nico Kostas and Nicholas Castle. Don't you think those names sound similar?"

"Don't know. Don't care."

"I understand that one of your fellow abductors had a phoenix tattoo on his left forearm."

Larry cleared his throat.

"Interestingly, both a man named Nico Kostas and a man named Milo Sanchez have the same exact tattoo. I'm talking identical, on the left forearm, and both got the tattoo at a shop in Snow Creek. Do you find that odd at all?"

"Can't say that I do." He cleared his throat again. "Listen, I don't have to talk to you."

"No, I suppose you don't. But I'm not done here, so you stay seated."

"Why should I? What will you do for me?"

"How about this? I don't talk to the guard over there, and you don't get murdered in your bed tonight."

Larry widened his eyes for a moment, but only a split second. A-ha. That got to him.

"I see you've already been having some trouble with your fellow inmates. Trust me, it could get worse. Much worse."

He pursed his lips into a thin line.

"So you will sit here and talk to me until I'm done."

He nodded.

"So far you've been a huge help," I said sarcastically. "Are Nico Kostas and Milo Sanchez the same person?"

"And I told you I don't know."

"Was Milo Sanchez one of the abductors?"

His mouth remained closed, his lips set.

"How about this? Whose idea was it to take Talon?"

"Talon was never meant to be taken."

"So you say, but we've come into some new information. From Wendy Madigan."

His brow lifted slightly again.

"Wendy seems to think Talon was taken on purpose, for ransom, by enemies of my father. Tell me, Uncle. Who were these enemies of my father?"

"I don't know what you're talking about." He sounded genuinely confused. "Talon was never meant to be taken."

"That's your word against hers, then. You're a psychopathic child molester, and she's a respected newswoman. Who should I believe?"

"She's not who you think she is."

I'd already decided that for myself, but now my uncle had confirmed it. "Who is she, then?"

"Nobody. She's nobody."

"What was her role in all of this? Was she my father's lover?"

Larry's brows nearly jumped off his forehead. But he said nothing.

That was all the proof I needed. I'd be investigating Wendy Madigan further. However, I did know one thing for certain. Wendy was not one of Talon's abductors. They were all men. So this line of questioning wasn't going to get me any closer to the two we hadn't caught.

Time to try a different avenue.

"The last time we were here, you had some advice for my friend Bryce. And also for me, I believe. You said not to go searching for the truth, that it was overrated. What did you mean by that?"

"I think that speaks for itself."

"Perhaps, but I want to know why you said it."

He glared at me. "You *know* why, don't you?"

Yes, I did. And now Larry knew that I knew. "Tom Simpson, the mayor of Snow Creek. Bryce's father. Is he one of the abductors?"

"I won't roll over."

"I know about his birthmark. Talon remembers it, just like he remembers the phoenix tattoo, and he remembers that you were missing a little toe. It's amazing what therapy can do for repressed memories. Things you thought were long gone come screaming back into your head. That happened for Talon. And that's what helped us catch you. Believe me, we will catch the other two. However, if you help us, we can help you."

Larry said nothing for several seconds. Then, "They'll kill me."

"What makes you think they won't kill you anyway? They already tried once, didn't they? After you let Talon go. Remember? You ended up in the hospital, on the brink of death."

"See what I mean?"

"Look, you're in here. They're out there. They can't get to you in here. But *I* can."

"Believe me, they can too."

"What are you saying? That the reason you've been getting gangbanged is because of them?"

He nodded.

"Then what does it matter? We get them into custody, and they can't make any more trouble for you from the outside."

"Don't be naïve. They could make a lot more trouble for me from in here."

"Look, I need some answers here. There's a girl who allegedly committed suicide because her uncle abused her—an uncle who went by the name of Milo Sanchez, which just happens to be the name of a man who had the same tattoo as one of Talon's abductors. It's possible that this young woman didn't kill herself, but that she was murdered. I need to know where to find that man. And as for Tom Simpson? He has disappeared."

Larry widened his eyes again. "He has?"

"Yes. About a week ago. No one's seen him or heard from

him. Do you have any idea where he might be?"

"If I did, I wouldn't be able to tell you."

"Because they'd kill you?"

"Yes."

I felt kind of caught between a rock and a hard place. I wouldn't mind seeing Larry get the shit kicked out of him, but I also needed him alive, to answer my questions. Problem was, so far he had refused to do so. If only we were sitting at the table, right in front of each other. I'd be able to play with his head a little better.

I opened my mouth to speak, but he spoke first.

"So have you told your friend about your suspicion?"

"You mean about his father?"

Larry nodded.

"No, I haven't. Not yet."

"Your brother?"

"Not yet. I need proof. That has to come from you."

No response.

"The mayor told me that you and he go way back. That you went to high school together in Grand Junction."

"That's right."

"Any chance Theodore Mathias went to that same school?"

No response.

"Nico Kostas? Milo Sanchez?"

No response.

"Larry, you've got to give me something here."

"I don't have to give you anything."

Christ. Either this man was terminally stubborn, or he truly was afraid for his life.

"Fine." I stared straight at him, through the glass, into

his vacant blue eyes. "One last thing. You might want to do something before you go to sleep tonight."

"What?"

"Say your fucking prayers. It'll be a long night."

CHAPTER THIRTY-SIX

Melanie

Jonah had gone into the city, so Talon came over in the late afternoon for our session. I needed an enclosed space, where we could have quiet, so I decided on one of the vacant bedrooms. Unfortunately, Talon was used to sitting in my recliner during his sessions. The best I could do was either a rocking chair or a bed.

"That's fine," Talon said. "I'll lie on the bed."

"Are you sure? You never wanted to lie on the couch in my office."

"Yeah, but that was when I was new to therapy. I'll be fine. I no longer feel so...vulnerable. Plus, lying on a shrink's couch—that's just so cliché."

"This will seem a little different because we're not in my office, but it will basically be the same thing. I'll take you back to the beach, like the other times. Then we'll go from there. Is that all right?"

"Yes. Whatever you think is best." He sat down on the bed and pulled his legs over, laying his head on the pillow. He squirmed and fidgeted a bit.

"Let's get you a little comfortable first," I said. "How are things going? With the ranch? Jade?"

"Good. I'm still taking terrible advantage of my foreman.

He's been really understanding about the extra workload. I love having Jade at the house. We talk every night after dinner."

"How's her work going?"

"She's overworked. There's only one attorney, so everything falls on her. And now, with the mayor missing, she has even more going on."

Of course. The mayor was missing. Bryce had told Joe and me earlier. In fact, I was possibly the last person to have seen him in the Snow Creek hardware store before he disappeared.

But I couldn't tell Talon any of this. At least not yet.

"The mayor's missing?" I said.

"Yes. He just up and vanished sometime last week. Now a lot of his stuff has fallen on Jade as well."

"He doesn't have a deputy mayor?"

Talon laughed. "Not in a town this small, Doc."

I returned his laughter. "How are you feeling otherwise? Are you still having dreams?"

"Yeah. About once a week. I try not to let them bother me, though. I've kind of trained myself to wake up before the dream gets bad. I lie there for a few minutes, listening to Jade breathe beside me, and then I'm able to go back to sleep."

"Good."

"Do you think they'll ever stop altogether?"

"They may. And they may not. The important thing is to handle them well, which you seem to be doing."

"This is never really going to go away, is it?"

I sighed. "Therapy can't erase what happened to you, Talon. I only wish that it could. The best therapy can do is help you heal, help you deal with the fact that it did happen, help you accept that it wasn't your fault and that it doesn't change who you, as a person, are. You've come a long way. You're definitely one of my biggest success stories."

"I suppose. I know I want to live now. I look forward to every new day, and for a long time I never thought that was possible." He cleared his throat. "I'm really sorry about your other patient. The girl."

"Every therapist—every doctor, whatever his specialty—has patients who don't make it." I tried to sound nonchalant.

"I'm sure," he said. "That doesn't make it easier, though."

"No, it does not. But let's get back to you."

"Okay. Sorry."

"No problem. Are you ready?"

"Yes. I need to figure out if I can remember anything at all that might help us catch the other two guys."

"All right." I flipped the speakers on from my laptop and started playing the ocean sounds.

"Close your eyes. You're on a lounging chair on the beach. I want you to scrunch your toes up and then relax them. Feel the tingle. Feel the sun shining on you, as you hear the waves rolling in. The birds chirping here and there. Now tense up your calves, and then relax them. Feel the tingling and relaxing sensation from your knees out to your toes. The sun is shining its warmth on your face, a tiny breeze blows over you, and you welcome the coolness of it..."

★ ★ ★

Look around. Do you see anything on the walls?

The walls... They're caving in on me. It's dark... I am shivering. And so cold. Always cold.

Warm yourself. You have woolen gloves on your hands. You're wearing a warm fleece jacket and fleece pants. Snuggly slippers on your feet.

So, so cold.

You have mittens, fleece. You're not cold.

The walls are caving in. So frightened.

You know the walls can't move. They're inanimate objects.

The bird. The bird with flames for wings. It's on the wall, *staring at me, taunting me.*

That's your imagination. You know it's your imagination. Now look around the room.

Just gray walls. Gray concrete floor. Never any light except when they open the door up the stairs.

There are no windows in the place?

No. No windows. They open the door, and the light hurts my eyes.

Look around the room. Is there anything you can identify?

Just gray. Cold, dark, gray.

And then someone opens the door, and there's a sliver of light?

Yes.

Who comes down?

He feeds me.

Yes, the one who's missing a toe on one of his feet.

Yes, that one. He always wears his mask, but sometimes, when the others don't come, he doesn't wear black.

What is he doing today?

My eyes adjust. He brings me a sandwich. Peanut butter and jelly, I think. He sets it on the floor in front of me, and then he takes the bucket upstairs. He brings it back empty.

Does he say anything to you?

No. Not when he comes alone. He only talks when the three of them are together.

Are you going to eat the sandwich?

Yes, I always eat what he brings me. Even if I'm not hungry. I'm never really hungry.

So there's nothing in the room itself that you can recognize?

No. Just dark, cold, and gray. Dark, cold, gray.

Look at the steps. Look at them the next time someone enters. What do you see?

Just steps.

Are they carpeted?

No. Just wooden steps. They're painted gray, I think. Everything is gray.

Remember the day you escaped. The one when he left the door open.

Yes. I'm so tired. Weak. I can hardly walk. All I have is my T-shirt. No pants. But I have to try. So I get up the stairs.

And what do you see when you get to the top of the stairs?

I'm in... Is it a kitchen? A little kitchen. I don't know. I look around a little. I think I pick something up...but then I run. I'm so scared, and I run. I run out the first door I find, in the kitchen.

Go back. Go back to the kitchen. You said you looked around. Do you see anything in the kitchen? Anything unusual?

I... I see a briefcase.

Good. What color is the briefcase?

It's brown. Brown leather. Like my saddle at home.

Anything else?

Yes. Masks. Black ski masks. Sitting on the table next to the briefcase. And something shiny.

Do you stop to look at these things?

Not for very long. But I like shiny things. I pick it up. It's gold. It's a circle. It has letters on it.

You mean it's engraved.

Yeah. Letters. T. And something else. I don't remember.

Look around the kitchen once more. Do you see anything else?

No. I drop the shiny thing, and I run.

Where do you run?

There's a door right by the table. A screen door, and then another door that's locked. But I can unlock it from the inside, and I open it, and I run.

Again...where do you run?

I just start running. I'm in grass. I run and I run and I run... And then it's different. I'm in a field, and now I have clothes on, and I see a house.

You escaped. But I need you to go back to the house, back where they kept you.

No! No, I won't go back there. You can't make me go back there!

You have to if you want to find anything else.

Nothing else! I won't go back! No! No! No!

Everything is fine. You never have to go back. You're not there. You're on the beach, lying in the sun...

★ ★ ★

"Relax," I said. "You're not there, Talon. You're here. In Jonah's house. And you're safe. Relax and count back with me. Nine, eight, seven..."

"Six, five, four, three, two, one." Talon's voice became calmer.

"You're safe here. Now open your eyes."

He opened his eyes and then sat up, clearly agitated. "Oh my God. I didn't know what that thing was at the time. I was just a kid. But it was a cuff link."

"It was?"

"Yeah. It was a gold cuff link. I wanted to keep it. If I found it anywhere else, I would've put it in my pocket. But I didn't have a pocket."

"Instead you left it there."

"Yes. I threw it on the ground."

"You said it had letters on it. One was a T. Can you remember anything else? Maybe the other letters?"

He shook his head. "I can't believe I haven't remembered that until now. It's all clear as day. There was a T, and then I got scared and threw it down."

"Are you sure there was more than one letter?"

"Yes, I think so. Damn!" He rose from the bed and paced around the room. "Why didn't I stop and look harder?"

"Because your first thought was getting out of there, as it should have been. Don't berate yourself. You were ten. You did the best you could."

"Could T be an initial of one of my abductors?"

"I don't know," I said. "But it's certainly something to look into."

"But not Nico Kostas or Milo Sanchez. Neither of the other guys who got the tattoo has those initials either." Talon raked his fingers through his hair and let out a heavy sigh. "God, Doc, it could be nothing. It could be fucking nothing."

"You're right. It could be nothing. But you did remember something. I tried having you look around the room where they kept you, but you kept saying dark, gray, cold. You were focused on Larry bringing you food, so there really wasn't an opening for me to get to one of the other guys. So I had to go up the stairs, and we got something. We got another clue."

"Yes, I suppose so. What I was really hoping for, though, was to get more physical characteristics. Something to identify the other two."

"You're being too hard on yourself, Talon. You were ten years old, a scared little boy, and all you remember about that place is that it was cold, dark, and gray. It's a miracle you've remembered the things you have. These men were all in black, and it was dark. You may have to face the reality that you may not remember anything else visible. Because it was dark and you were scared, there are a lot of things you probably didn't notice."

"Take me back, then. I'll try harder. I'll look around more. I'll—"

"Talon," I said, "I think you need to face the facts that you've remembered everything you're going to remember."

"No. There's got to be something more."

"Maybe. But probably not. It's pretty amazing that you've been able to recall what you have. Remember that today all you said about the area was that it was cold, dark, gray. I couldn't get you to go any further until you went up the steps. Up the steps there was light. You could see. You were frightened, and you wanted to get out of there, but still, you noticed a few things on the table. That's huge."

"But it's not enough."

"It's a leather briefcase and a cuff link with a T on it. It's what we have, Talon."

"I need more. I need to figure out who the hell these guys are. I need to find them."

"Calm down. You need to focus on your healing. I think it's time we really focused on that. I think you need to take a break from trying to figure all this out."

That was easy for me to say, since Jonah had already figured out who one of them was. Once Talon knew that, he would feel better about the whole thing, and maybe he'd decide to give up this quest and focus solely on the life ahead of him.

"You have a beautiful future with Jade. The future is what's important. Not the past. Don't take your eyes off the prize."

"I haven't, Doc. I haven't."

"Have you popped the question to Jade, yet?"

He shook his head. "No."

"Why not?"

He sighed. "You know why. Because we're knee-deep into this investigation into the rose and the business card. The thing with Felicia. And now what has happened to you, and how it might be all related... It's just so much to deal with."

"And again, you're losing focus on what's truly important."

"This is all important, damn it."

"I'm not saying it's not. But what is constant, whether you figure the rest of this out or not?"

He closed his eyes. "My family. Jade."

"That's right."

He opened his eyes. "You always have the right answer, Doc."

"I'm not so sure that's true," I said. I hadn't had the right answer for Gina, apparently. Though now I wasn't so sure.

"It's true for me."

I opened my mouth to respond when the doorbell rang.

"I'll see who that is," Talon said. "I don't want you answering the door after what you've been through."

"I'm fine—"

He gestured for me to stop. "Nope. I'm getting it."

I followed him out anyway. He opened the door to a young man dressed in jeans and a button-down shirt. "I'm looking for Melanie Carmichael."

"I'm Melanie Carmichael." I walked to the door.

He handed me an envelope. "This is for you. You've been served."

CHAPTER THIRTY-SEVEN

Jonah

I didn't like doing it, but I dropped a few Franklins to a guard, asking that Larry be roughed up a bit in the next week. I had no idea whether it would get done or not. I didn't rightly care. Maybe I was just padding the guards' pockets, and I was okay with that too. They were more than likely underpaid for their thankless work.

I probably didn't need to go to the trouble. Some of the inmates had obviously been taking care of Larry. Child molesters didn't usually do too well in prison.

I was pretty okay with that, too.

I let out a sigh. I had a job to do, one I'd put off for too damned long. I was going to drive back to Snow Creek and stop in town to see Bryce. Our talk was long overdue.

★ ★ ★

Although Bryce had rented an apartment on the outskirts of town, he was still staying at his parents' house since his father had gone missing.

Evelyn Simpson answered the door. She looked pale. "Hello, Joe. What can we do for you?"

"I'm looking for Bryce. Is he here?"

She nodded, holding the door open for me. "Come on in."

"How are you holding up?" I asked her.

"All right, for the most part. I just don't understand what could have happened to Tom. It's not like him to up and disappear." She grabbed a tissue out of her pocket and wiped at her eyes.

Rage seethed inside of me. Evelyn Simpson was a nice woman. She'd fed me many times as a kid, and she continued to do a lot for her family and the community. She didn't deserve what was about to go down in her life.

She didn't deserve it at all, and neither did Bryce.

"How's the baby doing?" I asked.

That got sort of a smile out of her. "He's good. He's the only sunshine in my life these days."

Hell of a lot of pressure to put on an innocent baby, especially with what was coming. I wasn't sure what to say to her comment, so I changed the subject. "Is Bryce back in the nursery?"

"No, he's out back. Henry's napping."

"Okay. Thanks." I walked through the house and out to the deck.

Bryce was sitting at the table, reading. I never knew Bryce to be much of a reader.

"Hey," I said.

He looked up. "Oh, hey, Joe."

"Sorry to interrupt."

He set the book down. "You're not. I've read the same fucking page twenty times. I'm trying to get my mind off of my dad, but I'm not having much luck."

"Your mom doesn't look good," I said. "I'm sorry."

"It's taking its toll on her. And me. Thank God for Henry, or I wouldn't be able to focus on anything."

Again the baby. I was really glad that Bryce had Henry. Evelyn too.

"So no news on him, then?"

Bryce shook his head. "None. I've got some PIs on the job. Thanks again for the loan."

"Don't worry about it. And it wasn't a loan. It was a gift."

"I don't take charity, man."

"It's not charity, and you know it. I have more than I need. If I can help my oldest friend in the world, I'm going to do it."

His PIs wouldn't find Tom, though. Mills and Johnson hadn't unearthed him yet, and they were the highest paid investigators I'd ever come across. They'd get him eventually. I had no doubt.

"Thanks, bro. I *will* pay you back, but you're the best."

You're the best. Would he still think that after I dropped the bomb that was hovering over his head?

"Hey," I said. "You want to go over to Murphy's and have a drink?"

"Nah, not much in the mood. But if you want something, I'm always pouring."

"No, I'm good." I just didn't want to have this talk with him with his mother inside the house.

But since he wasn't moving, and since I wasn't leaving his presence until this was done, I was going to do it whether I liked it or not.

"I've been wanting to talk to you for a while now." I drew my gaze away from Bryce. How could I look my best friend in the eye? How could I look anyone in the eye and tell him that his father was a maniacal child molester iceman?

And of course I had no solid proof, other than Tom Simpson's birthmark. That was proof enough to me, and I knew it would be for Talon. But for Bryce?

"I know, bro. Seems like there hasn't been a lot of time for us to get together. We keep getting interrupted."

I'd been happy for those interruptions. They had given me a reprieve from this job I faced now. Something I could no longer put off.

"I know. I've been focused on the ranch, not to mention Talon's situation. And Melanie."

"That's great. I'm happy for you, man. You seem to have something very special with her."

I nodded. "I do." Another truth I had to tell. I hoped my relationship with Melanie would survive when I told her that I had neglected her phone call the day she was taken.

"So what is it you want to talk about? Need advice on your love life?" Bryce chuckled.

God, I wished it were that simple. "This is pretty serious, Bryce."

"All right. You're freaking me out a little."

"I'm afraid you're going to be more freaked out by the time I'm done."

Bryce clenched the book he was holding. "Okay, now you're scaring me."

Scared? He *should* be scared. He'd been living with a psychopath a lot of his life.

"We think we've identified another one of Talon's abductors."

"Really? That's great."

"You see, Talon remembered something about one of his abductors during his therapy."

"Yeah? What?"

"One of the guys had a birthmark."

Bryce's eyes widened. "What kind of birthmark?"

I cleared my throat. The time of reckoning had come. "A tan birthmark on his upper arm, right below the armpit. Shaped like the state of Texas."

"Wow, that's—" Bryce stood. "No way. You're not trying to tell me that you think—"

"Sit down. Hear me out. Please."

"You're accusing my father? The fucking mayor of Snow Creek? One of our finest citizens?"

"Please. I don't make these accusations lightly," I said. "If you have any respect for our friendship of thirty-five years, please sit down and hear me out."

"Respect for our friendship? You're the one with no respect for it. You really think my father could've done such a thing? My father raised me. He never laid a hand on me my entire life, even when I was a little piece of shit. This is my *father*. The man I trust with my life. With my *son's* life."

God, Bryce's son. Every time that baby had been left alone with the Simpsons, I had chills. I wanted to drive over to that place and grab the kid and never let him set foot in the house again.

"I know this is hard to believe. But look at Larry Wade. He was the city attorney. No one believed it of him either."

"You're really going to compare my father to Larry Wade? That sick motherfucker?"

"If what we suspect is true, your father is just as sick, maybe sicker, than Larry Wade."

"You, of all people. When my father has been missing for a week now. You want to lay this on my doorstep?"

I rubbed at my forehead. My head was starting to ache. "Did it ever occur to you to question why your father might be

BURN

missing now? He knew we were onto him. He's probably gone into hiding somewhere. We think we've identified the third abductor as well, and we haven't seen hide nor hair of him in months."

"Oh, yeah? Who's the third abductor? Your milkman? Maybe an elementary school teacher?"

"No. He's a man named Nico Kostas. You've heard me talk to Larry about him. He was dating Jade's mother, and we think he tampered with her airbag, trying to kill her for insurance money."

"You've lost it, Joe. Are you listening to yourself? Do you and Talon have such a need for vengeance that you've decided to write your own story? This poor Nico Kostas is probably as innocent as my father is."

I shook my head. "Your father is not innocent, Bryce. Who the hell else has the exact birthmark Talon described? No one."

"That's not evidence. It's circumstantial. I bet a lot of people have a birthmark like that. Talon probably saw my dad's once and made it up. You're trying to frame my father. What the fuck did he ever do to you?"

Rage boiled under my skin, and I stood. I had to stop myself from punching my best friend in the jaw. *Cool it, Joe. He's defending his dad. You expected that.*

I took a deep breath and walked toward Bryce. "What did he ever do to *me?* Nothing. But he kidnapped and raped my brother, man. He killed his own nephew. Open your eyes, Bryce. Your father is a psychopath, and you're better off now that he's gone."

Bryce backed away. "I never expected anything like this from you. We had the kind of friendship that stories are written

266

about. We could go for years without seeing each other and then get together, and it was like no time had passed. We were up to our old antics, finishing each other's sentences, laughing at each other's stupid-ass jokes. That's the kind of friend I thought you were, Joe." He shook his head. "I can't believe I was so wrong." He raised his fist.

I stalked toward him. "You want to hit me? Think that'll make you feel better? Go for it. Then I'll hit you back. And neither one of us will feel better. You think I like what your father has done? You think I like having to tell you? I've been dreading this since I figured it out. I haven't even told Talon yet because I thought I owed you the courtesy of letting you know first."

Bryce dropped his fist, his whole body tense. "I can't fucking believe it. You of all people."

"Look, if you believe in our friendship—"

"Friendship? We no longer have a friendship." Bryce raised his fist again, shaking, and then lowered it. "You're not worth it, Steel. Get the fuck out of my house."

He turned and walked inside.

I sighed. The conversation had gone about how I had expected. I sat back down, resting my elbows on the table, my forehead in my hands. Next, I had to see Melanie. I had put off being honest with her for too long as well. I stood and walked around to the front of the house to my car.

And then my goddamned phone buzzed.

I recognized the number. At least it wasn't my stalker this time.

"Hey, Mills," I said into the phone.

"Got some good news for you," Trevor Mills said. "We've located your mayor."

CHAPTER THIRTY-EIGHT

Melanie

The young man turned and walked away quickly.

"What is it, Doc?" Talon asked.

"I have no idea." I tore open the envelope.

And my heart sank.

Gina's parents were suing me for malpractice.

How dare they? They'd lied to their daughter, and now it wasn't even clear if she'd indeed committed suicide. I nearly lost my footing.

Talon caught me, taking the paper from my hands. He helped me into the living room and onto Jonah's brocade sofa.

He scanned the paper. "What the fuck? Haven't they already filed some sort of complaint?"

"They filed a complaint with the medical board. They can go after my license that way. This is a civil lawsuit for malpractice. Now they want money."

"Well, we've got that. Joe and I will pay them off to go away."

I had no doubt he meant every word he said, but I couldn't take his money. I ran my fingers over my hair. Couldn't I catch a damned break?

Not in this lifetime, apparently.

"You can't fix everything with your money, Talon."

"The hell I can't."

"Really? You think you can? You couldn't fix yourself, could you?"

I regretted the words as soon as they left my mouth. I was his therapist, his safe place. I shouldn't have said that, no matter how true it was.

"I'm sorry." I shook my head. "I shouldn't have been so harsh. But the words are true. You couldn't fix yourself solely with your money, and you can't fix this situation either. You can't bring Gina back to life."

He sat down next to me and looked me in the eye. "I know I can't. But you can't either. So why are they suing you?"

I opened my mouth, but he held out his hand.

"I'll tell you why. They're suing you for money. And we Steels have plenty of that."

"I don't need your money. I have malpractice insurance."

"I'm pretty sure we can pay more than your policy limits."

"I'm sure you can. But I've paid those premiums for years. Might as well put the policy to good use."

My phone rang from the kitchen where I'd left it so I wouldn't be disturbed during my session with Talon. "Excuse me," I said to Talon.

I walked to the kitchen, but was too late to get the phone call. It was from the insurance agent taking care of my claim on the loft. I didn't have the strength to deal with him just now. I made a note to call him back tomorrow.

Then I noticed a text from Jonah. It had come in a couple hours ago.

Visit with Larry amounted to nothing. I'm going to see Bryce. I'm going to tell him. I love you.

Dear God... I could only hope Bryce Simpson could

see his father for who he truly was. Otherwise, Jonah would be home soon, and he wouldn't be in a good mood. I quickly texted him back.

Good luck. I love you.

★ ★ ★

Jonah came home looking somber. I went to him immediately and pressed my lips to his. "How did it go?" Although I was pretty sure I knew the answer.

He shook his head. "About how I expected. The man is devoted to his dad, who, apparently, was a really great dad, despite his other faults."

"I'd hardly call those other things 'faults,'" I said. "Sit down. I'll fix you a martini."

Jonah raked his fingers through his hair. "I can't, Melanie. I can't sit down and pretend like everything is all right with you."

"What do you mean? Everything is fine with me."

He paced back and forth across the kitchen floor. "You don't understand. There's something I need to tell you too, only I've been too much of a coward to do it."

Me? What on earth could he have to tell me? He had given me a place to live when I couldn't bear to walk into my loft again. He'd hired private investigators to help me figure out the situation with Gina while he was still working on figuring out his own family's issues. I opened my mouth to say as much, but he gestured for me to stay quiet.

"I love you," he said. "God, Melanie, I love you so much."

I touched his cheek. "I love you too. More than anything. So whatever this is, we will get through it together."

"No, not this. I failed you." His fist came down on the table. Hard. "I fail everyone, Melanie. Don't get close to me, or I'll fail you. My brother, my best friend, and now you."

"First of all, you didn't fail your brother. You were a kid, Jonah. A kid. And you didn't fail your best friend. It's not your fault his father is a psychopath. You were only letting him know. And me? You've been nothing but good to me. So get off of this and—"

"No!" His fist came down on the table once more. "I have to tell you this. I have to. If we don't have honesty, we have nothing."

My heart stampeded. What was going on? He had something to tell me, and I couldn't imagine what it could be. But it wasn't going to be good.

"You weren't lying about your feelings, were you?"

"Lying about what feelings?"

"That you love me?"

And down came his fist once more. "Goddamnit, no. I love you more than anything. You're everything to me, Melanie. The fact that I'm about to lose you is killing me."

"You're not going to lose me," I said shakily.

"You... You just don't know."

"I do know. There's nothing you could do to make me walk away from you."

"You're not getting it. I failed you." He clenched his hands into fists, the muscle and sinew in his gorgeous forearms tightening. "That night when you were taken. I got your call, and I ignored it because I was angry with you for leaving me at my house that night, for not saying good-bye. I was fucking petty, and you went through hell because I didn't take your goddamned phone call."

My heart nearly stopped. My lips trembled. "I don't understand."

"What don't you understand? I didn't pick up the goddamned phone, Melanie. I was pissed off at you."

"I called you because I thought you would help me. Freaking 9-1-1 was busy. Busy!"

"Don't you think I know that? I know the whole fucking story. And I've been dying inside a little bit each day, knowing that I did that to you. That I'm the reason you went through hell."

"My God..."

"Great, huh? The woman I love went through hell because I was too petty to pick up the goddamned phone. The brother I love went through hell because I couldn't be bothered to go with him when all he wanted was to investigate the disappearance of his friend. I fucking hate myself right now."

I cleared my throat, willing myself not to break down. Was I angry? Yes. Hurt? Yes. But... "I...don't know what to say." I looked at him, at the man I loved, as I fingered the beautiful diamond choker he had put around my neck.

"No, keep it," he said. "No one else could wear it now."

"I didn't mean—"

He silenced me with a gesture. He was distraught, on the verge of tears, and I longed to run to him and comfort him, to tell him everything would be fine.

But my feet wouldn't move.

Damn it, feet. Move!

Now he did shed a tear. "You don't have to say anything. I see it in your eyes. We're over." He raked his hands through his hair once more and walked out of the kitchen. He looked over his shoulder. "I'll be out late. That gives you plenty of time to pack up and get out of here. I know you won't want to stay here. But I need to know you're safe, so I talked to Talon. You are welcome there, and he has plenty of room at his place."

"Why are you putting words in my mouth? And when did you talk to Talon? I was just with him a few hours ago."

"I called him after I left Bryce."

"Jonah, please, I don't want—"

He gestured for me to stop. "I was selfish. I wanted to keep you anyway. Even though I'd failed you. But I know I can't." He walked away.

I stood, numb, watching the man who meant everything to me walk out the door of his own home, to give me time to leave.

I hadn't said I wanted to leave. I hadn't said anything. He hadn't given me a chance.

Lucy swished around my legs, looking for attention, but somehow I couldn't even bend down to pet her. My body was still numb as I stood in the kitchen, wondering what I should do.

Jonah had already given up on us. Why hadn't he told me sooner? And why wasn't he willing to stay? To fight for us?

Was he truly not the man I'd thought he was?

No. This was his guilt, pure and simple, and goddamnit, I wasn't going to let him walk away from us.

Yes, he should have taken my call, but he'd been angry, and why shouldn't he have been? I'd walked out on him.

And now he'd walked out on me.

Emotions rolled through me. Anger, sadness, fear...all swirling around and through love.

I stood for a few timeless moments until finally I knelt down and petted Lucy. Perhaps leaving for a day or two wasn't a bad idea. I needed to take my life back, take myself back. I couldn't depend on Jonah's protection forever. Or Talon's, for that matter.

I walked slowly to the guest room where my things were. Packing wouldn't take too much time. I hadn't wanted to bring much from my apartment. The big problem was my file cabinet. It was heavy and bulky, and I wasn't sure I could move it by myself. I put all the papers pertaining to Gina in a box. Those, at least, were going with me.

Within a half hour, I'd loaded my car with everything but my filing cabinet.

I started driving.

I wasn't going to Talon's.

I was going somewhere to take myself back.

CHAPTER THIRTY-NINE

Jonah

Nothing.

I had nothing.

My family didn't need me. I'd done nothing but fail them, especially Talon. Bryce sure as hell didn't need me. He didn't think our friendship was worth a fuck. And Melanie... I hadn't had the strength to stick around and watch her leave me. Again I was a coward. I had been a coward, waiting so long to tell her the truth, and now I was even more of a coward, unable to stay and watch the outcome of my decision—watch the woman I loved walk out of my life.

So I drove. And though I didn't think consciously about where I was going, in the marrow of my bones I knew.

Trevor Mills had given me an address.

★ ★ ★

Two hours later, I arrived in the small town near the New Mexico border. The address hadn't shown up on GPS, so I had to drive the roads of the town until I found what I was looking for. It was a cracker box house on the outskirts of town. A one-car detached garage sat off to the side.

Tom Simpson's hideout.

I parked a block away to hide my car and then walked

stealthily to the small abode.

I didn't bother knocking, just turned the knob on the door. Oddly, it was open. I walked in. A nice enough home, sparsely furnished.

"Tom? Come out here, you sick son of a bitch."

No response. Not that I thought there would be. I walked through the living area, down a hall, to a couple of bedrooms. One was clearly being used, but no one was there. The door to what turned out to be a bathroom was also closed, but I opened it and walked in, not caring if I might catch Tom Simpson in the middle of a crap. But it was also vacant.

On the other side of the bedrooms was a small kitchen. Supplies had clearly been laid in. One more door. I opened it. It led to a dank basement surrounded by dark concrete walls. As I descended the stairs, eerie fingers seemed to crawl over my body.

The steps. The walls.

I inhaled, nearly gagging. Waste. Whether it was human or animal, I didn't know.

I looked around once I got to the bottom.

My heart nearly stopped. It was exactly how Talon had described it. I could almost see the phoenix on the dark gray walls, taunting him.

I had just walked into the cave-like cellar where my brother had lived for two months when he was a child of ten.

My skin tightened around me. I could hardly catch my breath. Was there no oxygen in this place?

I suppressed my fears as best I could and looked around. No windows, which was odd, and the room was pitch black. I waited for my eyes to adjust, feeling the wall for guidance, and I checked out the space. The rough concrete walls scratched at my—

I jerked.

A groan had come from the corner. I inched forward slowly, and a heap of blankets emerged in my field of vision. More groaning.

Someone was here. Someone in this basement where those three psychos had kept my brother.

I didn't dare speak. I made my way slowly and quietly to the blanketed lump on the floor and removed the dirty covers.

The body, bound and gagged, recoiled away, whimpering. My God.

It was alive.

"Hey, hey," I whispered. "I'm not going to hurt you."

It was a male, naked, his bony body streaked with blood and grime. His head had been shaved.

"I want to help you. I'm a friend. I'm going to take the gag off of you, but don't scream. All right?"

The man whimpered and nodded.

I removed the gag carefully. "Who are you?"

He groaned, muttering unintelligible words.

"It's okay. You don't have to talk. I'm going to get you out of here." As quickly as I could, I unbound his ankles and wrists.

I startled when a sound like a board creaking came from somewhere upstairs. Tom must have come back. I threw the dirty blanket over the sickly man. "Shh," I said. "Don't let him know I've untied you. I'll take care of him. If I don't come back for you in half an hour, find something to use as a weapon, and get the fuck out of here."

I hated leaving him there, but he'd at least be safe while I was in the house. I'd told him to leave if I didn't return, but he was so bony and sickly-looking, I wondered if he'd be able to get up the stairs.

But he would. Talon had gotten up those very same stairs.

"I'll be back for you. I promise."

I hoped I'd be able to keep that promise.

I walked toward the stairway, the dark walls seeming to pulse and close in.

My God, how had Talon survived this?

And who was the man in the cellar?

I willed myself to get a grip and ascended the stairs slowly. I had come here alone and unarmed. I hadn't thought about protecting myself. I could kick the shit out of Tom Simpson with a look, and if he had a knife, I could easily disarm him.

But if he had a gun...

The man was a killer. A cold-blooded killer. And God only knew what he'd done to this poor man in the cellar.

Bile nudged up my throat. That was a crock. I knew exactly what Tom had done. The same thing he'd done to my brother.

I shut the door of the basement quietly and walked through the small kitchen. The doorknob to the front door turned slowly.

A man entered, carrying a bag of groceries. As far as I could tell, he was unarmed. The hair on his head was dyed dark brown.

But the eyes...

A maniacal smile crossed my face. I had him.

Finally.

Finally, I would avenge my brother.

My smile became wider.

"Hello, Tom."

Jonah and Melanie's story continues in

Surrender

Coming May, 16th 2017

MESSAGE FROM HELEN HARDT

Dear Reader,

Thank you for reading *Burn*. If you want to find out about my current backlist and future releases, please like my Facebook page: **www.facebook.com/HelenHardt** and join my mailing list: **www.helenhardt.com/signup/**. I often do giveaways. If you're a fan and would like to join my street team to help spread the word about my books, you can do so here: **www.facebook.com/groups/hardtandsoul/**. I regularly do awesome giveaways for my street team members.

If you enjoyed the story, please take the time to leave a review on a site like Amazon or Goodreads. I welcome all feedback.

I wish you all the best!

Helen

ALSO BY HELEN HARDT

The Sex and the Season Series:
Lily and the Duke
Rose in Bloom
Lady Alexandra's Lover
Sophie's Voice
The Perils of Patricia (Coming Soon)

The Temptation Saga:
Tempting Dusty
Teasing Annie
Taking Catie
Taming Angelina
Treasuring Amber
Trusting Sydney
Tantalizing Maria

The Steel Brothers Saga:
Craving
Obsession
Possession
Melt
Burn
Surrender (Coming May 16th, 2017)
Shattered (Coming August 29th, 2017)

Daughters of the Prairie:
The Outlaw's Angel
Lessons of the Heart
Song of the Raven

DISCUSSION QUESTIONS

1. The theme of a story is its central idea or ideas. To put it simply, it's what the story *means*. How would you characterize the theme of *Burn?*

2. What new things are revealed about Jonah in this book? About Melanie?

3. A big change occurs in Melanie in this book. Discuss her character, how she has changed, and why? What can we assume about her past?

4. Who do you think is responsible for Melanie's abduction?

5. What do we know so far about Gina's parents, Rodney and Erica Cates?

6. Only one set of fingerprints has been positively identified on Colin's business card. Who do you suppose the other two sets belong to?

7. Discuss Brooke Bailey, listing both good and bad characteristics. Is she the one stalking Jonah? If not her, who might it be?

8. How do you feel about Melanie's initial decision to shred Gina's letter?

9. How do you feel about Melanie's theory that Gina might

have been murdered?

10. We learn more about Jonah's sexual desires in *Burn*. Do you think Melanie will be able to fulfill them? How do you feel about Dominant/submissive relationships? What about Master/slave relationships, which is what Jonah's past lover Kerry wanted?

11. Why does Jonah wait so long to tell Melanie that he avoided her phone call because he was angry that she sneaked out of his house at the end of *Melt?* Was he right or wrong to do this?

12. We meet two new women in *Burn*—Melanie's neighbor, Lisa O'Toole, and Officer Ruby Lee. What do you think of these characters, and do you think they'll have more significant roles in future books?

13. Who is the man in the basement?

14. Where do you think Melanie will go when she leaves Jonah's house?

15. How might Gina's death factor into the whole Steel Brothers storyline?

ACKNOWLEDGEMENTS

Burn was empowering to write. Melanie is a phenomenal woman, but like so many of us, she sees herself as merely average, despite her intelligence and success. Unfortunately, her plight is all too common among women. I was thrilled to be able to show the beginning of her transformation as she stepped outside the box and saw herself for what she truly is—strong, determined, and beautiful. As she transforms, she is more ready than ever to accept Jonah for all that he is—darkness and all. They're so in love, but can their love triumph? Stay tuned.

Thanks so much to my amazing editors, Celina Summers and Michele Hamner Moore. Your guidance and suggestions were, as always, invaluable. Thank you to my line editor, Scott Saunders, and my proofreaders, Claire Allmendinger, Audrey Bobak, and Amy Grishman. Thank you to all the great people at Waterhouse Press—Meredith, David, Kurt, Shayla, Jon, Yvonne, Robyn, and Jeanne. The cover art for this series is beyond perfect, thanks to Meredith and Yvonne.

Many thanks to my assistant, Amy Denim, for keeping my social media alive while I was in the writing cave. I couldn't do it without you!

Thank you to the members of my street team, Hardt and Soul. HS members got the first look at *Burn*, and I appreciate all your support, reviews, and general good vibes. You all mean more to me than you can possibly know.

Thanks to my always supportive family and friends and to all of the fans who eagerly waited for *Burn*. I hope you love it.

Thanks to my local writing groups, Colorado Romance Writers and Heart of Denver Romance Writers, for their love and support.

I'm excited to conclude the love story of Jonah and Melanie in *Surrender*. I hope you'll find it worth the wait!

ABOUT THE AUTHOR

New York Times and *USA Today* Bestselling author Helen Hardt's passion for the written word began with the books her mother read to her at bedtime. She wrote her first story at age six and hasn't stopped since. In addition to being an award winning author of contemporary and historical romance and erotica, she's a mother, a black belt in Taekwondo, a grammar geek, an appreciator of fine red wine, and a lover of Ben and Jerry's ice cream. She writes from her home in Colorado, where she lives with her family. Helen loves to hear from readers.

Visit her here:
www.facebook.com/HelenHardt

Keep reading for an excerpt!

CHAPTER ONE

Seventeen years later

"He doesn't look so tough," Dusty said to Sam as she eyed El Diablo, the stud bull penned up outside the Western Stock Show grounds in Denver. She winced at the pungent aroma of dust and animals.

"No man's been able to stay on him more than two seconds, Dust," her brother said.

"He just needs a woman's touch." Dusty looked into the bull's menacing eyes. Oh, he was mad all right, but she had no doubt she could calm him. The ranchers in Montana didn't call her the Bull Whisperer for nothing.

"I don't know. I'm not sure you should try it. Papa wouldn't like it."

"Papa's dead, Sam, and you can't tell me what to do." She pierced her brother's dark gaze with her own. "Besides, the purse for riding him would save our ranch, and you know it."

"Hell, Dusty." Sam shoved his hands in his denim pockets. "I plan to win a few purses bronc busting. You don't need to worry about making money."

"I want to make the money, Sam."

"That's silly."

"No, it's not."

"Look, you don't need to feel any obligation. What happened couldn't be helped. It wasn't your fault. You know that."

"Whatever." She shrugged her shoulders and turned back to the bull. "Besides, if I ride old Diablo here, I can make five hundred thousand dollars in eight seconds. That's"—she did some rapid calculations in her head—"two hundred and twenty-five million dollars an hour. Can you beat that?" She grinned, raising her eyebrows.

"Your math wizardry is annoying, Dust. Always has been. And yeah, I might be able to come away from this rodeo with half a mill, though I won't do it in eight seconds. Besides, Diablo's owner will never let a woman ride him."

"Who's his owner? I haven't had a chance to look through the program yet."

"Zach McCray."

"No fooling?" Dusty smiled as she remembered the lanky teenager with the odd-colored eyes. Yes, he had tormented her, but he had been kind that last day when the O'Donovans left for Montana. At thirteen, Zach had no doubt understood the magnitude of Mollie's illness much better than Dusty. "I figured the McCrays would be here. Think they'll remember us?"

"Sure. Chad and I are blood brothers." Sam held up his palm. "Seriously, though, they may not. Ranch hands come and go all the time around a place as big as McCray Landing."

"It's Sam O'Donovan!"

Dusty turned toward the deep, resonating voice. A tall broad man with a tousled shock of brown hair ambled toward them.

"Chad? I'll be damned. It *is* you." Sam held out his hand. "We were just talking about you, wondering if you'd remember us."

"A man doesn't forget his first and only blood brother."

Chad slapped Sam on the back. "And is this the little twerp?"

"Yeah, it's me, Chad." Dusty held out her hand.

Chad grabbed it and pulled her toward him in a big bear hug. "You sure turned out to be a pretty thing. " He turned back to Sam. "I bet you got your work cut out for you, keeping the flies out of the honey."

"Yeah, so don't get any ideas," Sam said.

Chad held up his hands in mock surrender. "Wouldn't dream of it, bro. So how are you all? I'd heard you might be back in town. I was sorry to hear about your pa."

"I didn't know the news made it down here," Sam said.

"Yeah, there was a write up in the Bakersville Gazette. The old lady who runs it always kept a list of the hands hired at the nearby ranches. Once she discovered the Internet five years ago, there was no stopping her." Chad grinned. "She found every one of them. Needs a new hobby, I guess. So what are you all up to?"

"Here for the rodeo. Dusty and I are competing."

"No kidding?"

"Yep. I'm bronc busting, and Dusty's a barrel racer. And..." Sam chuckled softly.

"And what?"

"She thinks she's gonna take Diablo here for a ride."

Chad's eyes widened as he stared at Dusty. Warmth crept up her neck. Clearly her five-feet-five-inch frame didn't inspire his confidence.

"You ride bulls?"

Her facial muscles tightened. "You bet I do."

Chad let out a breathy chortle. "Good joke."

"No joke, Chad," Sam said. "She's pretty good, actually. But she's never ridden a bull as big as Diablo. She's tamed some pretty nasty studs in Montana, though never during competition."

"I hate to tell you this, Gold Dust, but this rodeo doesn't allow female bull riding."

"I'll just have to get them to change their minds then," Dusty said.

"Good luck with that," Chad said. "In fact, can I go with you? I think the whole affair might be funny."

"Fine, come along then. Who do I speak to?"

"Honey, why don't you stick to female riding? I'm sure the WPRA will be happy to hear your pleas. But this here's a *man's* rodeo."

Dusty's nostrils flared as anger seethed in her chest. "I'm as good a bull rider as any man. Tell him, Sam."

"I already told him you're good."

"But tell him what they call me back home."

"Dust—"

"Tell him, or I will!"

"They call her the Bull Whisperer. She's good, I tell you."

"Bull Whisperer?" Chad scoffed. "So you're the Cesar Millan of cattle, huh? Ain't no whisper gonna calm Diablo. Even Zach hasn't been able to ride him, and he's the best."

"Yeah, well, he hasn't seen me yet." Dusty stood with her hands on her hips, wishing her presence were more imposing. Both her brother and Chad were nearly a foot taller than she was. "I'm going to ride that bull and win that purse!"

"Seriously, Dusty," Chad said, "I was teasing you. But you can't try to ride Diablo. He'll kill you. Trust me, I know. He damn near killed me. I was out all last season recovering from injuries I got from him."

"I have a way with animals," Dusty said.

"So do I, honey."

Sam rolled his eyes, laughing. "Whatever you say, McCray."

"Hey, dogs love me," Chad said.

"I'm not surprised," Dusty said, smiling sardonically. "I'm sure you make a nice tall fire hydrant. Now tell me, who do I need to talk to about riding the bull?"

"You need to talk to me, darlin'."

Dusty shuddered at the sexy western drawl, the hot whisper of breath against the back of her neck.

"And there ain't a woman alive who can ride that bull."

Continue Reading in Tempting Dusty

Visit www.helenhardt.com for more info!

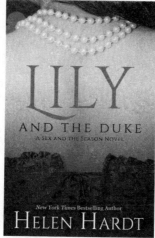

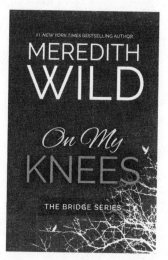

3567405667411Z